WARLOCK HOLMES

A Study in Brimstone

Also by G.S. Denning and available from Titan Books

WARLOCK HOLMES

The Battle of Baskerville Hall (May 2017)

G.S. DENNING

WARLOCK HOLMES

A Study in Brimstone

TITAN BOOKS

Warlock Holmes: A Study in Brimstone
Print edition ISBN: 9781783299713
E-book edition ISBN: 9781783299720

Published by Titan Books
A division of Titan Publishing Group Ltd
144 Southwark Street, London SE1 0UP

First edition: May 2016
10 9 8 7 6 5 4 3 2 1

© 2016 G.S. Denning
Illustrations © 2016 Sean Patella-Buckley

A CIP catalogue record for this title is available from the British Library.

Printed in the USA.

To my wife, Amanda, for all her support.

To my kids, who I hope get a giggle from this someday.

To my parents, who had the grace not to suggest I get a real job.

CONTENTS

A STUDY IN BRIMSTONE

PART I

FROM THE JOURNAL OF DR. JOHN WATSON

1

THE DOMINION OF MAN IS DRAWING TO A CLOSE. THE age of demons is upon us. This, I recognize, is largely my fault and let me take just a moment to apologize for my part in it. I am very sorry I doomed the world.

Really, just... absolutely, horribly sorry.

And yes, I do realize my apology fails to come up to the occasion. I am not accustomed to expressing regrets of this magnitude. In fact—this being the first time the world has been doomed—I can safely say that no man has *ever* had to craft such an apology, so let's all agree to give me a break, shall we?

It's not as if my words could save any of us, in any case.

No, I'm afraid the only useful commission remaining to me is to chronicle the history of our fall. If this book survives to be read, if any survive to read it, I hope this volume will make clear that Warlock Holmes—though powerful almost beyond description—was merely a dupe. That Moriarty, whose name is unknown to the species he betrayed, was our true nemesis and architect of our destruction. That I am...

well… not so much of an idiot as might be supposed.

How is it, some might wonder, that a London doctor chose to share his lodgings with a sorcerer? Is this the same John Watson who once demanded a new room at medical school, just because "Splitty" Winslow kept that damned yappy dog? Yes? Then why did he fail to move out of 221B when he noticed the walls were bleeding? In what way is a howling, demon-filled void preferable to a schnauzer?

These are fair criticisms, but there were extenuating circumstances. Believe me, if fortune had not contrived to doom me to the company of Warlock Holmes, I would not have endured it. You see, I do not enter into this story as a healthy, well-moneyed London gentleman. I enter it as a ninety-two-pound typhoid-wasted wreck secretly rifling his wallet in a cheap pub. I was sure—*sure*—I had another shilling. I could not have miscounted. I had not spent every night of the last month agonizing over the ever-dwindling pile of coins just to lose count. Where was that damned shilling?

Had I put it in my waistcoat pocket? I had! There I found it. I gave thanks for small mercies, withdrew the coin and snuck it into the leather sheath our waiter had brought with our bill. It was my last shilling. I had only three coins left to my name: tuppence, sixpence, ninepence. Starvation could not be far off. On the one hand, it was folly to be paying for a meal out for Stamford and myself. I hardly even liked the man and if it were not for a chance encounter on the street and the burdens of London gentility I would not have made the offer. On the other hand, why not? My choice as I saw it was this: If I did not purchase lunch, I would starve to death in a London gutter, in two weeks' time. If I *did* purchase lunch, I would starve to death in only one week's time, but just before I succumbed, I could turn to the next beggar over and tell him with my dying breath, "If you ever find yourself at the Holborn, don't bother with the beef consommé; it's somewhat overrated."

Without taking my eyes off of Stamford, without respite in my continual "Oh yes, quite,"-ing agreeing and nodding, I slid the sheath to the edge of the table, hoping our waiter would claim it the next time he passed and that Stamford would not notice. I needn't have worried; Stamford was not known for observational acuity.

"I have the worst luck," he was saying. "Just the damnedest luck! Why such misfortunes should flock to me, I will never know!"

"Oh yes, quite," I agreed, nodding.

In the years since we'd worked together at St. Bart's, Stamford had done nothing to cure the tediousness for which we'd all shunned him. He had been holding forth for ten or fifteen minutes about his troubles, which seemed to revolve around nothing more than making an ill-advised promise to help some chap he knew at the hospital. At last he came to the end of his diatribe and settled on a topic I enjoyed even less.

"I say, Watson… I don't mean to be rude, but you look like you may have had a bit of misfortune yourself. I've rarely seen a man so changed. Do I miss my mark, or…"

"No. You are quite right, Stamford. I was shot."

"Shot?"

"Through the shoulder."

"But how did you manage to get shot in India? Nobody gets shot in India—nobody British, anyway."

"Exactly why I elected to go there," I told him, "but then the army realized it had been nearly forty years since our last disastrous invasion of Afghanistan. I was sent to Maiwand."

"Maiwand? Afghanistan? As in the Battle of Maiwand?"

"The same."

"But we lost that one, didn't we?"

I winced.

"Well, you know, I missed the end. Still… the last bit I remember… it looked as if we weren't doing all that well."

Oh yes, I'd say we lost that one. I choked back memories—visions of my friends and comrades being hacked to sauce all around me.

"Oh… well… you got out all right, though, eh?" Stamford stammered. "So… getting shot—that's what made you so skinny?"

"Eh? Oh, no. Enteric fever. My orderly Murray got me back to the hospital at Peshawar before I bled to death, but the conditions were filthy. The fever killed off half my ward before it relented."

Memories: piles of corpses, baking in the sun. The doctors too busy, the soldiers too sick, the natives too wise to dig our graves. I tried to think of something else besides the big black wasps that laid their eggs in our dead and dying. Puppies, perhaps? Christmas? Ponies? Big-eyed puppies riding ponies home for Christmas?

"Ah… So sorry to hear it, Watson," said Stamford, visibly regretting the zeal he'd just employed complaining of workplace trivia. "What is next for you? Are they sending you to India?"

"They are not sending me anywhere. The army has reconsidered our partnership. I suppose I wasn't the most useful doctor they've ever had…"

"What are you going to do, Watson?"

What could I say? The truth was I had considered myself a goner from the moment I was struck. The better soldiers had the sense to be unconscious before they hit the ground and dead two minutes later. I, it seemed, was determined to stretch the ordeal out.

"I don't know," I whispered. "I suppose I ought to be seeking a job or… common living arrangements of some sort, but…"

I looked up expecting to see pity in Stamford's eyes. Instead, I found him wearing an inscrutable expression that encompassed both hope and guilt. He licked his lips and mumbled, "So many misfortunes, Watson… Ought I to add one more? It is cruel, yet it also seems you may have been sent as the remedy to my own woes."

Let me admit that I didn't care for his tone. I said, "Add to my misfortune? What an extraordinary thing to say. What are you speaking of?"

"Well… that man I was complaining about before, at the hospital. Oh, he is the damnedest fellow, but if you need an inexpensive place to rest yourself, he may be just the man you need."

"If he is, that would not be adding to my misfortune, it would be an unexpected boon," I said. "Tell me about him."

"Awful fellow. A loner and a skulker. Loves the macabre. Always breaking into the hospital to hang about in our morgue. He has a devil of a time getting anyone to lodge with him. Well... trouble keeping them, I suppose. He was complaining of it only this morning. I said I would help and I made a promise I should not have and I got myself rather tangled up in the whole affair. I've been drifting about all day, wondering how to get out of it."

For a moment, the man sounded revolting to me. Yet, as Stamford spoke, I began to reflect that I myself was far from an ideal living companion. Not many Londoners craved the company of a shoulder-shot, gut-sick invalid who would mope around the house, complaining of life's treatment of him, occasionally screaming when he heard a loud bang or suffering an attack of nerves if he realized his blanket was Afghan. Also, having become destitute over the concern of this one meal, my need was dire. I swallowed my pride.

"Stamford, I am intrigued. I would very much like to meet this... what did you say his name was?"

"Warlock Holmes," Stamford replied, wincing as if the name alone were enough to undo all my interest.

It was not. "I should very much like to meet this Warlock Holmes. When might it be arranged?"

A look of profound relief broke across Stamford's face

and he turned to the wall clock above the bar. "If we rush, we might intercept him now!" he said. "Hurry, hurry! Get up! Let's go!"

I was loath to hurry. I had no money for a hansom cab, and no strength for the walk. I related this regret to Stamford and suggested that perhaps I should come around the next day and that our current attentions were best devoted to lunch.

"No!" he cried and slapped the soup spoon from my hand, spattering the table with second-rate beef consommé. All heads turned. He immediately demurred and added, "Ah… what I mean, Doctor, is… why waste a day? Certainly, I would be happy to provide us with a cab. Wait here. Don't move. *Do not leave this spot*, do you hear me?"

He disappeared out the door, only to reappear a few moments later, feverishly beckoning me to follow. One side of his suit was torn and dirtied. Apparently the fastest way to get a cab on High Holborn was to run into the road and be struck by one, then insist that you would summon the police unless the driver took you where you wished to go. As soon as we were settled in his ill-gotten cab, Stamford shrieked that he would like to be taken to St. Bart's Hospital as quickly as possible and shoveled the driver twice the usual fare. Once, during the ride, he gave the man an extra shilling, enjoining him to hurry, lest we arrive too late.

Alighting at the hospital, Stamford practically shoved me down a small flight of brick stairs, through an aged side door, towards the morgue. As we neared it, the sound of an argument came to my ears, though I could discern only one of the participants' voices.

"Absolutely not! Brains are the natural property of the individual in whose skull they reside. They are the seat of our very identity. A man's brain is his kingdom!"

The voice had a high, strident timbre to it, but lacked the haughtiness of a true gentleman. In a few moments, I heard it again, saying, "I have already told you: I am unwilling to part with it. Good day, sir."

A second later: "I said *good day*, sir!"

Something crashed to the floor and the sounds of a distant scuffle reached my ears. The voice said, "Unhand me! You have your own brain! Be content with that, can't you? Ouch! You cad! Very well, you have brought this upon yourself!"

Now the combat began in earnest; a series of bangs and wet, fleshy thuds echoed down the corridor. Stamford, who had grown ever more nervous as we approached the source of the noise at last suggested, "You know, Dr. Watson, perhaps tomorrow would be a more ideal time…"

I disregarded him and pushed past, intent on discovering the nature of the disturbance. I rounded the final corner into the morgue and beheld, for the first time, my future friend, Warlock Holmes.

He was an excessively tall man, easily the better of six feet. His face was hawkish and thin. He stood in his shirtsleeves, his long jacket discarded across a nearby chair, his sleeves rolled to his elbows to keep them from interfering with his current study. His striking green eyes were wide with the physical effort he was engaged in, which dewed him, brow and arm, with sweat. On the table before him lay the corpse of a gentleman who must have perished in the last week or so. He already displayed the bloating and discoloration that comes as decomposition sets in. The hospital winding sheet on which he lay was spattered and stained with almost every bodily fluid one could name. Some of it may have leached out naturally, but you didn't have to be a doctor to see there was a more immediate cause for the majority of it. Holmes was repeatedly striking the corpse across its chest and face with a dented cricket bat, crying, "Stay down! Stay down! Stay! Down!"

"By God! Whatever are you doing, man?" I gasped.

Holmes froze for a moment, mid-swing. His guilty eyes locked with mine and his mouth began to move as if to formulate a response, but no sound emerged.

Stamford stepped in, offering, "Holmes is a scientist... of sorts... greatly interested in forensic studies. Doubtless, he is conducting some... experiment or other to... erm... Ah! To determine whether and to what extent bruising can be caused, post mortem. Isn't that right, Holmes?"

Holmes stood frozen a moment more, cricket bat raised. A look of consternation crossed his features and he wondered aloud, "What *are* you talking about, Stamford? What was all that?"

"The perfectly reasonable, scientific explanation for your *extraordinary behavior*, Holmes!"

"Oh! Yes! So it was. Yes... thank you, Stamford."

Holmes began to look about the room, searching—I suppose—for somewhere he could lay a battered, bloody

"Stay down! Stay down! Stay! Down!"

cricket bat, where it wouldn't look out of place. Finding none, he lowered it to the floor and slid it under the autopsy table with one foot, as casually as he could manage. Once this was accomplished, he gave me a half-convincing smile of welcome and said, "You see? There. It's gone. Now... um... who is this, Stamford?"

"Ah! This is Dr. John Watson. He has given me to understand he has an immediate need for shared lodgings."

At this, Holmes's bright green eyes flashed up at me and for a moment I had the sensation of being held in place by a giant but invisible hand. When I next exhaled, it seemed to me as if it contained not only discarded air, but the complete truth of my person and position as well.

"Dr. John Watson," Holmes intoned, his voice suddenly two octaves deeper than it had been, his expression remote as if lost in thought or struggling to hear a conversation being held at great distance, "late of the British Army, having been wounded in the left shoulder in Afghanistan, currently residing at the Hotel d'Amsterdam, on the Strand."

The feeling of restriction left me, but I stood aghast nonetheless. After a moment I breathed, "By God... By God, how did you do that, man? Why, it's almost supernatural."

"What? No! Supernatural? No, no, no," said Holmes.

Again, Stamford endeavored to explain. "No. It isn't. Holmes is particularly observant. With the merest glance he can glean facts that elucidate a man's entire history. Though it may *seem* supernatural, it is an entirely explainable phenomenon. Isn't that right, Holmes?"

"Oh. Yes. Of course, that's it. Why I merely observed,

my dear Watson... I merely observed..." he gazed at me searchingly, almost desperately, "your left arm hangs limp, but not stiff, indicating a wound, but not to the arm itself. The shoulder then. You have a sad expression, so of course, you must have been to Afghanistan. Any doctor recently wounded and recently in Afghanistan is bound to have been attached to the British Army. As to the Hotel d'Amsterdam... well... Ah! Observe the red mud caking your left shoe, sir! It is of a very specific type, unique in London to one particular puddle, just outside the Hotel d'Amsterdam, on the Strand."

He gazed at me with an expression of triumph and relief. My eyes wandered to my left shoe. It was indeed caked with mud, but not of a reddish hue and definitely not from my hotel. In fact, it was from a wet patch that Stamford had dragged me through, just outside the hospital. It occurred to me that a truly observant man might have realized that it was still wet. As it was not a rainy day, this small quantity of mud would surely have dried on the journey from the Strand. Nevertheless, he had guessed exactly and I had no means to refute him.

"Ahem... Holmes?" Stamford interjected, "I think you said you have already found lodgings?"

"I have," said Holmes. "A fine suite of rooms at 221B Baker Street."

My heart sank. Though Baker Street was not the most fashionable area of London, its central location and proximity to Regent's Park assured it would be beyond my meager means. Nevertheless, with flagging hope, I inquired, "What should be my share of the rent?"

"Oh, a sovereign," Holmes replied.

What did he mean? A sovereign a month would be nice, but so would having a passing leprechaun present me with underwear, woven of solid gold. The two phenomena were equally unlikely. Most probably, Holmes meant a sovereign a week. Yet, the more I reflected on it, even that figure seemed optimistic. Surely not one per day, I hoped.

"A sovereign... how often?" I asked.

"Just once," he said. "One sovereign, once, and you may stay however long you please."

My jaw dropped. Surely, he was strange company, but what other company was I fit for? And here—here on the proverbial platter—was presented to me the cure to all my present woes. The leprechaun, it must be said, failed to appear. Yet might that not be a blessing, too? When one considered the advantages of cotton over gold, as an undergarment material: durability, breathability, ease of cleaning... not to mention the difference in weight...

"However," Holmes continued, "there are some circumstances you should know. Are you averse to the smell of strong tobacco smoke?"

"Not at all," I said.

"What about sulfur?"

This, I presumed, would be a result of his scientific pursuits, so I nodded my agreement and informed him that—should I establish a medical practice—I might also need to bring home odorous chemicals or medicines. He agreed immediately.

"Let's see… let's see… what are my other faults?" he said, beginning to pace. "You must be constantly wary of poisons, for I seem to have some always about. I am sometimes the victim of periods of melancholy or elation that have no apparent cause. Also, I play the accordion. When I say I play it, I mean with no warning, at whatever hour I must. I shall endeavor to keep this to a minimum, and make it up to you if I should begin it at untoward hours, but… well… there is the truth of it. What do you say, can this arrangement be satisfactory?"

For the cost of one sovereign's rent—ever—I should not have cared if he had the entire London Philharmonic strapped to his back, perpetually blaring "Aunt Petunia's Pepper Pot."

"Absolutely," said I, then blushed to have to mention this in front of Stamford, "except that… owing to a few outstanding obligations, and the daily demands of my belly… ah… it may take me almost two weeks to raise the sum of… a sovereign."

Even as I said it, I could scarce believe it, but that was the fact of the matter. But it did not seem to bother Warlock Holmes in the least.

"That is of little consequence," he said, "so long as you are willing to move in at exactly midnight tonight and agree to step backwards over the threshold the first time you enter."

Hmm… Odd… Odd but not impossible and—as my own situation seemed more desperate every time I stopped to consider it—I agreed that I could. At this point,

Stamford leapt between us, jabbed his finger into Holmes's chest and declared, "I think you must admit, Holmes, that Dr. Watson here outstrips me in every criteria that is of value to you!"

"Indeed," Holmes agreed. "I doubt you should have lasted the week."

"Take him then," Stamford urged, "and release me."

Holmes fixed me with his searching, green-eyed gaze and asked, "You'll do it then, Dr. Watson? You'll move in tonight? At midnight? Backwards?"

"I shall," I said, with more relish than I felt.

"Then, Stamford, you stand unbound," said Holmes with a dismissive wave.

Stamford released a profound sigh, turned to me, grasped both my hands and said, "Dr. Watson! Thank you! Oh, by God, thank you! And… I'm sorry."

With that, he turned and fled the room. Holmes watched him go with a knowing grin, and then turned his gaze on me. Strangest thing, his eyes grew softer and his smirk transformed into a genuine smile.

"Yes. Thank you, Dr. Watson," he said. "I am an excellent judge of character and I can tell already that you are perhaps the most suitable companion I might have found in all this wide city. I am glad of you. I am… not well suited to being left alone for any great period of time."

We shook hands and parted. I had more than ten hours to fill before midnight and precious little to do. I forced my feeble legs to drag me back to the Strand, packed my few possessions into two steamer trunks, cajoled the landlord to have them delivered to Baker Street the next day, and sat down to rest. I left for Baker Street early, lest my progress was slower than hoped. On the way out, it occurred to me to scan the grounds for Holmes's unique red puddle. I found none.

I arrived shortly before midnight to find Holmes standing just inside the threshold of his rooms, expounding on how glad he was that I had come. As eager as he seemed to welcome me, he nonetheless stood in the doorway—all but a door himself—barring me entry until the clock in the hall struck the hour.

I was weary with walking and almost broke my neck, tripping backwards over the threshold as I entered. Nevertheless, I was thrilled when I saw the place. I had not thought to inquire as to furniture and indeed, if there had been none, I was scarce in a position to remedy the situation. Happily, I entered a well-appointed sitting room—not ostentatious, not cramped. There was a dining table and chairs set by the small back windows, and before the front window that looked out onto Baker Street were two overstuffed armchairs and a small sofa. They sat before a clean brick hearth upon a tasteful rug (which I admired, despite the fact it was clearly Afghan). Off the main room was a hallway, which ended in a bathroom with—to my great relief—indoor plumbing. On opposite sides of the hallway stood two doors. The bedrooms I presumed. I inquired as to which room was mine.

"Ah, I am only just arrived myself," Holmes said, "so I am not yet installed. You may take whichever you please."

As I examined them, my heart fell. On the Baker Street side, the room was large, airy and luxurious. The room across from it might easily have been mistaken for a closet, if it were not for the fact that it *had* a closet. There was no fireplace in the small room and only one tiny window, which gave no visible sign that it could even be opened. The room must have been designed by a sadist—sure to be sweltering in summer, freezing in winter and cramped all year round. 221B, it seemed, had been intended to accommodate one gentleman and one wretched slave. Which room did I prefer? Of course, there could be only one answer.

And yet, my total contribution to this venture was to be one sovereign. Ever. Just one. I took a deep, doleful breath and announced that the smaller room was ideal for my needs.

Warlock's face drew into worried lines.

"You may have your choice, of course," he said, "but if one is as good as the other, to you... well... I would be obliged if I might be allowed that room."

"The smaller? That one?" I asked, incredulous.

"I have always preferred having walls close by me," he said. "And besides, that large room has a western window! Oh, I do not care for so much light, Watson. I don't know how I'd abide it. I know we have only just met, but... you would have my enduring thanks if..."

Scarcely believing my luck, I entered into by far the more luxurious of the two rooms and flung myself upon its excellent bed. I had meant only to test it, but before I realized what was happening, I was fast asleep.

2

THOSE FIRST DAYS IN BAKER STREET WERE A PROFOUND comfort to me. It seemed as if all the perils that assailed me had dissolved into luxuries overnight. They hadn't, of course. In point of fact, I had just moved in with one of the most dangerous creatures ever to walk the face of the earth—perhaps *the* most dangerous. Still, the threat that Holmes represented was slow to reveal itself.

His peculiarity, on the other hand, was apparent right from the start. Though he was kind almost to a fault, there were a thousand social niceties Holmes stood ignorant of. His every meal consisted of toast and soup. I never saw him eat anything else. I couldn't even be certain the man slept. I never caught him at it.

He packed his tiny room with the most extraordinary quantity of books. He had a desk in the corner, upon which he kept a kit that resembled nothing so much as a sixteenth-century alchemical workshop (which, indeed, it was). He also had a bed. That was all. The remainder of his floor was covered in books. He had gigantic tomes and single-sheet leaflets. Some were ancient and some contemporary, but they were present in such numbers as to fill his room from floor to ceiling. Such was their weight that the floorboards frequently groaned when anybody stepped in Holmes's room, or even in the hallway before it. They groaned with a strangely human voice—one might almost discern words. The only area not covered by these books was a cramped path that led from his door to the bed, with a minor spur that diverted to his desk.

This setup granted the impression that Holmes was living in an overfilled storage shed. I several times enjoined him to trade rooms with me, as my own possessions were few, but he refused. He loved his little hideaway. He was like a hermit crab that had found the perfect little seashell for itself. Often he would retreat there when he felt threatened or solitary. When his mood was foul, I could hear him in there, holding whispered debates with... well... with the walls, or nobody, I presumed.

Just as common as his depressions were periods of ecstatic mania, during which he would leap about the sitting room with strange vigor, stopping now and then to say how happy he was of my company. In these moments, he was apt to scoop up the battered accordion he kept on the mantelpiece and launch into some antique war shanty or other, singing along with such abandon that you would have thought he, himself, had won the battle in question.

One morning I woke to find him leaning over my bed.

"Watson," he cried, "if anyone calls and says they are

the physical embodiment of Amon-Ra, I am *not in*!" He then disappeared into the confines of his bedroom and slammed the door. I was sure I could hear him barricading himself in there, piling his innumerable books against the door. We had no callers.

Then again, on days when we *did* have visitors, they were strange ones. Holmes would often beg use of the sitting room, preferring to send me to a teashop or Regent's Park, rather than allow me to sequester myself in my room. I would not have minded so much if these visits had not come at all hours and without warning. There was a little old lady from Dorset who came with the dawn one Saturday. A few dock workers stopped by over the next days. We had numerous visits from a peculiar little man named Lestrade—a Romanian fellow, judging by his accent. He was in his mid-fifties, beady of eye, pale and hunched. He was one of those who had a complaint for every occasion and seemed even less able to abide sunlight than Holmes.

My first overt clue as to Holmes's true nature came two weeks after we'd moved in, the day he sprang from his room, interrupting me in the middle of my luncheon.

"Watson! What a fine day, don't you think?"

I agreed that it was, despite the drizzle I could see through the window. He seemed not to hear me at all. Instead, he grabbed me by the arm and hauled me to my feet, suggesting, "How about a walk in the park?"

"What? Now?" I asked, as he dragged me towards the door.

"Gods, yes! Right now!"

"What about lunch?"

"It can wait," he said, handing me my hat and walking stick. Only as he was pushing me out into the hallway did I realize that he had not dressed himself for an excursion.

"Are you not coming?" I stammered.

"Oh, I've seen the park before," he answered, gazing distractedly over his shoulder. "You'll tell me if anything has changed, won't you?"

Suddenly the quiet was shattered by a beastly roar, from the direction of Holmes's bedroom.

"Ah! Damn! Enjoy the park, Watson!" he cried and pushed me bodily into the hall. The door slammed behind me. I had no intention of allowing the situation to pass unexplained, so I reached for the door handle to let myself back in. It burned me! Somehow, it had been heated to the point where it was unbearable to touch, even with gloves. From behind the door, Holmes yelled, "Be gone! You are unwelcome here!"

"But… I live here!"

"Not you, Watson, obviously," Holmes answered. "Best run along to the park though, eh? Don't want to miss the… er… pigeons or whatever."

Anything else he might have said was drowned out by a second hellish roar and the thud of heavy footfalls. Whatever company Holmes had, it possessed the voice of a lion and the grace of a rhinoceros. I banged upon the door and demanded to know what was going on in there, but was ignored. At last, lost for better options, I huffed my annoyance and left, ignoring the sounds of battle behind me. I allowed myself the expense of a paper from the boy at the corner and a cup of tea at a nearby café.

When I returned, an hour and a half later, I found Holmes contrite and welcoming. He asked as to the state of the park and I told him I had elected to go to a café instead. He said that sounded pleasant. I could not help but notice that half his face was bruised and swollen and that he seemed to have developed a limp. Our dining table had fared little better; one leg was broken and had been clumsily glued back together. The wastepaper basket was full of the remains of my lunch and the shards of the plate that had held it. On the table lay an ineptly prepared replacement lunch at which Holmes fired occasional nervous glances, hoping, no doubt, that I would fail to realize this was not the original.

"Holmes, what has happened here?" I demanded.

Sheepishly, he mumbled, "Look now, Watson, I think both of us would be happier if you could develop the habit of ignoring these little occurrences, eh? I shall replace anything that is damaged. I shall make things right, I promise. These matters are... private."

I hope you will not think less of me, dear reader, but I took his advice to heart. I buried myself in purposeful ignorance and did my utmost to ignore these oddities and outbursts. In this, I was merely displaying the common human reaction to unbelievable events, which is—just as the phrase implies—not to believe them. I did my best to carry on as if they had not occurred. And besides, was it not in my best interest to deny these perils? My clearest alternative to living at 221B Baker Street was to live in the gutter, just outside. My petty debts were almost cleared (notwithstanding the single sovereign I still owed Holmes) which engendered in me a love of this new situation, which no amount of domestic peculiarity could eradicate.

Indeed, my chief nemesis in those days was not Holmes, but our landlady, Mrs. Hudson. She was a tough old spinster, as advanced in age as she was regressed in height and interpersonal skills. She had the eyes of a weasel, the heart of a shrew and a scowl to rival any of the grand inquisitors who had so troubled Spain in the 1400s. She stood at about four foot nothing, in battered pink house slippers. Several times, as I prepared to leave our rooms, I would sweep the door open only to find her standing there, waiting to assault anybody who appeared with her disapproving stare, as if they had just done something unspeakable. What this crime against her sensibilities might be, I could not guess. Nor could I imagine how long she must have stood there, her nose all but touching the door, just waiting for someone to scowl at. Sometimes I feared she might have been there for days. I think she must have been a very lonely person. The only things she had for company were the hundreds— or perhaps thousands—of French romance novels she inexpertly concealed about the house. There was nothing *romantic* about them, merely biological. In fact, these books contained such a highly refined brand of smut as to render them illegal in each and every civilized country. Such was our hatred and fear of this hovering dwarf that Holmes and I formed a silent accord to release Mrs. Hudson from her contractual obligation to provide us with meals. Instead—at my direction and Holmes's expense— we built the little alcove beside the dining area into a proper pantry, jammed with cupboards, an icebox and a preparation table. The fireplace had a pivoting crane, from which we could hang a kettle, a pan, a pot, or even a grill, if needed. Usually though, Holmes's toast racks had pride of place.

It was a damned inconvenient way to get sustenance, yet infinitely preferable to dealing with Mrs. Hudson. We limited our reliance on her to the washing-up of dirty dishes. We would pile our used settings on a tray and leave this on the landing, outside our door. Occasionally, we would peep out and find that they had disappeared, or that they had been returned to us washed and quite often broken, out of sheer spite.

Regardless of these precautions, the peculiarity of our eating habits did attract her notice. One Thursday, after surviving a particularly vicious Hudson-scowling, Holmes slunk into our sitting room and muttered, "I think our landlady takes it amiss that I survive on toast and soup, Watson."

"I suspect she does," I said. "It is a most unusual trait."

"Well, damn! What am I supposed to do? Toast and soup quite suffice to provide all the nutrition I require!"

"Indeed."

"Why are people so particular about what they eat? Where do they find the time to worry over such things?"

His expression was one of animal desperation. I made no answer except to shrug. He paced the room for a few moments, sparing me an occasional nervous glance until— having worked up his courage, I presume—he approached and asked, "I say, Watson, I don't suppose... you'd help? That is... if you wouldn't mind... you could go down to the grocer and furnish us with some more suitable food? You know what people are meant to eat, don't you?"

"Of course I do."

"Well then, go get some, won't you? Have them deliver it here some time when old Mrs. Hudson is watching. Tell them they can present the bill to me. May I count upon you, Watson?"

"You may," I replied.

Later that day, I set off. At first I approached our nearest greengrocer, but at the last moment, a cruel idea occurred to me and I resolved to carry it out.

You see, I still had no notion as to Holmes's occupation or the source of his funds. Despite this, he seemed to have no concern over money, nor indeed did he place much value in it. When he needed me to go out so he could conduct his private business, he would often dispense a few shillings and encourage me to visit one of the local teashops. I don't know which I resented more: the fact that he did this, or the fact that I always accepted. Thus, I decided to test the limits of his fiscal disregard.

I directed my steps south to Fortnum & Mason's,

on Piccadilly. I knew of no other place so aloof, elite and criminally overpriced. I bought everything I could think of: the finest Ceylon tea, cakes, crumpets, French cheese, Italian wine, German beer, cold meats, greens and a truly singular marmalade I had admired once while lunching with the dean of my medical school. These I ordered in unnecessary quantities and asked that they be brought round at about two that afternoon. I hardly made it back before that hour myself, my legs being still uncertain. I pulled one of our sitting-room armchairs closer to the front window into a suitable vantage point to observe the coming exchange, sat and waited.

Promptly at two, Mrs. Hudson ushered up a pair of porters who deposited two large hampers on our dining table. I had ordered even more than I realized. The quantity was such that the two of us could scarce eat it all before it spoiled, and the bill would have raised eyebrows at Buckingham Palace. Warlock did not mind in the slightest. He paid without complaint, smiling all the while, then as our landlady retreated grumpily down the stairs, he called out, "I say, Mrs. Hudson, you must come around some time and join us for one of our *perfectly normal meals!*"

He then spun on his heel, whistled a cheerful jig, stepped over to our fireplace and proceeded to make himself his usual: toast and soup. He seemed to have no desire to examine his newly acquired mountain of victuals or even remove it from the table. He may not have been tempted, but I certainly was and, I confess, I proceeded to eat him out of house and home.

Thus it was that, on that fateful Saturday, Holmes interrupted me in the middle of my fourth consecutive marmalade crumpet. I had been stuffing myself insensible for three days running. Holmes stepped out of his bedroom, gave me a nod and opened his mouth to mutter some pleasantry or other. Yet, it never came. All of a sudden, he stiffened as if stricken. His spine arched, his face contorted, he threw back his head and his eyes shone with such an intense brightness that I swear they illuminated a circle of the ceiling above him. In that strangely deep voice he had used the day we met, he intoned, *"On the eleventh hour of the fifth day of the month of nine, thou shalt receive a dire messenger! The sea hath refused him—his sheep cast loose upon the waves to wander uncommanded. Fear him, for in his hand lies the mark of the reaper! Death brought him hither and discovery shall be thy fate, Holmes, if thou darest attend his challenge!"*

At that moment, his spine lost all its rigor and he crumpled to the floor in a heap. Tossing the crumpet to my plate, I ran to attend him. I found him shaking, sweating, even more pallid than usual.

"What is wrong, Holmes? What has happened to you?"

"Oh... why... nothing, Watson..." he stammered, his voice weak and uncertain, "I was... I was practicing for a play, you see."

"A play?" I demanded, incredulous.

"Yes. Yes. A play, that is all."

"Much as I wish to believe you," I said, "I cannot help but reflect that the only people who rehearse for plays are those people who are actually *in a play*. Which you are not, I think you will recall."

"Ah... yes. Well, no," he spluttered, "but I hope to be. I practice this play, every year, in case some theater mounts it. Then I shall be ready to audition."

"What is the name of this play?" I pressed.

"Uh... *The Dread Messenger*, of course," he answered, then changed the subject. "I say, Watson, what day is it?"

"November the fifth," I said.

"And what time?" he asked.

"Ah... three minutes to eleven."

"But... that makes no sense, does it?" Holmes wondered aloud. I was sure he hoped I'd failed to notice his fell prognostication, but such was his confusion with his own message that he could not help but stop to puzzle it out. "Month of nine? September?"

"There was some curious word choice, you know," I reflected. "September may be the ninth month, but it is named for the Latin-derived term for seven: *sept. Oct* is eight; *nov* is nine; *dec* is ten. So, though the months are effectively named 'Sevenmonth,' 'Eightmonth,' 'Ninemonth' and 'Tenmonth,' their numbers no longer match their names."

"Curious," said Holmes. "So, if it means the ninth month, then this warning relates to something that happened two months ago or which will happen, nearly a year hence."

"That is correct."

"Yet, if it relates to the proper name 'Month of Nine' or 'Ninemonth,' then it references an event which will occur..."

As I could see he was having difficulty with the mathematics, I chose to inform him, "Roughly two minutes from now."

"What? Oh! Wonderful! *Wonderful!* Thank you for the *ample* warning, Moriarty," he howled, then, "Watson, help me up! I must reach the window."

I pulled him to his feet and towards the armchair by our front window, thinking to deposit him in it, but he had no intention of resting. He propped himself on the windowsill and scanned the street below.

"There," he said, pointing. "That man there."

"That man?" I asked, peering at the large, hunch-shouldered figure he indicated. "Who is he?"

"He is a retired sergeant of the Royal Marines," Holmes said. "He's coming here."

"Why?"

"There has been a murder, I think."

3

THE CARRIAGE BOUNCED ALONG, OVER THE COBBLESTONE streets, shaking the already pale Warlock Holmes where he slumped in the corner. He looked as one who is in the very depths of pneumonia, but he had absolutely refused rest. Our strange visitor—who had indeed been a recently retired sergeant of the Royal Marines—had come to deliver a letter. This proved to be the oddest missive I had ever seen, but the messenger seemed afraid of Holmes and would not tarry to explain it. As soon as he left us, Holmes resolved to set out immediately. He tottered to the hook by the door, donned his long tweed coat and that peculiar hat of his. I had never seen its like. He said it was called a soulstalker. Still unsteady on his feet, he asked to borrow my walking stick—which I happily lent him—then sent me into the street to hire a cab. Holmes asked the driver to hurry to 3 Lauriston Gardens and collapsed into the corner of the carriage.

"Holmes," I said, "you look terrible. Why are we rushing to answer this strange summons?"

"Because Moriarty told me not to," he said, staring out the window at the gray streets.

"And who precisely is this Moriarty?" I inquired.

"Nobody you ought to have any dealings with, if you can help it."

"Well, so you say, but it is a very strange business and I don't understand—"

"Yes, it is a strange business, but it is *my* business," Holmes interrupted, "and the mere strangeness of it cannot contrive to make it any other man's!"

I demurred. This is a plea that cannot be ignored by an English gentleman, under any circumstances. The day an Englishman turns to any other and says, "Isn't it strange that none of us get married until our thirties, yet when we do, it is to enjoy the 'pleasures of the hearth,' rather than out of fifteen to twenty years of pent-up sexual frustration? On what I'm sure is an unrelated note: I can't help but notice our streets are choked with 'flower girls,' yet I never see anybody carrying newly purchased flowers. In fact, you yourself seem to visit the flower girls two or three times a day, but you never bring flowers to work. Or home. Or to the doctor's office, where you go twice a week to combat your magnificent array of venereal diseases..." Well... that would be the day all our lies unravel and our society collapses. Thus, we doggedly afford each other the luxury to conduct our own matters.

"As you say," I conceded.

"Read me the letter again, won't you?" Holmes asked—to change the subject, I think.

I leaned over, pulled the letter from Holmes's hand and read:

bey warlok

Fownd a ded guy. whys he ded? I cant
tel. Dont look like no one smote him
or nothin. No ax. No hamr. Emty room.
Emty house. whys he ded? I em hungry.
you help. Numbur 3 Loristin Gardins.

Blud and onur
Torg Grogsson

I rubbed the letter with my thumbs, wiping away
smears of dirt, blood and strawberry jam, musing, "This
has to be a hoax."

"It is quite genuine, I assure you," said Holmes,
shaking his head gravely.

"But who would... who would write such a thing?"

"Torg Grogsson, just as it says."

"Well yes, but what manner of man..."

"He is a detective inspector at Scotland Yard," Holmes
said.

"Surely not!" I began to laugh, in spite of myself.

"He is, I assure you," Holmes shot back, "and a quite
effective one at that. Perhaps he is not the finest example
of reason or observational prowess, but there is more to
police work than just that, Watson. When you meet him, I
think you will realize why."

"Why?" I pressed, unwilling to wait.

"The last word of that letter—before his name—which

you read '*on-uhr*,' is in fact '*honor*.' It is the topic dearest to his heart. When you meet him, examine him carefully and ask yourself what might become of you if Torg Grogsson ever caught you in a lie."

Warlock turned to the window, threw his arms across his chest and settled into one of his sulks. I realized I had insulted a friend of his. As luck would have it, I had another topic I was all too willing to address.

"Holmes... that messenger..."

"Yes?" he snapped.

"How did you know him to be a retired Royal Marines sergeant?"

A look of extreme weariness crossed his features and he looked over at me as if he were a nine-year-old lad whom I had just found with one hand on my teacake and the other in my wallet. His eyes bespoke exhaustion and they sought mine, begging with a glance to be excused the labor of explaining. I said nothing, so he heaved a sigh and began, "Simple observation, of course. His left boot was spattered with a unique red mud, particular to a puddle outside the Royal Marines... sergeants'... pension... dispensing office, or whatever they call it."

"Is this unique red mud akin to the sample which told you I was staying at the Hotel d'Amsterdam?"

"Don't be cynical, Watson."

"I think his boots were clean, Holmes."

"I assure you, they were not."

"There is no sense arguing about it," I said. "It is an easily settled matter. When we get home, we shall see if there is any dried red mud upon our carpet."

That upset Holmes. He began to stammer, "I wonder, did you note the tattoo on his left forearm?"

Holmes seemed to have forgotten that our guest had been wearing a greatcoat. Either that or he'd forgotten greatcoats have sleeves.

"I didn't," I said.

"Well he had one and it was a large blue anchor and it said 'Royal Marines, Sergeant, Retired, 1869–1880.'"

I was sure our visitor had had no such thing, or at least that Warlock would have had no opportunity to see it.

"Really?" I pondered. "That's a peculiar tattoo, don't you think?"

"He was a peculiar man," Holmes said.

"What would drive a man to get such a tattoo, do you suppose?"

Holmes shrugged.

"Perhaps he was concerned that if ever he should die, and be discovered with no identification on his person, that the coroner would be unable to establish his *previous occupation?*"

"Look here, Watson, I cannot surmise what drove the man to favor such a tattoo; I merely observed that he had one."

"Odd that I overlooked it."

"Hardly," Holmes countered. "Most people *see*, but they do not *observe*. There is a difference between seeing a thing and observing it."

"I know," I told him. "I'm a doctor."

But he continued unabated. "For example, Watson, how many times would you say you had traveled up or down the staircase from our rooms to the street?"

Having been now about three weeks in his company, I estimated, "Fifty or so."

"Then you have *seen* those steps fifty times, Watson. I wonder, have you ever *observed* how many there are?"

"Seventeen."

"There are, in fact, seve—oh… yes. Seventeen."

For a moment, he sunk back into his sulk, then jerked towards me with sudden vigor. He fixed me with a hideous grin, his green eyes burning, and demanded in his deeper voice, "But tell me, Watson, do you know their true names? If ever you should have to call upon the power, the loyalty of those steps, what name would you call them by, mortal?"

I confess, I cried out and shied back towards the opposite corner of the carriage, sputtering, "Ah! Holmes! Really! Really now, I'm not sure such a thing as steps should have names."

"Ro'glugh!" he shouted.

"I say!"

"Griegh'eh!"

"What?"

"Mek-ek, Fef, Uhl," he continued.

"Holmes, are you quite all right?"

"Hregah, Vie, Doff, Seff, Geg'ar, Zhess, Jierg, Bhe'dei, Mur, Mech'hel, Jekh'hel and *Squeeee-errk-ka-reeek*!"

"The creaky one, third from the top!" I gasped.

"Your instinct serves you well," he said and began to issue a slow, deep laugh.

"This is highly irregular, Holmes!" I said, but he would not cease his morbid laughter. Seizing the initiative, I demanded, "I wonder, would you say that a retired Royal Marines sergeant had been refused by the sea, leaving his sheep to wander uncommanded upon the waves?"

"*I* would not," he laughed, vaguely.

"And yet you did."

"What? Did I?"

"Just before the man appeared," I said.

"Out loud? Damn!" The fire in his eyes cooled and he drooped once more into his seat, muttering, "I hate that Moriarty..."

We rode along in silence for a while. His breaths came ragged and tired. I stared at him. He was my deliverance from poverty, and I quite liked him, on a personal level. I had the sense he needed me. Still, there was so much of the inexplicable and dangerous about him, I half thought I should throw myself from the cab, take to my heels and not stop until I found myself master of a Jamaican cotton plantation. I told myself I would if the need arose, and gazed out the window to distract myself from the unwelcome thoughts that flooded in upon my repose.

The morning was dreary. Though the rain of the past evening had abated, the low, oppressive clouds hung heavy with the threat of more. There is something malicious about November drizzle in London. It is always cold, unwelcome and delivered at the most fiendishly inconvenient times.

The cab-horse was a veteran of some years' service, with the rhythmic gait to prove it, but even he stumbled once or twice over irregular cobbles.

"Why did we come?" I asked.

Holmes said nothing.

"Why does a detective inspector of Scotland Yard ask the help of a... of you?"

Still staring out his window at the gray mass of London, Holmes admitted, "I am a sort of... consulting detective."

"But, what does that mean? What is a consulting detective? I have never heard of such a thing."

"No, well you wouldn't have. I am the only one. It means that when certain individuals encounter a crime that they cannot solve, they call upon my powers.

"Of observation!" he quickly added.

"Quite," I said, but I couldn't help reflecting, "You know, Holmes, Scotland Yard has always seemed to project such an air of superiority that if God himself were to descend and offer to help them find the Holy Grail, they'd ask to see his badge."

Holmes nodded and agreed, "I don't work with the Yard often. Or anyway, I don't work with most of them at all. But if Grogsson or Lestrade need my help, I must answer."

"Lestrade? That queer little man who comes to visit?"

"The same," Holmes said.

"And they pay you for your help?"

He sighed again, heavily. "No."

"Ah, then you are credited with solving the crime, which helps build your reputation for private practice?"

"No."

"Then, Holmes, why are we going?"

"Understand, Watson, the Yard and I... we get on rather poorly."

"Why?"

"It can hardly have escaped your notice that I am an unusual sort of man."

"It has not," I agreed.

"To their way of thinking, I am a guilty outsider if ever there was one. Whenever there is a crime with... unusual characteristics, I must solve it as rapidly as possible, or expect to be accused of it, in short order."

"I see," I said, "and you assume this to be such a crime?"

"No," he shrugged. "Or rather, I don't know. It's just that Grogsson and Lestrade are... unusual gentlemen themselves. Despite their positions, the rest of Scotland Yard seems to harbor almost as much suspicion of them as they do of me. Yet, these two are my only friends there. It is of some importance to my continued freedom to ensure that Grogsson and Lestrade remain the most effective inspectors on the entire force. So long as they continue to solve cases the others cannot, they are safe and so am I. So no, Watson, there is no money in this for me and no recognition, only safety. That is why I am going."

He settled back into his thoughts for a moment then suddenly sprang up and exclaimed, "Oh! Hey now! Why are *you* going?"

I was embarrassed to admit I didn't quite know. I'm

sure I must have said something about abandoning a friend or the duty of a doctor to see to a seizure victim. But that was not the truth of it.

Why was I in that cab?

I had always considered myself a creature governed by reason; clearly, I had seen enough to know that Holmes was dangerous to me and dangerous to the fundamental foundation of my worldview, as well. Yet that, I suppose, was the very bait that had caught me. I realize that most men will shy away from a thing that contradicts their understanding. I admit I had done it too, ignoring Holmes's supernatural nature for as long as I could manage. But eventually, awe and wonder overruled my fear. There is nothing so intoxicating to the scientific mind as the weird and unfamiliar.

The fundamental basis of scientific thought is that an observed truth that undermines one's understanding is yet the truth. If the observation is not flawed, one's previous understanding must be. To the open mind, this is not a crisis; it is an opportunity to form a new, more perfect understanding of the world. Did I ever abandon science for a belief in magic, as some people may accuse? Never. Rather, I included magic in my understanding of the physical phenomena that shape our world. Science is a path to knowledge—one that must include and explain every observable fact, embracing all and rejecting none.

So, there is the professor's answer. To the reader who cares not a whit for science or the scientist, let me say: curiosity. That's why I went. I was curious, all right?

Of course, that day in the cab, I had no ready answer. All I could do was stammer half-truths until I looked out the window and noted, "Lauriston Gardens! We're practically there, Holmes."

Holmes rapped on the ceiling with my walking stick and called, "Driver, stop here."

4

I WALKED CALMLY DOWN THE STREET TOWARDS 3 Lauriston Gardens. Holmes did not. On the pretense of investigation, he ducked behind every single hedge we passed. Occasionally, he would break a leaf between his fingers and examine the sap, or rub his finger against a brick in one of the neighbor's walls and say, "Yes, that's all very well, but I wonder…" The closer we got to Number 3, the slower his pace became. At last, he eschewed the pavement altogether and slunk from lawn to lawn, hopping over the walls when he thought himself unobserved. I waited patiently in the street. Or rather, let us say, I waited in the street. I deduced that Holmes must have some compunction about actually arriving at 3 Lauriston Gardens, but could not guess what it might be. It remained a mystery, until the constable guarding the front door saw him pop up over the garden wall.

"Oi! It's you!" the officer shouted, face reddening. At Holmes's chest he leveled one finger—it shook, nearly bursting with the strain of containing so much vehemence and accusation.

Warlock stopped, halfway over the wall, frozen like a deer in a hunter's sights. "No it isn't!"

But the constable's whistle was already at his lips. He blew three sharp blasts and shouted for his fellows, then turned to Holmes—who was engaged in extricating his trouser leg from the wrought-iron railings that topped the wall—and cried, "Warlock 'olmes, I charge you stand in the name o' th' lawr!"

Warlock didn't stand. Instead he toppled backwards into the neighbor's azaleas, shrieking. When at last he was free of both masonry and shrubbery, he endeavored to take to his heels, but accomplished no more than three steps before being tackled by two burly constables. A third arrived a few moments later, huffing and panting. He must have been embarrassed to have missed the apprehension, for he made a point of re-tackling Holmes, right out of the arms of his comrades.

My walking stick bounced free of the melee and clattered into the street. I made sure to recover it before wading in to save my friend. It is good to have something to lean on when dealing with constables—they can be tiring.

"Wait! I didn't do it this time!" Warlock was protesting as I approached. "Oh! I mean: ever! That's what I meant to say: I didn't do it, ever!"

"Officers, what is the meaning of this?" I inquired, in my most imperious tone.

"We har hengaged into th' haprehension of this suspicious hindividual! Stand haway, sir!" One of the peculiarities of London's police force is that they are all recruited from areas of Britain where folk use no h's at all, or far too many.

I almost protested that Warlock Holmes was not a suspicious individual, but caught my tongue just in time; it was not an argument I could have won. Instead, I told the red-faced constable, "This gentleman, whom you have just collared, is here on the particular request of Detective Inspector Grogsson, to assist in the solution of this crime."

"I don' know habout that," he said. I rolled my eyes at the man, reached into Warlock's overcoat and withdrew Grogsson's letter. I presented it to the constable, who glared at it for the barest instant before huffing his disapproval and waving his friends away.

"We don't need none o' 'is mumbo-jumbo," one of them protested, as he wandered back to his post. Warlock gave me a look of deep relief and sidled away towards the garden path, by the side of the house.

"Hand 'oo might you be then, my fine friend?" the constable barked at me, as if the murderer might make the mistake of approaching the police to argue the innocence of other suspects.

"My name is Dr. John Watson; I am here as a friend of Warlock and to lend my knowledge to the case. You may want to take note of my name and address, Constable, in case anybody asks you to identify me later."

He nodded curtly, as if to say that was going to be the next thing out of his mouth (which it was not, of a certainty) and began searching his pockets for a notebook and stub of pencil. He took down my information and even ventured to get a little free work done, which is a hazard of my trade.

"Medical doctor, then?" he inquired.

"I am."

"Hi wonder 'f you'd take a look at me back, Dr. Watson, sir. Pains me somethin' hawful now."

"No need, man. There are three courses of cure for you: take the clerk's position the next time they offer it, spend more on shoes, or spend less on pastries," I said, gazing around his bulk towards the door.

"Hoi! Wait there! I said me back!"

"Your back is in sad shape because you have been walking your beat far too long in cheap shoes on cobblestones. The whole situation is not aided, Constable, by the fact that you have doubled your weight since joining the force—observe the stretch marks on your neck and your original-issue academy stockings, which are swollen almost to bursting. This has ruined your feet and the waddling gait you have adopted to pamper them has begun to work upon your spine. I am told that should a constable break his leg, it's considered poor form to take him out behind the station house and shoot him. Instead, the force finds desk jobs for its physically unsound members. If they haven't offered you sedentary employment already, they soon shall. Accept it. Now, I feel I must reclaim my friend and address the matter of the day, if you please."

"Very well, Doctor," he replied. "And here's some hadvice in payment: you need to consider more carefully the comp'ny you keep."

I found Warlock crouching over a patch of mud by the garden path, absorbed in the examination of some characters scrawled in the dirt. Some of it was in our Roman alphabet, but in pseudo–Latin phrases that made no particular sense. Much of it was symbolic in nature—drawings of little stick-figure constables with daggers stuck in them.

"Look, Watson!" Warlock enthused. "*Someone* has inscribed symbols of ancient power, right here, beside the crime scene!"

"Have they?" I inquired, observing his muddy index finger. "What is the meaning of it, do you think?"

"Who can say, Watson; who can say?" he piped, springing to his feet. "Well, I suppose we ought to examine the scene, eh?"

"Let's," I agreed and we strode past the angry constable at the door and into the house.

We found ourselves in a gloomy hallway, which led us to an equally dank sitting room. There was a dead man, lying face up with eyes wide and a rolled piece of paper jutting from his mouth. Disconcerting to some, perhaps, but I had seen dead men before. There was blood on the floor, but a doctor is no stranger to such sights.

No, the thing that stopped me cold in my tracks was Detective Inspector Torg Grogsson. The room seemed barely able to contain him and his clothes had an even harder job of it. He stood at least seven feet tall. I could not swear to the exact measurement, for at that moment he was bunched up against the ceiling, unable to straighten to his full height.

His shoulders were broader than most men are tall and every seam of his brown tweed suit stretched and groaned to contain the muscles that bulged against them. Through many of these belabored seams jutted tufts of spiky brown hair, which I suppose must have covered most of him, in the fashion of an ape. The stubble on his chin looked as if it would serve as sandpaper and he scraped at it constantly with a silver-plated straight razor. His fists were wrapped in cloth as a prizefighter's and upon his head was perched a battered bowler. When we first met I could not imagine what might work such ruin upon an innocent hat, but I soon discovered the source of the damage. In spite of his height, Grogsson had a habit of failing to duck under doorways. The lack of care he took with his own head was alarming.

When he saw my companion, his jutting brow relaxed and he grumbled, "Warlock! Good! You're come!"

"Good afternoon, Inspector," Warlock said, then turned to the shadowy corner behind us and added, "Inspector Lestrade."

I hadn't noticed at first, but there was our queer little Romanian visitor. He lurked in the darkest corner over one of the pools of blood that dotted the floor. He had traces of that blood on his fingers and on his lips. He was entirely silent. I would have been prepared to swear he was not even breathing, until he drew air to say, "What is this, Holmes? Have you brought your fellow lodger?"

"I have, Vladislav. You may trust him. He is sympathetic to peculiar individuals," said Holmes, then grinned at me and added, "Surprisingly sympathetic, I must say."

I smiled, wanly. Lestrade smiled back. I nearly cried out. His lips drew back much further and higher than a normal person's ought, revealing a maw of overlapping fangs. As I watched, they grew, sliding from his gums until each of his teeth, from the front to the very rear, was a curved white knife. At least I understood why he had always been so tight-lipped when he spoke.

"Well then, let us bid farewell to the world of men," Lestrade suggested, but rather than embark upon a mystic journey to a faerie realm, he simply shut the sitting-room door.

In all my strange adventures with Warlock Holmes, that is the moment I came closest to washing my hands of the whole business. Perhaps if I had not been too terrified to move, I might have run away and never more associated myself with Warlock or his "peculiar" friends. I didn't. I stayed. And in that moment, my illusions fell from me. Despite what I believed to be true about my world, despite all my medical knowledge, I was forced to admit that the room certainly appeared to contain an ogre, a vampire, a warlock and a dead man. Oh, and myself, of course. Ignorant of Holmes's true powers, impotent against Grogsson's strength, no more than a tasty treat to Inspector Lestrade—there I stood.

5

I CANNOT RECALL WHAT I EXPECTED TO HAPPEN NEXT. Did I anticipate some sort of black mass? That my hideous companions would fall upon the corpse and devour it? Creeping shadows? Chanting? Perhaps I was too involved in my terror to anticipate anything at all.

In any case, I was heartily relieved when they started doing police work. It was in no way supernatural and it was also in no way... competent. Grogsson seemed unable to talk about the corpse without giving it a derisive little nudge with his foot, quite disturbing the crime scene. Vladislav Lestrade had a professional demeanor, compared to the others, but could not stop himself dipping his fingers in the congealing pools of blood and sucking at them greedily. Warlock raised a magnifying glass to his eye and began looking all about the room.

"What is that device for?" I asked.

"Ah," he said, as if divulging a great secret, "only look at my face and you shall know! It makes one of my eyes look large and disconcerting!"

That it did. Though nobody asked me, I endeavored

"It makes one of my eyes look large and disconcerting!"

to help. Understand, I had no knowledge of investigative practice. At least, I had no knowledge of investigating *a crime*. Then again, what does a doctor do but *investigate* illness? Each disease leaves its mark—its signature—for any man with the wit to spy it out. My instinct was to approach crime-solving with the medical method; to observe the symptoms, their effects and aftermath, and from that data, determine the cause. By happy chance, this proved to be an apt method.

I began with the object most familiar to me: the human body. This particular specimen was approximately forty years of age and utterly without friends. I assumed this last part, but his expression, even in death, was one of an insufferable, self-centered blowhard. I cannot explain what gave this impression, only that upon entering the room and beholding him, one got the feeling that he was much more fun to be around now than he had been while living. There were no visible wounds on his body. I concluded that, if it were not for the note in his mouth, there would be no reason to judge this a murder. It had every appearance of a heart attack. The only strange thing about the body was the smell. It reeked of alcohol, but there was something else as well, a bitter tang not native to corpses, whiskey, or any food I knew. Poison, I surmised.

Despite the lack of wounds upon the corpse, the room contained a notable quantity of blood. There were no spatters upon the walls, such as one might expect from a sword-swing or gunshot. Rather, it was spread across the floor, mostly in small droplets. There were a few puddles of it, one only a few feet from the corpse, near the door. I guessed it must be the murderer's blood, unless there was another victim. Probably this man's killer had some slow-bleeding injury or other and the puddles represented spots where he had stood for a time. He must have paused by the door to watch the victim expire. The blood was O negative, as I learned from Lestrade, who practically moaned, "Rare. This is rare. Such blood would sustain any human into whom it was suffused. This blood is the purest; bringing life to all, death to none. Oh, rare…"

A search of the man's pockets revealed more clues. He had personal cards; they listed no occupation, but gave his name as Enoch Drebber. He had a wallet, with several banknotes still in it (until Grogsson snatched them), so theft was clearly not the motive. Nor had the killer taken much care to obscure the victim's identity.

"I think he was American," I mused. "See here, he carried his wallet in his back pocket, in the American style, rather than in his breast pocket. And look, it is stamped with the motif of a bull's head within a star. I can think of no people barbaric enough to fashion such a monstrosity; none but the Texans."

Yet, the best clue—and also the most baffling—was the paper in his mouth. I drew it out, employing my surgical practice of slow and steady hands. It is well I took such care, for the artifact was fragile in the extreme. It was wax paper, yellowed and brittle with age. It bore the marks of having been carefully folded and kept for some time. Unrolling and then unfolding it, I beheld the faded logo of

Hall and Sons' Bakery, St. Louis, Missouri.

"That!" Warlock cried. "Give me that! I had nothing until now, but this—this is precious to someone."

"How can you tell?" I asked.

"Oh... well... you know... observation?"

Since his tone was so desperate, I elected to bail him out. "I see. You suppose its good condition, despite its fragility and age, means someone has gone to pains to see it preserved, thus proving that it is not rubbish, but treasure to them?"

"Quite right, Watson, quite right," Warlock said, with a relieved sigh. He turned the paper over and over in his hands, folded it gingerly and placed it in his breast pocket, saying, "He should not have left it; I'll have him now."

Precisely how he intended to lure the murderer with a baked-goods wrapper was beyond the reach of my reason. Then again, I realized that reason would only carry me so far, in this present company. I began to examine the room and, after only a moment, gave a cry of discovery.

"Look here!" I called to my companions. "Here, scrawled on the wall, in blood. It's a word! Somebody has written '*Rache*.'"

"No!" insisted the vampire Lestrade. "Not possible. It was not there before; I would have smelled it."

"I shouldn't pay much attention to that," Warlock said. "It has nothing to do with the murder."

I was quite taken aback and demanded to know, "How can you say that, Holmes? '*Rache*' is German for 'revenge'! Surely this is a fine clue!"

"No. It isn't," he said.

"Revenge." Grogsson smiled; it was one of his favorite words.

"This was not here when you came in," Lestrade insisted.

"It must have been," I said. "None of us has been near this wall. And anyway, why would we wish to write 'revenge' in German, in blood, on a wall?"

Holmes turned on me, wagging his finger, and said, "Dr. Watson, *if* you recall, before you moved in with me, I distinctly warned you that certain objects, notably walls, are likely to bleed in my company. When I listed my faults as a living companion, I told you to expect bloody messages to appear in German, Latin and Sanskrit."

"Excuse me, you did not!"

"Oh. Did I not?" replied Holmes, with a sheepish look. "I ought to have. Anyway, it's nothing to do with the murder. Lestrade, you can have it, if you like."

"I'll not be touching that," he said, staring at it as if it were... well, the word 'revenge' scrawled in blood. In retrospect, I suppose revulsion should have been a common reaction and unusual only for Lestrade.

"Ahem... well... I suppose we must try to determine who he was," I suggested, indicating the body of Enoch Drebber.

"Easier said than done," Holmes shrugged. "I suppose we—"

He did not finish, for in that moment, his spine spasmed and stiffened. He threw back his head and his green eyes lit the ceiling once more. Quicker than I thought possible, Lestrade's hands flashed to his pocket and emerged holding a notebook and pencil. With these, he took notes in a positive blur as Warlock recited, "*He is Enoch, of the Latter Day Saints, fallen from grace, fallen from life, soiled and sotten, spoiled before he fell. From the dry dusts of wild Mojave, he is come in company. Seek ye Joseph, Son of Stranger; their steps lie side by side, their fates intertwined. Enoch the master; Joseph the man. Clerk. Secretary. Brother in faith and blackest crime!* Rache! Rache! *Justice comes upon the wicked! The finder knows! He that beheld the work beheld him that did the deed!*"

This must have represented his entire opinion on the matter for, as soon as he had finished venting it, Warlock gave a satisfied little smile and then collapsed, face first, to the floor. Lestrade must have been used to such spectacles, for without moving to see to Holmes at all, he began to read over the strange speech he'd just transcribed into his notebook. He tapped his horrid fangs with the end of his pencil and muttered, "So, two of them, then. American— just as you guessed, Dr. Watson. Enoch Drebber, we have; now for this Joseph Strangerson…"

"Did we… did we have a last name?" I asked from where I crouched, a comforting hand resting on Warlock's twitching shoulder.

"Son of Stranger," Lestrade said. "That's 'Strangerson,' almost certain. Spend more time with Holmes and you'll start picking up on these things."

It boggled me, but I began considering. "If what Holmes said is true…"

"Yup," Grogsson grunted. "Always true."

"Well if they are American visitors, they must be staying somewhere," I reflected. "Can you Scotland Yard fellows figure out where?"

"Maybe," Grogsson said, distastefully. "Lots uh work."

"Ah!" I said, snapping my fingers. "The finder! He that beheld the work! Who found the body? Is he still here?"

Lestrade flipped through his notebook for a moment and said, "A constable, John Rance. He went home. Got his address here, if you want it."

"I want it," I said. "Perhaps on the way back to Baker Street, Warlock and I might stop by to see if he really did behold him that did the deed!"

6

THIS IS HOW I KNOW MYSELF TO BE A MAN OF NO GREAT intelligence: in the cab, I was giddy with anticipation. When I was surrounded by doctors and nurses, who wished me to heal, I had been sullen and disconsolate. Now, surrounded by monsters and corpses, tracing the steps of a murderer, I could not have been merrier. The streets between Lauriston Gardens and Audley Court were every bit as dreary as the ones we'd journeyed through earlier. Yet somehow, in spite of the cold grayness of London, everything seemed to sparkle with possibility and intrigue. If we had not had a cab, I should have run to John Rance's house.

46 Audley Court was a humble dwelling, but I liked John Rance immediately, he being one of only three London constables who understood the letter H. Rance was tired. After all, he'd just come off an extra-long shift, with the added stress of having discovered a murder. He didn't wish to speak to us at first, insisting he had already given a full report and police business was not to be disclosed to strange men who knocked upon your door just as you were beginning to dream. I'll admit, he had me there. I began

to despair of having any help from him, until his eyes fell and locked upon the half-sovereign Warlock was fidgeting with as he waited for me to conclude my business. Rance looked away from it when he addressed me, but his eyes always wandered back to the coin. He licked his lips. I had an idea.

"Warlock, you should put that away, lest you lose it," I said.

"How would I lose it? It's right here, in my hand."

"It is, but what if we went in and sat down with John, here? Suppose we sat in his kitchen and discussed what he saw. Why, when you got up again, you might well forget it and leave it on his table."

"Unlikely," he scoffed.

"Very likely," said I. "In fact, I am *certain* that is exactly what is going to happen."

"Really?" asked Holmes.

"Yes," I said, eyeing Rance.

Holmes regarded me with wonder and asked, "How can you tell?"

In the end, Rance and I induced him to realize that we meant it as a bribe. I did feel a pang of guilt. Not only was I corrupting a constable (only slightly, I suppose), but I had also been rather free with Holmes's money the previous week. Still, it was a coin well spent, for it yielded quite a story.

Rance told us how he was drawn into the house at 3 Lauriston Gardens by the sight of a burning candle. His beat carried him past the house every day, so he knew it ought to be vacant. Drebber was quite dead when Rance found him and the room was empty of furniture and feature, other than the dead man with the note in his mouth and the pools of blood. Rance then ran back to the street and blew his whistle to summon the nearest fellow constable. When his comrade arrived, Rance sent him running to the local station for help while he himself stayed to guard the scene. It was well he did, for that is where his story took an interesting turn.

"And what did you see after that?" I asked him.

He shrugged. "Naught worth notin' if you take my meanin', sir. Rain fallin', dargs barkin', drunks swervin'."

"Drunks?" I asked.

"Just one drunk, I guess."

"Tell me about him."

"Well... he was drunk," Rance began, lamely. "Come up to me cryin' bout this donut of his."

"Donut?" I wondered. "Exactly what is that?"

"Some sort of pastry they've got over in the United States," Rance explained. "I take it to be somethin' like a real sweet crumpet, with a hole poked in, cooked in hot oil."

"A hole?"

"Yeah, right through the middle."

"And exactly why," I wished to know, "would any man in his right mind wish to pay another man to poke a hole in his crumpet?"

Rance shrugged again. "Might be some advantage to it..."

"Such as?"

"Well, just think: you could hang fifty of 'em on a rod

or a wire. Dip 'em in and cook 'em all at once, then pull the rod up and hang 'em all up to cool, neat as you like."

I gasped. I suppose I may have shed a tear then, for England and her empire. What hope was there for us? Against a people who would destroy the stately majesty of our favorite breakfast treat; a people who had actually *industrialized the crumpet*—how could we compete? The decline of our empire was thus presaged to me—as plain as a hole in a crumpet.

"Monstrous," I muttered.

"Anyways," Rance continued, "that drunk was lookin' for one. Said he left it somewhere thereabouts and missed it summat terrible. Wanted me to find it, or any trace of it. Asked if I'd seen the wrapper, even."

Warlock and I exchanged a loaded glance. I asked Rance, "What did you say to him?"

"Told him to stumble off, didn't I? Had other worries last night, I did."

"I wonder, Constable Rance, did you examine the note in the dead man's mouth?"

"No, sir! I don't go messin' with no scene of no crime, not when 'spector Lestrade is comin'! He'd have my skin, he would. Mind, if Grogsson's got the case, you might as well rifle the body, rob the place and draw a moustache on the corpse; he wouldn't mind."

"I suppose not," I agreed, then asked, "What became of the drunk?"

"Oh, he didn't want to go. I had to load him back into his cab and send him on his way."

"He had a cab waiting?"

"No, sir, it was his cab. He were the cabby. Lots o' them fellows drink more than they ought."

I had a growing doubt that the man had been drunk at all. Perhaps he'd been faking to seem less suspicious, or perhaps had been overwrought with emotion, having just killed a man. No, the actions of this killer—this poisoner—were calculated and sober. The fact that he had asked after the wrapper did make me suppose that Warlock's prognostication was correct and this cabby had indeed been the killer. I asked Rance, "What had he been drinking?"

"How should I know?" he replied.

"Surely a constable on a beat like that knows the smell of whiskey! And wine, and gin. Which was it?"

"Er... I don't recall smellin' nothin' like that, sir."

This was as I had expected, though I could hardly take it as concrete proof that the man wasn't drunk. John Rance, though well-meaning and dutiful, was not an especially observant patrolman. Even his physical description of the subject was lackluster. The man had been large and athletically built, he recalled, with ruddy hair and an unkempt beard. His clothes were of standard workman's cut and quality. Rance remembered the man had an unusual accent, but couldn't place it. In the end, there was nothing to do but thank him and be on our way. As we left, I told Holmes, "I think we have it right; given Rance's description, the fact that the wrapper is from Missouri and the murderer's use of the word 'donut,' the overwhelming likelihood is that we are looking for an American-born cab driver."

Holmes nodded and said, "I too believe I have discovered a fact that will be pivotal to the solution of this case."

"And what is that?" I asked.

Holmes smiled. "That my new friend, John, is really good at this sort of thing."

7

EVEN IN MY PRIME, THE DAY'S EXERTIONS AND excitement would have caused me some weariness. But I was not in my prime; I was still recovering from my shoulder-shot, gut-sick Afghan misadventure. Thus, the instant we reached 221B Baker Street, I collapsed into my armchair before the hearth and slept.

I woke at a quarter to eight, famished and bedewed with my own drool. It was not my hunger but the slamming door that stirred me from my rest. Holmes rushed in with the evening paper in his hands and a look of terror upon his face. "On your feet, Watson, the game is afoot and the wolf at our door! Or anyway, he should be at our door in as little as fifteen minutes."

Rubbing the sleep from my eyes and spittle from my chin, I asked him, "Whatever can you mean, Warlock?"

"I think I owe you an apology," he said and flicked the newspaper into my lap. It was open to the classifieds; one of the advertisements was circled in black ink, that I might identify the source of our strife.

FOUND: one bakery wrapper, in the street outside No. 3
Lauriston Gardens. If the owner wishes to reclaim, I shall
be in my rooms at 221B Baker Street, alone, unarmed and
probably drunk from 8 p.m. until 9 p.m. I am physically
feeble and my neighbors cannot hear loud, violent noises.
Inquire Dr. John Watson, MD. Mother's maiden name:
Constance. Lloyds Bank account number: 8720764.

"What the deuce is this, Holmes?" I howled.

"*The Times*," he said.

"No, this advertisement! How has this happened?"

"Well, I posted it myself, to lure the killer here."

"When?" I demanded. "It takes days to get an
advertisment in *The Times*!"

"I know. I think it was four, maybe five days ago that I
submitted it."

"Ridiculous! How would you have known what to say?"

"It was a surprise to me as well, I assure you," he
replied. "Though, I must say, it is nice to know what it
means. I remember being quite baffled at the time."

"Why have you included my bank account number?"

"Well, how should I know, Watson? To grant you
increased verisimilitude, perhaps? This way, the killer can
stop in at the bank and learn that there is indeed a Dr. John
Watson residing at 221B Baker Street."

"And clean me out while he's there, I suppose."

"Oh come now, Watson! Everybody knows you have
no money to steal. I'm surprised that *that one detail* is what
should concern you in any case! What is the theft of a few

shillings, compared to the prospect of your murder? Well,
I suppose I had better go."

"What? Go where?"

"To get Grogsson, of course. We'll want him here to
intercept the killer. He's just down the street. Shouldn't
take me more than twenty minutes, if the streets are clear.
Back in a tick!"

Holmes was already at the door, hat in hand.

"Warlock! I may be dead by then!"

"Nonsense, Watson," he scoffed. "The poison
probably takes a few minutes, don't you think? Stall him
for us. Shoot him, if you must. You've got a gun."

That was true; I had my service revolver. I was already
mid-lunge, heading for the case I kept it in, when Warlock
added, "I stripped it all down and cleaned it for you."

"Where did you put it?"

"Why it's… hmm… where did I put it?" he mused.
"Ah! I recall that the chamber is on the bathroom sink. Ta-
ta, Watson. Good luck!"

The chamber? I went pale. How clearly my mind's
eye could picture it: Holmes in a fine mood, humming
one of his absurd little ditties, cheerily cleaning this pistol
component and then the next, carelessly discarding one
the instant he was ready for another.

If somebody had asked me that morning whether I
might be able to ravage all our rooms in eleven minutes,
I should have said no. I would have been right, too. In
thirteen minutes I could have done it, I think, but I ran
out of time. I had the chamber, the carriage, the barrel,

both halves of the handle, the revolving pin, the advance mechanism, the trigger and four bullets when I was interrupted by a knock at the door, promptly at eight. No hammer. I had no firing hammer. I let the pieces drop onto the dining table and called, "Yes?"

"Dr. Watson?" said Mrs. Hudson, poking her head in at the door. "Lady here to see you, Doctor."

She swung the door wide. There, framed against my only reasonable route of escape, was a "lady" with a bulging purse and a copy of *The Times*. She was a strapping six-footer with well-muscled shoulders and a prominent Adam's apple. Obviously she'd had some hurry getting here, for her face still bore traces of the lather she had used when shaving off her beard. The dress could not have been hers, for it was made for a person barely half her size, but the bonnet actually did suit.

I'd say the disguise was insufficient to fool anybody, were it not for the fact that Mrs. Hudson had been taken in entirely. She fixed me with the first friendly smile I'd ever seen her perform and chirped, "Well, I'll be off then. I hope you'll not be wanting anything, Dr. Watson. It's scrap-metal night and I'm just off to fire up the grinder. No, I won't hear you call, I don't think. Why, that old contraption would beat a brass band, wouldn't it? Anyway, sure it'll drown out any noise you two could make up here. Night all."

For a second, I thought Mrs. Hudson was leaving us alone because she would be happy to see me murdered, but the spritely glint in her eye gave me to realize she had other reasons. The idea that young, unmarried doctors might be willing to rendezvous with aged spinsters, unchaperoned in their quarters at night, was a source of great hope to her. Doubtless, she had several scandalous novels that began in exactly that manner. Her rusty old heart swelled with optimism, she tripped lightly down the stairs and was gone. The killer smiled and stepped through the doorway.

Realizing my only hope lay in playing along, I croaked, "Good evening, Mrs…?"

"Sawyer," the killer said, effecting a pathetic impersonation of an elderly crone. "I come about the advertisement. Do you still got that wrapper?"

"Just there, on the table; you're welcome to it," I said, nodding my head to where the bakery wrapper lay, beside the ineffectual pile of pistol parts.

"Oh, God-a-mercy, thank 'ee, good sir."

"You're very welcome. Good day."

"It belongs to me daughter, you see," the murderer continued, visibly counting off his rehearsed speech on his fingers, point by point. "She married that Tom Dennis—regular fellow, he is, so long as he's not in his drink. He's true enough at sea, but in port, well, the women and the liquor they get the better of him. Oh sure, my good daughter was due for a savage beating had you not recovered her missing wrapper."

"How lucky that I did. Please, take it back to her."

"She lives at 3 Mayfield Place, Peckham and I live at 13 Duncan Street, Houndsditch. She was on her way to a circus that night, when she dropped the wrapper."

"Ha!" I cried. "3 Lauriston Gardens does not lie between Mayfield Place and any circus that was open on the night of… Wait… I don't care. Please take it."

"Sally Sawyer, that was her name; now Sally Dennis since Tom Dennis wedded her. I have their marriage license here, if you care to see."

"Not necessary, please…"

"Now 'ave a look, sir, and ye'll know I speak true."

"Please, I believe anything you say, no matter how preposterous!" I pleaded. "I have no intention of fact-checking any of this! Just take the wrapper and go!"

But he ignored me utterly and continued, "It was a token of their love you see."

I gave a deep sigh and muttered, "How odd, yet perfectly credible."

"It's off the first donut what he bought her."

"I'm sure it was a very nice donut," I said, which turned out to be a terrible mistake.

The killer's face went pale. A look of remorse and longing that would have drawn sympathy from the very stones crossed his face for a moment, but was chased away by a flood of vengeful hate that froze me where I stood. He howled with a rage so intense he managed to drown out Mrs. Hudson's scrap grinder for a moment, then turned away to punch the wall. His fist shattered lath and plaster and sank in so deep I half fancied he'd broken through the opposite side as well.

"That it was," he told me, all pretense of the fictional Mrs. Sawyer gone from his voice. "The best one ever."

He closed his eyes, hung his head, withdrew his fist from the wall, then promptly plunged it through again, setting a second hole just six inches from the first.

With trembling hands, I picked the wrapper up from the table. Inch by inch, though terror gripped my heart, I approached him. A sudden inspiration took me; as stealthily as my unsteady fingers could manage, I tore a tiny corner from the wrapper and placed it in my pocket. I forced myself across the room to where he stood, with his fist in the wall and his petticoat all in disarray. I placed the wrapper in his free hand, closed his fingers over it and squeaked, "It's yours."

In my heart, I prayed he had not seen me tear away the corner of his precious wrapper. His back was to me. How could he have noticed? I hate to think what would have occurred if he had.

"Thank you," he said. Strange how heartfelt his gratitude seemed. He sounded as if I had just saved him from the gallows and I had an instant of guilt when I realized I intended to do just the opposite. Without another word, he drew his fist from the wall and disappeared through the door. The moment he was gone, my knees gave out and I would have plunged to the floor, except I knew I must observe all I could about the man, in the hope of catching him later. I staggered to the window and sagged into the very armchair I had thought to deposit Warlock in just that morning. The killer walked into the street, approached a waiting cab and called out loudly, so that all the street might hear, "3 Mayfield Place, Peckham, driver."

All this in spite of the fact that there *was* no driver.

After shooting a fleeting glance up and down the street, the old crone bounded up into the driver's seat herself and whipped the horse into a gallop.

At least we had it right that the killer was a cab driver.

The urge to collapse overcame me. I staggered across the room to the brandy decanter, then back to the chair before the fire. Here at last, I allowed my legs to buckle and I fell in a heap, interrupting my tremors, from time to time, to pour a healthy draught of brandy down my throat.

It was nearly an hour and a half before Warlock returned. By that time, I had already turned away two other callers. One was some sort of insane baked-goods collector. The other had just come from my bank and claimed to be a Nigerian prince, in spite of the fact that he was clearly of Chinese descent. His family fortune had been seized, he said, and if only I would deposit a thousand pounds in my own bank account (the number of which was written on a crumpled piece of paper, clutched in his right hand), this would somehow allow him access to his own monies, ten thousand pounds of which he would immediately pay to me. Exhausted and by no account sober, I told him I would. The instant he left, I made a note to open a new account at my earliest convenience.

At last, Warlock burst through the door, in high spirits. He clucked, "Hi-ho, Watson! I've just had a merry chase. I quite forgot: Grogsson was headed out to the theater this evening! I checked a few, but never found him. Any luck here?"

I nodded.

"Did you encounter the killer?"

Again, I nodded.

"Tell me all, Watson! Tell me all!"

I shook my head.

"Perhaps tomorrow, then. You look quite undone, I must say."

He leapt into the other armchair and poured himself a snifter of brandy. He had no intention of drinking it, I knew, but would often pour himself one whenever anyone else had a glass, so he could pretend to be joining in. He settled back, smiling, but then jerked forward, his reverie interrupted by sudden remembrance. After rummaging through his coat for a few seconds, he withdrew a small metal curio and said, "By the by, Watson, I found this queer little device in my pocket. Have you any idea what it can be?"

I can hardly describe the wave of fury that washed over me. If I had not been in an alcoholic stupor, I think I would have leapt from my seat and throttled him. Yet, in my current state, there was nothing I could do but say, "That, Holmes, is the firing hammer of a Webley-Pryse .455 revolver."

His face contorted in a mixture of amusement and wonder. "Is it?"

"I am fairly certain."

8

I AWOKE MUCH LATER THAN USUAL THE NEXT MORNING —just before 10 a.m. I had not meant to sleep so long, yet the body is always master of the mind and my own physical form was still in feeble shape. Having wasted so badly since being wounded, it was in no condition to receive the quantity of stimulation the previous day had yielded, and not half the brandy. I had the impression that my slumber had been deep and profound and I realized I had no idea what had wakened me from it.

Mrs. Hudson's next shriek reminded me. Danger! Screaming! That was it. I rolled from bed and stumbled for the door, still dressed in the crumpled remains of yesterday's suit. By the time I reached our sitting room, Warlock was already at the door to the hall, shouting, "It's quite all right, Mrs. Hudson, they are here by my invitation! Really, I hope in the future you will keep a more civil tongue in your head when you address my guests."

In principal, I agreed. In practice, I had no time to voice an opinion on the matter before I began screaming myself. In through the door streamed a swarm of rats—probably a hundred of them. They swirled into our sitting room. They scuttled over our table and into our cupboards, quite devouring the last of my crumpets. You must not think less of me for screaming at the sight of them. I am a grown man and have certainly seen rats before, but none like these. Each was afflicted in some unique and horrifying way. One had eight legs. One was the size of a dog, yet colored like a cow. One was inside out. One stopped upon my shoe and turned its eye up at me—it had only one, in the middle of its head.

A hand upon my shoulder stopped my screaming and I turned to behold Warlock who, with a hurt expression, said, "Watson, please, a little kindness to our guests, don't you think?"

"What the hell are they?" I demanded, quite forgetting to be kind.

"Nothing so out of the usual," Holmes responded. "These are some of the rats that live on Baker Street with us."

"But, what's wrong with them?"

"Watson! How rude! They are merely unusual. Rats, like people, are subject to accidents of birth. And just like people, the unafflicted members of society—the regular rat folk—quite unfairly disdain these good rodents you see here today."

"So all these rats are…"

"The Baker Street Irregulars."

I recoiled towards a chair, but it was occupied by a rat with long whip-like tails in place of ears and another with tiny stigmata. Reeling about the room with some care not to step on our strange visitors, I sought an unoccupied spot to rest myself, but found none. Holmes did not even try to mask his disappointment. He tutted loudly and turned to the one normal-looking rat in the room, saying, "There, Wiggles, do you see? Do you see what a stir they make? I am sorry, but in the future, you had best come up alone. The rest of you lot must wait outside, I fear."

The normal rat looked up at him for a moment, then began to shift. The bones moved about beneath its skin. Its hair grew back into its hide, even as the body began to expand and contort into a bipedal form. In two winks, a young street urchin stood before me, clad in rags, with a battered cap in hand.

"Yes, sir, Mr. Holmes, sir," he said and smiled at me, devilishly.

I grasped my chest and fell into the nearest chair, sending six-eyes rat and open-sores-that-smell-like-chocolate rat scurrying for safety. Warlock asked the rat-boy, "Anything to report yet, Wiggles?"

"Nuffin' yet, sir, beggin' yer pardon. I gots all the boys gathered up and we're on the streets. We'll have him for you, sure as we're breathin'."

"I never doubted it," Warlock confided. "Here is one day's wages, in advance."

From one of his pockets, Warlock produced twenty or thirty pounds of rotting cabbage (by means I still cannot explain) and began casting it about the room to the waiting Irregulars.

"Very gen'rous, sir," Wiggles said, with a tip of his cap. "We'll be off, then. Oh, brought yer paper, sir."

Wiggles gave a nod to big-as-a-dog-but-colored-like-a-cow rat, who began a rigorous campaign of retching and choking. At last, with a final spasm, he regurgitated our paper onto the table, gave himself a congratulatory nod for a job well done, then turned to join the swarm as it scurried out the door and down the hall. I watched them go with horror and disbelief vying for control of my wits. Warlock only turned to the paper, wiped off some stomach acid and chewed-up cabbage, and began scanning the first few pages. Suddenly he piped, "Watson, look! We're famous!"

After perusing the article for a few moments, I was inclined to disagree. Though the case was causing quite a sensation, I was relieved to find neither Holmes nor I were mentioned by name. In fact, Holmes was mentioned by the wrong name, when the writer declared that the unwelcome consultant, Mr. Rache, had once again appeared and scrawled his name in blood on the wall. Lestrade and Grogsson fared even worse. It was clear the author believed one or both of them were guilty of the crime. He complained that they would probably "solve" it, as they usually did, finding a party who would prove more guilty than they, even if he seemed less. The article included a wealth of information, much of which we had previously lacked. The reporters had already uncovered the name of the deceased and the fact that he was traveling with one Joseph Strangerson, his secretary. Further, they had information as to where the two had been staying—Madame Charpontier's boarding house in Toruay Terrace—although they had checked out the evening before the crime. The paper even detailed the last time Drebber and Strangerson had been seen together: just after quarter past nine on Friday night, arguing on the platform at Euston Station. The two men had then walked off in separate directions. On a whim, I flipped through the paper until I found the schedule for the trains. Likely as not, the two of them had just missed the Liverpool train. The question was, where had they gone after missing the train? Why not head back to the boarding house together? I was forming a strategy of investigation, when Holmes—sitting in his armchair by the window, picking cabbage from his shirt front—muttered, "Oh dear. It looks as if Grogsson has read the paper this morning."

Rushing to the window, I beheld the massive form of Torg Grogsson coming down the street. He was beaming broadly, face alight with self-satisfaction, in spite of the fact that he was practically naked. His left fist was closed around the collar of a battered corpse, which he dragged to our door, before ringing the bell. Presently, Mrs. Hudson began her second screaming fit of the morning and a moment after that, Grogsson himself flung open our sitting-room door and shouted, "I win!"

He triumphantly tossed the body into the center of the room. Only when it gave a groan of protest did I realize the man was still alive. I bolted to my bedroom for my medical bag and then back to attend to him, while there was still time. One side of his face was half stove-in. I later learned that Grogsson had hit him—only once, with his fist—very nearly killing the man.

"Torg find killer," Grogsson declared, jabbing himself in the chest with his thumb. "Is best 'tective evar!"

No. The man on my floor was younger, shorter and entirely less threatening than the killer had been. I had no idea who he might be, but I knew who he wasn't.

"Good job, Grogsson," said Warlock. "I had hoped Watson and I would capture him, but you've bested us entirely. Come in, why don't you, and tell us how you did it."

Torg Grogsson proudly recounted his morning's adventure, but I will not relate the conversation. It was so riddled with grammatical and pronunciation errors, so horribly tainted by the most rudimentary attempts at speech, that I hope it is never committed to paper. Instead, I shall offer you my own version of events, reconstructed as best I could manage from Grogsson's account, witness statements and the police report that Madame Charpontier later filed against him.

It seems Grogsson had arisen at roughly half past seven that morning and proceeded to read the paper (a feat I still can barely bring myself to believe him capable of). When he came to the mention of Madame Charpontier's boarding house on Toruay Terrace, he became particularly excited; he knew the place. In his eagerness to apprehend the killer, he had neglected to dress and bounded into the street in his nightwear. Unfortunately, this consisted only of underpants, his bowler hat and a tie. After twenty minutes of running through the streets of London, howling his battle cry, he arrived at Madame Charpontier's. Or rather, near it. He'd forgotten exactly which door was hers, so he frightened a number of her neighbors by bursting in upon them, before chancing upon the correct address.

Madame Charpontier was not overly glad to make his acquaintance, nor was her daughter, Alice, who was also present. This daughter must have been quite pretty, for Torg spoke of her much more than the story warranted, sometimes leering like a maniac, other times tracing delicate patterns in the air with his goat-sized hand, as if softly stroking her cheek. I was sure there was just the hint of a tear in his eye.

At first, communications were strained. Madame Charpontier—assuming herself to be under attack by a rampaging monster—shot Grogsson twice, in the chest. Only after he mentioned it did I realize this was true. One of the bullets had not even penetrated his tough, hairy hide. The other had left a comically small hole and a trickle of thick blood. Torg would not allow me to examine him. He protested that such things happened to him all the time and, in truth, it didn't seem to have injured him much.

After plucking the offending revolver from the landlady's grasp and bending it to useless scrap, Torg demanded to know where Enoch Drebber was. It seems he'd momentarily forgotten Drebber was dead and had come to apprehend him. Madame Charpontier also had a copy of the paper handy, and used it to convince Torg that Drebber was… no longer in residence. Torg does not respond well when his plans go awry (even though they usually do), so he began making quite a lot of noise at that point and smashing furniture. Odd as it may sound, this proved to be an adroit strategy. It turns out that if someone of Grogsson's size, temperament and state of undress begins doing this in one's company, one will tell him almost everything one knows, in the hopes of finding some tidbit of information that will please him enough to end the rampage.

Madame Charpontier related that Drebber and Strangerson had checked out Friday night and that she was almost as glad to see them go as she would be to see Grogsson leave. Strangerson was a reasonable enough fellow, it seemed, but Drebber was prone to drink and carousing. Happy as Madame Charpontier had been for the near-criminal pound per day she had from each of them, she made it clear that they were not welcome to return. They had both left on Friday, just after eight in the evening to catch the train to Liverpool at a quarter past nine. (I took some satisfaction that I had guessed their purpose.) Some hours later, Drebber returned, much the worse for drink. It seems the two had missed their train by the matter of a few minutes. Strangerson had left for alternate lodging, thinking to meet Drebber there. Drebber had returned to Madame Charpontier's boarding house claiming to have forgotten one item: Alice Charpontier. What Drebber lacked in sobriety, he made up in obscenity, offering a few choice suggestions for an... unconventional courtship.

Upon hearing this, Torg swore to kill Drebber (already dead) and, according to some sources, proposed marriage to young Alice once the deed was done.

She declined.

However, during this polite rebuff, Alice Charpontier let certain interesting facts come to light. Her honor had already been defended, she said. It seems the exchange with Drebber had awakened her brother Arthur. He was on leave from the Royal Navy and had turned in early, as the military schedule had become his custom. Though he had missed the earlier conversation, Arthur soon caught the gist of it and escorted Drebber out with some alacrity. In the street, Drebber offered a few parting comments that sent Arthur back inside to fetch the family cudgel. Arthur then claimed to have chased Drebber all the way down the street and halfway back up, until the latter staggered into a cab and made good his escape.

All of this was related to Torg, who gleaned nothing from it, except that Arthur Charpontier had motive, means and opportunity to kill Drebber. He elected to take young Arthur into custody, a process that consisted of a single blow to the face and a long drag across town to our place. It never occurred to Grogsson to take him to the police, his urge to brag being a larger portion of his character than his grasp of judicial process. Most of all, he seemed eager to talk to Lestrade.

"Stoopid Lestrade! Stoopid!" Grogsson laughed. "Him think Strangerman did it. Him chasing all over town when Torg have criminal! Torg!"

I had to approach my next sentence very carefully. "So, Grogsson, it is your opinion that Mr. Charpontier here *poisoned* Mr. Drebber?"

"Yah!"

"With a cudgel?"

"What you talking, Watson? Stick for hitting."

"That's right, Torg," I agreed, "but remember: Drebber was not found beaten to death; he had been poisoned. Probably not with a stick."

Torg stood for a moment. Blinked.

"NOOOOOOOOOOOOOOOOOOOOOO!"

He raised his giant fists to smash the closest piece of furniture he could find—likely our table—and, for the first time, I got to see Warlock employ his gifts on purpose.

"Stop," said Holmes, and Grogsson immediately did so, but not by choice. Understand that no visible force restrained him—it is hard to conceive of one that could. Not chains, but merely the *shadows* of chains sprung from the darker corners of the room and twined themselves not around Grogsson, but *his shadow*. He roared in frustration and strained with all his might, but could not move an inch.

"We're not going to have any of that in here, Grogsson," said Holmes. "Watson raises a fair point. Also, I like that table. Now, I'm going to let you go and we're not going to have any more of this nonsense, are we?"

"But… but Lestrade make fun of me!" Grogsson complained.

"He may indeed," Holmes agreed. "He'll be here soon. He's coming. I can feel him."

Looking out the window, I realized he was correct. Lestrade was turning the corner onto Baker Street.

"No, he won't make fun of you, Grogsson," I told

the giant. "I don't think I've ever seen him so downcast. Something has happened."

"Oh!" said Holmes eagerly. "The plot thickens."

How nice for Mrs. Hudson that she got to answer the door once that morning to someone who didn't make her scream. The third time is the charm, they say. I listened for Lestrade's step on the landing but could not detect it. Nevertheless, he soon stood in the open doorway, wearing a hangdog look. I began to welcome him, but Warlock clapped a hand across my mouth and said, "Lestrade, how good to see you. You have permission to enter, *only once*, for the purpose of solving this case."

Stepping through the doorway, Lestrade gave a resentful look and muttered, "You've no reason to fear me, Warlock."

"Caution is its own reward, Lestrade. Now tell us, why have you come?"

"The same reason as always: some fool has got himself done in. I'm afraid I've located our Mr. Strangerson."

9

I MADE TEA. IT WAS A DREARY SORT OF DAY AND BOTH of our Scotland Yard friends had nothing else to savor but the bitter broth of professional defeat—a perfect day for Ceylon tea. Soon Warlock and I held steaming cups. For Grogsson, I filled our never-used watering can, though it still looked small in his hands. Lestrade also had a teacup. He held it close, as if treasuring the heat, but I never saw him drink. Arthur Charpontier didn't touch his, either. As soon as we were all arranged in the sitting room, Lestrade sighed and began to recount his effort.

"I don't mind telling you, I suspected Joseph Strangerson of the murder of Enoch Drebber. The two were from out of town. Who here would even know Drebber, much less where to find him? Would any Londoner have had the time to form a vendetta? It seemed to me Strangerson was my man. I began looking for him. I went about by night, peeping in windows and knocking on doors. I went to public houses, taverns, hotels and rooms to let, hunting him, always hunting. The dark hours fled, but still I searched, beneath the cursed sun. At last, I came to Halliday's Private Hotel, on Little George Street. When I asked for Strangerson, the desk clerk said, 'Finally, you're here. He's been waiting for you all day and all night.'"

"Oh? You told him you were Drebber?" I asked.

"No, but he assumed so and I saw no need to correct him. He was perfectly willing to take me up to the room, despite the early hour. We had not made it to the top of the stairs before I realized something was amiss. That wonderful smell... that rarest of blood. Most of the blood was Strangerson's—a common brew, I'm afraid. But the killer's blood—that most perfect draught—was there as well. I had the clerk open the door. Strangerson lay by an open window, still in his nightshirt, killed by a single stab wound to his left side. The murder weapon was still lodged in the body—a pearl-handled knife with an eight-inch blade. It struck him right to the heart."

"Ha!" yelled Torg, who loved a good killed-in-a-single-blow story.

"Stabbed?" I cried. "But our man is a poisoner. Could it be there are *two* killers on the loose?"

Lestrade shook his head and insisted, "Same man. It would be strange indeed to find two killers with that same rare blood. Besides, look what I found in Strangerson's mouth."

Lestrade began divesting himself of Mr. Strangerson's personal effects, which he had purloined from the crime scene, preferring our help to his colleagues' at Scotland Yard. Sure enough, there lay the aged bakery paper.

"It is the same kind," Lestrade said.

"It is, in fact, the same one!"

I went in triumph to the cupboard and withdrew the tiny corner I had torn from the wrapper. It fit exactly.

"By Jove," breathed Holmes.

Grogsson seemed to care not at all. Lestrade was wonderstruck. "How on earth did he get it back?"

"Ask Holmes," I said bitterly, adding, "And this time, we are keeping it! I've had quite enough of entertaining murderers, thank you."

"As you wish, Watson," smiled Holmes.

"So, you have seen the killer?" Lestrade asked.

"Rather."

"Well, we are in luck," Lestrade said. "He was also observed leaving the scene of the crime. A milk-delivery boy noticed a ladder propped against the wall of the hotel, under Strangerson's window. He saw a man come down the ladder and run off for a nearby cab. Perhaps we can determine if it was indeed the same man. The milk-boy said he was tall—over six feet…"

"He was," I answered.

"…red-faced and ruddy-haired…" continued Lestrade.

"Indeed."

"…in a red and white gingham dress."

"That is our man."

"How fortunate," said Lestrade. "We almost missed the witness entirely. Until I questioned him, the milk-boy assumed the killer was simply a cross-dressing carpenter of some sort, performing window maintenance in the dark."

I made a mental note, on my sister's behalf. Her son was so simple she worried he might never be employable. Perhaps he should become a milk-boy. "What is the rest of this?" I asked Lestrade, indicating the pile of personal effects he had deposited on the table.

"Everything except his clothes," said Lestrade. "Almost five pounds still in his wallet, so we know it was no theft. Identification and papers—he was American, like Drebber. A novel. A pipe. There was a glass of water on the bedside table, but I left it there, thinking it was the hotel's…"

"What is this little box? Anything in it?" I asked.

"A few pills," said Lestrade with a shrug. "His medicine, I suppose."

I froze. No. Not likely. The box was old and battered; it bore every sign of having traveled far and wide, for some length of time, probably in someone's pocket. It was not the type of pillbox dispensed by a doctor, but a wooden keepsake box, such as one might purchase at a curio shop. There was no label stating what kind of medicine lay inside, but I thought I knew. With trembling hands, I opened the box. Within lay two pills, irregular and crude—clearly homemade.

"The poison," I said.

Everybody drew closer to stare at the pills, Warlock asking, "I say, Watson, are you sure?"

"No," I had to admit, "but these are like no

professionally made pills I have ever seen. I suspect that this box belonged to the killer, and that he planned to poison Strangerson. Perhaps Strangerson resisted, so the killer stabbed him. This is just conjecture, of course. I can't be sure this is poison until we test it."

"Good idea," said Warlock. "I'll be right back."

"Wherever are you going, Holmes?" I asked.

"A test, Watson! A test!" was all he said, before disappearing out our door.

Only when he was gone did I realize how very uncomfortable I was in the company of Grogsson and Lestrade. Grogsson stared at me, silently, challengingly. Lestrade's eye kept wandering to the helpless form of Arthur Charpontier. I suppose I should have offered them food of some sort. Then again, the Baker Street Irregulars had eaten most of what we had and Lestrade still hadn't touched his tea. Something in me recoiled from the notion of offering to feed a vampire.

I must have stared too long for, without turning to me, he gave a pained grin and grumbled, "You aren't about to start asking foolish questions about garlic, are you, Dr. Watson?"

"No. No. I… Pardon me for staring."

Lestrade shrugged. "You have nothing to apologize for. In fact, I must congratulate you: you are doing very well, Doctor."

"Why, thank you. It turns out that ferreting out a criminal is much the same thought process as diagnosing illness, so—"

"I was not thinking of the case," Lestrade interrupted, "though you seem to have a deft hand at that, as well. No. I am referring to how well you have dealt with *us*."

I had nothing to say.

Grogsson grunted out a laugh at my discomfort. Even Lestrade allowed his regular dourness to fall away for a moment. He chuckled, shook his finger at me and said, "You are a man of science. I would have thought you incapable of operating amongst such a profusion of abnormal creatures."

"It hasn't been easy," I said, my voice hoarser than I'd intended.

"No," Lestrade agreed, "but rest assured, Doctor, I intend you no harm. Humans who speak with our kind are a rare commodity. Humans willing to live with Holmes are even rarer. That ought to keep you safe from Grogsson. I have encouraged him to remember how *very cross* Warlock would be if Grogsson lost his temper with you."

The comment caught me off guard and I laughed at the silliness of it. Grogsson turned his head towards me and bellowed, "Not make fun!"

"No! I'm sorry! I don't mean to insult you," I protested. "I only... I can't imagine... I mean, Warlock is not a brave man; I just can't see him standing up to you, Grogsson, that's all."

Grogsson turned away from me and mumbled, "Thought doctors wuz smart."

Lestrade smiled, "Well, Torg, I suppose that just means he hasn't really *met* Warlock Holmes yet."

Grogsson gave a wry snort. Lestrade crossed one leg theatrically over the other, pressed his fingertips together and said, "Let me tell you something you ought to know. Suppose the three of us decided to murder Holmes in his bed tonight. Suppose he had no warning, no weapon and you brought that service revolver of yours. I tell you this: tomorrow morning, Warlock Holmes would wake up, safe as a babe in arms; there would be a bubbling pile of molten pistol on the floor and no such thing as Grogsson, Lestrade or Watson."

This speech had a strange effect on me: I became lonely. Though I did not understand how the unassuming Holmes could be a match for either Grogsson or Lestrade, I did not doubt the news. Rather, it had the effect of removing my last confederate. Though I knew him to be unusual, I still perceived Holmes as basically human, like myself. Somehow, Lestrade's words had removed him from that sphere and left me the only man amongst monsters. It hadn't been so bad, until I was alone. I hung my head and mumbled, "I don't know what I'm even doing here. Can I be of any help at all? I am only a man…"

My thoughts were interrupted by a thunderous crash—Grogsson had smashed the table. When I looked up, I beheld him staring at me with a primal rage in his eye. He bellowed a challenge and balled his fists. I shied back and fell from my chair. In an instant, Lestrade was between us, shouting, "Torg! No! Remember! He doesn't mean it. He doesn't know."

I think I was beginning to form some words of thanks, when Lestrade rounded on me. I was surprised to see his face alight with anger, as well.

"I think you should apologize, Dr. Watson," he said.

"For what?" I asked, drawing another cry of rage from Grogsson.

Lestrade gestured for him to calm down, but his gaze made it clear he thought me the stupidest creature on earth as he said, "Look out that window, Doctor. What do you see? Is London peopled by vampires? By Grogsson's kind?"

I made no answer.

"I am sure that Grogsson or I might best twenty of you, but can we best two billion? No, Dr. Watson, the battle has been fought; the matter is decided. This is the realm of man. You are the most powerful force in the world—the undisputed masters of earth. How dare you best us so totally and call yourself slight? How dare you make us run and hide ourselves and obey your strange customs for fear of our very lives, then declare yourself 'only a man'?"

I sat stunned for a moment then said, "Well… I've never thought of it like that…"

"What luxury," Lestrade sneered, then grumbled to Torg, "You'd better tell Warlock you'll get him a new table."

My head swam. I understood what he was saying, but I wanted to protest that such treatment was not reserved for only monsters. It applied to all of us. How welcome were African tribesmen in London? Or Chinamen? Or anybody who dared to step outside his front door wearing the wrong hat? Wear a top hat to the lunch counter or a boater to the opera and you'd find out in a second exactly how much mercy London has for outsiders. None. Returning from the army, I myself—a native-born, well-educated doctor—had almost fallen through the cracks and found myself digested by this greatest of cities. I suppose I had known my society well enough to expect no pity. Yet, at the time, it did not seem unfair to me, or even unkind. Suddenly, mankind's policy of intolerance—which I had always obeyed but never much considered—made itself clear to me.

How total.

How cruel.

My thoughts were interrupted by Warlock, who returned at that moment, proclaiming, "Gentlemen, a test!"

In his arms was our neighbor's flop-eared puppy. Off guard as I was, this sufficed to jolt me back to my senses.

"Warlock, no! Surely not!" I protested.

Now, I am a man of the world. I understand that the medical knowledge I possess was built upon the corpses of many an unfortunate experimental subject, both animal and human. But this really was beyond the pale. Rocco was a three-week-old basset hound, blessed with the kindest disposition I think I have ever encountered in beast or man. But he also bore the dual curses of short legs and long ears. Either one of them, in isolation, is harmless; together they are burdensome. Rocco could not take two steps without treading on an ear and tumbling to the ground. It was the cutest thing I'd ever seen.

"You are not going to poison that dog!" I insisted.

"Watson, calm down. This animal is doomed," said Warlock.

"Because you intend to poison it!"

"No, no, Watson," he said, shaking his head. "I've been watching him for days. I can feel the pale reaper, following this poor little mutt. One way or another, I promise you, this dog will not survive the week."

"Preposterous!"

"I tell you, Watson, I am very in tune with this sort of thing. I don't know what fate awaits young Rocco here, but I know this: we can save him from it!"

"By poisoning him?" I cried. "Warlock, you are not feeding those pills to that dog!"

"Of course not," Lestrade agreed. "We need some for evidence. The dog can have half of each pill."

He already had a kitchen knife and was carefully sawing the pills in half. Before I could stop him, he tossed half of the first pill over to Warlock. I moved to snatch it from his hand, but Grogsson caught the back of my collar between his thumb and forefinger and held me as easily as you would a kitten.

"Here, boy! Here, Rocco!" Holmes cried, dangling the half-pill in front of the puppy. When Rocco was sufficiently excited, Holmes tossed the pill up in the air so Rocco could catch it. He wolfed it down happily and waited for more. We all drew close, rapt in morbid curiosity, waiting to see what would happen. The puppy sneezed. He barked twice. He leapt upon Warlock's knee and licked his nose, hoping to restart the game. When it became clear none of us were playing any more, he lost interest and began sniffing around the room, lost in the fascinating rat smell. Five minutes passed. Then ten.

"Hmmmm…" mused Lestrade, "some poisons take days, I suppose."

"Not the kind our man used," I said. "Remember, the killer stood and watched Drebber die. Do you suppose he poisoned him on Wednesday, then figured out exactly the correct time to pick him up on Friday, spirit him to an abandoned house and watch him expire? No. Our killer's poison is quick."

"Not work on dogs?" Grogsson suggested.

"Possible," I said, "but most acute poisons are deadly to a wide range of organisms."

"Perhaps it isn't poison," said Lestrade. "Maybe it *is* medicine after all."

I screwed up my face and shook my head. "They're too irregular to be professionally manufactured pills. If they are medicine, they must be homemade. But you have a point, Lestrade; perhaps they are something else entirely."

We all paused to wrack our minds for a moment. What other small, round edibles might somebody place in an unmarked box and carry on their person? Warlock snapped his fingers and crowed, "Ah! Perhaps they're candy!"

"CANDY?" cried Grogsson, lunging for the box. We tried to stop him, of course, but I think I might have had better luck trying to wrestle a carriage and six to a halt. He gleefully popped half of the second pill into his mouth and smiled for just a moment before making a face and spitting it to the floor, shouting, "Aaaaaargh! Bad candy!"

It was a good thing for all of us that he spat it out as quickly as he did, for it would have been no small task to move his body out of our sitting room. Almost before the half-chewed gob of poison hit the floor, a worried expression passed across Grogsson's face and he suddenly contorted. He fell to the floor, twitching awfully. Warlock and Lestrade stood stunned. I knelt down to sniff the pill. It smelled pungent, but not acidic. Nor did Grogsson grasp at his throat or belly as if they were burning.

"Get him to the bathtub!" I shouted and snatched up my medical bag. The three of us struggled to drag him into the bath and I poured my entire bottle of ipecac down his throat. For a moment I thought him too far gone to swallow and prayed he would not choke on it, but enough must have made it down to his gut to take effect. In seconds, the emetic properties of the syrup took hold and he began to… emit. I had not paused to consider how much food might be necessary to sustain an individual of Grogsson's size and energy, but let me tell you, it was an impressive volume. It was a good thing we hadn't taken him to the sink or commode; he could have overflowed them both. Equally impressive was the strength he possessed in his abdominal muscles, which caused him to void with such efficacy that, for a few moments, he might have been mistaken for the world's most revolting fire hose. Soon there was nothing left in him and his retching and twitching subsided. Warlock looked about the vomit-drenched ruin of our bathroom and noted, "We'll be wanting Mrs. Hudson to come up and do some cleaning, eh?"

We dragged Grogsson back to the sitting room and made him as comfortable as possible on the floor. We didn't give him the sofa because Arthur Charpontier was still recovering there and we couldn't have lifted Grogsson, in any case. It took him half an hour to regain his senses. His hands shook and he looked positively green. His first words after his ordeal were the same as his last words before.

"Bad candy…"

I fell back into one of the armchairs and wondered aloud, "Only one of the pills is poison? Why would the killer do that? Why carry two identical pills, one harmless, one deadly?"

"I think we shall soon know," Warlock said, smiling, indicating the clock. It had just struck noon and, in a moment, there came a scratching at the door. Well, it began as a scratching, but unaccountably transformed itself to a knock partway through. I listened in horror as the noise, which had begun at the lower corner of the door, slowly worked its way upwards until it was a pounding, just above the knob.

"Come in, Wiggles," said Holmes, "and report."

The door swung wide and there stood the urchin, grinning. "Afternoon, sir. Pleased to say we've found 'im."

"Capital!" Holmes cheered, crossing the room to deposit a handful of coins in Wiggles's hands. "Here's for the fare, and a little extra. Have him come round at half past one. Not here; he'll recognize the address. We'll use Grogsson's place. You know where it is?"

"That I do, sir. Half past one," Wiggles replied, and was gone.

Warlock walked to the prone figure of Grogsson and mused, "Hmm… He won't like us going to his house without him. And I hardly trust him here. What do you think, Watson, is Torg fit to walk a mile or so?"

I leaned over him, to assess. He was becoming responsive; his muscle movements were still unsteady, but voluntary, and his groans had taken on a melodramatic quality (the big baby).

"Well, he's been shot in the chest twice at point-blank range, and had a dose of deadly poison, all before lunchtime. Yet still… yes, I think he's fit to walk."

Warlock smiled and we all set to the task of getting the ponderous bulk of Torg Grogsson back up on his feet. As we grunted and struggled, Warlock noted, "Egad, Watson, you're right: lunchtime. I quite forgot."

I laughed. "Perhaps we can stop at a bakery and get an English muffin, to eat on the way."

"Well and good for you three," Lestrade complained.

"I don't suppose they'll have toast and soup?" Holmes wondered.

"An English muffin *is* toast. Round toast," Lestrade said. "I don't even eat food and I know that."

I paused a moment to reassemble my service revolver, while the others donned their coats. Thus armed and prepared, we set off to catch a murderer. On the way out, Grogsson trod on the dog.

"Told you so," said Holmes.

10

THE LIGHTEST SCENT OF LAVENDER GRACED THE AIR.
I sat upon a tasteful velvet settee, utterly in awe. Grogsson
owned a proper house on the edge of town—and by
proper, I mean *immaculate*. No speck of dust could be
seen. Framed prints of Europe's finest ballet dancers,
male and female, adorned the walls. No other subject was
featured in any of Grogsson's artwork. He even had a pair
of Marie Taglioni's shoes, preserved in a glass display case.
Warlock and Lestrade had known of this predilection, but
it was my first time in Grogsson's house. Grogsson stared
at me with a look that promised utter physical destruction
if I breathed a word to anyone, or dared to mock. In
fact, I had no desire to cast fun, but rather felt a swell
of sympathy for the hulking detective. Ballet dancers are
graceful, delicate, refined and beautiful. In order to make
the list complete, one need only add "well spoken" and
preface the whole thing with "Here are five things Torg
Grogsson will never be."

Warlock rummaged about in the attic for a few minutes,
returning with a battered trunk. This he took out onto

the front step and filled with large, decorative rocks from the garden. Lestrade and I helped him position it on the floor of the sitting room, near the door, as if Grogsson had packed for a trip and was preparing to depart. After that, there was naught to do but sit and wait.

It was agony.

I had never been present at the apprehension of a murderer before and it was not the sort of thing I was capable of approaching calmly. Lestrade looked eager. Holmes grinned like a schoolboy; his enemy was boredom and that nemesis would not be showing its face this day.

As it approached quarter past one, Lestrade became ever more bitter and agitated. As twenty past neared, Warlock turned to him and said, "Vladislav, my friend, I think perhaps we ought to chain you up, a bit. Just for safety, you know."

Lestrade made an awful face but nodded his agreement, saying, "I do not know if I could trust myself, if I had to lay hands on a man with blood like that. Grogsson and I both have irons."

"You fellows ought to try this type," Holmes said, drawing a pair of shiny handcuffs from his coat pocket. "I find them to be light, portable, and magnificently quick to fasten. Then again, I'm saving them for our friend. Let's use yours."

Holmes clasped one pair of cuffs around Lestrade's ankles so he might not run. The other he fastened to Lestrade's left hand and then the wooden arm of the chair he sat on. I can't say why, but this put me quite on edge. Perhaps I was simply unaccustomed to seeing people clapped in chains. More pragmatically, I was sorry to lose Lestrade's help. The walk had done Grogsson no good, so I had every impression that Warlock and I would have to face the murderer alone. Though each passing day improved me, I was still frail. I had my pistol, but I had never shot a man and—though I could not recall the specific wording—I was fairly sure the Hippocratic oath took a dim view of such things. Holmes I still had little faith in. Despite Lestrade's warning and the shadows that bound Grogsson, I could not picture Holmes as anything more than a well-meaning but bumbling buffoon. I steeled my nerve as best I could and waited.

Just before the half-hour, we heard hooves in the street outside. I placed myself with my back to the wall near the front door. It was all I could do not to draw my pistol. I never liked guns, even before my disastrous encounter with one in Afghanistan, but found I yearned for its comforting presence in my hand.

When the door opened I practically jumped through the ceiling, but it was only Wiggles. It was fortunate that I hadn't drawn my weapon. Such was my fright, I might well have blown the poor urchin's face off.

"Afternoon, Wiggles," Holmes said, beaming. "I wonder, would you ask the driver to come help me with my trunk?"

Wiggles disappeared down the path and in a few moments came scampering back, with the murderer at his heels. I meant to avert my gaze, lest he recognize me from the night before, but I could not help staring. When he came through the door, I saw a man transformed. He was wearing men's clothes this time, but that was not the chief change in him. Gone were his hate and his fury, replaced with a light stride and a wonder-struck torpor, as if he had just seen the world for the first time this morning, and found it beautiful. In his amiable daze, the killer failed to notice me. He stepped up to Holmes with a friendly nod and reached down to grasp the trunk.

In a flash, Holmes had the cuffs on him, one around his wrist and one about the handle of the luggage. The surprised murderer recoiled and tried to run, only to find himself chained to a hundred-pound trunk.

"Gentlemen," crowed Holmes, turning to address the room, "allow me to present the murderer of Enoch Drebber and Joseph Strangerson!"

One should never stop to count the spoils before the battle is done. Though his eyes flooded with rage and fear, the killer's mind remained unclouded. He simply reached down and unfastened the trunk's single clasp. He tipped it forward, sending a dozen dirty rocks clattering onto Grogsson's pristine floor.

"You didn't lock it?" I shouted to Warlock, who had time to shrug slightly before the murderer swung the empty trunk at his head. Warlock collapsed against the wall, blood streaming down his face. The killer turned for the door. I stood to block his escape, but I might have saved myself the trouble. He put his shoulder into me as he passed, knocking me aside as if I were a man of straw. I wound up on the floor, half indoors, half out. Holmes was shouting something.

"The cab! Watson! Shoot the cab!"

My gun was under me, stuck in my coat. I struggled up to one knee and yanked it clumsily from my pocket. It occurred to me to wonder what effect one pistol round might work upon a cab, but I had no time to ask. The killer was already on the garden path and nearly at the street. I knew I ought to shoot the horse, but the animal was blameless and it seemed unfair he should die for his master's sins. I resolved not to aim my first shot at him and squeezed the trigger with the cab in my sights. I felt the Webley buck in my hands and heard its report ring through the neighborhood. An instant later, the front of the cab exploded in a flash of purple flame. The horse must have been even more shocked than I was; it bolted down the street, dragging the ruins of its harness with it. The explosion had freed the animal from the cab, which lay sprawled in the road, with one wheel crushed and the cabin smashed wide open.

For the second time in less than twenty seconds, I was knocked to the ground— *much* harder this time. Grogsson had roused himself. He later admitted that he had been perfectly happy to let Holmes and me handle things, until he saw what the killer had done to his nice clean floor. His frailty forgotten, Grogsson stormed past like a maddened yak, with Warlock close behind, clutching his bleeding nose and shouting, "Alive! Torg! We want him alive!"

Though he might have preferred rougher alternatives,

Grogsson mastered himself enough to obey. He overtook the killer just as he sprang back from his stricken cab. Grogsson grabbed the back of his coat and the belt of his trousers and hoisted him easily off the ground, slamming him roughly into the side of the wrecked cab. The blow was enough to daze the killer, who went limp, the empty trunk dangling from his wrist. Warlock cheered. Grogsson roared in triumph. I might have joined them, if I had not been checking each of my teeth with my tongue, wondering how many would fall out later.

As soon as he recovered from the shock of being thrown against his cab by Grogsson, the killer held up his free hand in a gesture of surrender and said, "Enough. You have me."

Warlock removed the cuff that bound the trunk to the murderer's wrist and used it to fasten the man's hands together. This was not enough for Lestrade, who came down squarely in favor of binding him, head to foot. Having been released from his own bondage, Lestrade suggested we also use the other two pairs of cuffs—one around the prisoner's ankles, and the third between the other two, locking him in a bent-over position. Then, he said, we should chain the trunk full of rocks to him again, and drain enough of his delicious, wonderful blood so that he would be too weak to run away.

"I say, Vladislav, that seems a bit much, doesn't it?" Holmes asked. "Are we gentlemen, or are we not?"

"Well… probably not," Lestrade reasoned. Grogsson nodded that yes, he concurred with this assessment.

"You've no worry of me," the killer said. "I'll not run now. Ain't a point to it. I reckon I'm a deader this time tomorrow, no matter what. I'll confess all, but when I tell you why I done it, I think you'll find each of you would have done no different."

His account had to wait, however, for at that moment he burst into the most spectacular nosebleed I think I have ever seen. Lestrade went fairly ballistic and had to be restrained by Grogsson. The tiny Romanian would not stop struggling and we eventually had to lock him in the garden shed while we waited for transport. Yet I think things ended happily for Vladislav Lestrade—when our prisoner asked for a cloth to staunch the flow of blood, Holmes handed him a drinking glass instead.

Wiggles was immediately dispatched with the direction to hire two more hansoms to drive us to Scotland Yard. When these arrived, Warlock insisted that only he and I should be allowed to ride with the killer. He trusted neither Grogsson's fury nor Lestrade's thirst. Thus, our two monster friends were banished to the first cab. Holmes, the murderer and I followed in the second. Surprisingly, of the three of us, it was our prisoner who began the questioning.

"What kind of gun was that?" he asked.

Holmes smiled. "That depends. First you must tell me who you are and why you expect to die."

The killer shrugged and gamely answered, "My name is Jefferson Hope, out of... well... I suppose St. Louis was the last real home I had. That's in America. I ain't from here, as I'm sure you know. I followed Enoch and Joseph out here to do 'em in. As to why I ain't going to be around long… I got cardio-cranial narrative-sensitive exploditis."

Holmes turned to me and asked, "Doctor, are you familiar with that affliction?"

"No," I replied, "but the language is simple enough. It describes a condition in which some element of a story will cause this man's head and heart to… explode. That said, I have never heard of such an illness and I doubt its veracity."

"I don't," said Holmes, respectfully. "Mr. Hope, I'm afraid that you are quite right and not likely to survive much longer. I have always been able to sense impending doom and, if you will forgive my directness, you are ripe with it."

"I know it," Hope said. "I been wishin' doom on those two so long, I come to have a sense of it my own self."

"Why?" Holmes asked. "Why go to such lengths to ensure those two men's deaths?"

To my great surprise, the killer burst into tears. It took some moments for him to regain his composure enough to tell his tale.

PART II

NOT FROM THE JOURNAL OF DR. JOHN WATSON,
BUT FROM SOME NEBULOUS, UNDEFINED SOURCE THAT
IS SUDDENLY THIRD PERSON AND ALMOST MAKES YOU
THINK YOU'VE PICKED UP THE WRONG BOOK

11

SOUTH OF CANADA AND NORTH OF MEXICO LIES A LAND many Englishmen do not deign to speak of. For the triple crimes of bloodying our nose, stealing itself from our empire and eventually surpassing us at the industrial revolution that we ourselves started, it has been banished from the thoughts and vocabulary of our more conservative element.

Towards the western edge of that cursed land, lies a blighted waste called the Mojave. It is as if the hand of the creator, having formed the earth but not yet adorned it with flora and fauna, paused here. Unable to think of anything apt to draw, the immortal architect resolved to complete the rest of the earth first, then come back and finish up.

Except, he forgot.

Nothing of consequence lives here. In fact, any life that happens to wander into this sun-blasted hell usually dies before the day is out. This is the place where scorpions go to perish of dehydration.

Behold the Spring Mountains, unfinished and unadorned, which jut from the empty plain. These are naked heaps of rock, shoved up from the bowels of the earth just so there could be *something* here. East of them lies an open basin of sand and alkaline dust, an almost endless open expanse of *vegas* which the Spanish call *Las Vegas*. It is a place of madness, where the heat and the unending miles of sand have caused delusion in the few travelers who have managed to traverse it and live. Many report ghostly visions. They speak of a city of a million lights, rising from the sand. Some claim to have seen an ebony pyramid, capped in light, some a vast Italian villa that takes the tiny quantity of precious water that exists there and blasts it into the air in intricate patterns for no reason. One gent even insisted he came across a replica of Camelot itself, gone to squalor and disrepair. These reports are all sun-drunk fantasy of course. Such a city would be totally unsustainable. Who would consent to live there but madmen, insatiable gamblers and the Dutch?

One evening in 1870, this blighted wasteland beheld a rare sight. As daylight faded, a tiny spot of light sprang up upon the plain. It was a campfire. Beside it huddled three dark shapes. Men. Travelers. In those days, anybody who wished to prospect in California had their choice of routes. The wise ones went north, through Oregon Territory, though it was hundreds of miles out of their way. Those foolish few who decided to hurry along the most direct route ended here. These three travelers belonged to the latter kind and were beginning to wish they'd thought better of it when they'd had the chance. They had gathered a pile of the stunted brush that overgrows the plain and set fire to it—as much out of spite as anything. This campfire provided scant relief against the encroaching darkness and the mood of the travelers was strained.

Joseph Strangerson was the youngest, most handsome, best educated, kindest, most reasonable member of the party, but the novelty of these advantages had dried out a thousand miles ago. He was worn to a nub. He sighed. "Feels like I haven't seen a river this side of a week."

"No. Nor no pastry shop for a good while longer," Enoch Drebber groused, staring with unguarded greed at the dainty pink box that rested upon the lap of their companion.

Jefferson Hope's hard eyes fixed him with a warning glare. "Let's not have no talk like that, Enoch; you a'ready ate yers."

Joseph shook his head and kicked a rock into the fire. Enoch, whose temper had been growing shorter and shorter over the last few days, spat, "I sure did an' it was delicious, too! What the hell kind o' man wouldn't eat a donut if he got one? A fool, if y'ask me!"

"I may be a fool, Enoch Drebber, but not so much that I can't recognize when I'm holdin' a good thing. You kin take yer eyes off my pastry now, hear?"

Strangerson sighed again and sent another rock to the flames, saying, "He's got a point, Mr. Hope. If you ain't gonna eat it, you might as well share. Sharing is one of the seven cardinal virtues, you know."

"Ain't never heard of no seven virtues," Jefferson Hope said, his gaze fixed at the heart of the fire, "jus' the seven sins. One of 'em's greed."

"Goddamit!" shouted Drebber, springing up. "Eat it! Eat it right now or hand it over!"

Jefferson Hope's eyes rose slowly from the flames to clasp Enoch Drebber in their fell grip. "I'll eat it when I please, Drebber," he said, in a voice calm and quiet, but loaded with menacing promise, "an' there ain't no man nor beast nor god can make me take a bite afore I'm ready. I'm savin' it."

"Calm down, fellers," Joseph pleaded. "It's just a damn donut."

"No. It ain't. It's the bestest, most perfect donut what ever there was. I named her Lucy an' I love her an' that's all there is to it," Jefferson Hope insisted.

"Crazy, that's what you are," Enoch Drebber said, but they had reached that same familiar impasse they did every night. In the end there was nothing for it but to hunch down into their bedrolls and go to sleep.

The night was not four hours along and the moon not yet so high in the eastern sky when Joseph Strangerson awoke suddenly to find a hand clapped across his mouth. For a moment he thought to scream, but gazing up he saw the wide, earnest eyes of Enoch Drebber. He had a warning look about him and held one finger to his lips to signal silence. Drebber withdrew his hand and Joseph sat up.

"What? What's goin' on?"

"I mean t' have that donut," said Enoch.

"That ain't nothin' but crazy," Joseph said, and began to settle once more into his bedroll.

But Drebber shook him bodily and insisted, "I mean t'

have it, I tell you! An' you're goin' to help me."

"The hell I am," whispered Joseph, trying to pull himself free.

"You've got them light fingers," Drebber said. "Sure, I'm gonna eat that donut, but he's sleepin' on it again and I ain't got the art t' git it without wakin' him."

The two men looked over at Jefferson Hope. There he lay, with the peace of angels on his face and his arms curled around the pink box, which lay half under his bearded cheek. Joseph Strangerson heaved a sigh of resignation, like a man condemned as he mounts the gallows steps. He had not the bravery nor the brawn of his two companions, but he could see how this would all play out and he wanted it done with. He drew his long, thin knife from its sheath and crept towards the sleeping form of Jefferson Hope. Silently as he could, he slit the thin strip of clear tape that held the box top closed and cut down both corners of the box, from top to bottom. He scarce dared to breathe as he folded back the side of the box to reveal the precious wax-paper packet within. With steady hands, he pressed the scrubby remnants of a half-burned bush into the box, alongside Lucy, so as to stop it collapsing when the pastry was withdrawn. Then he slipped the long blade underneath the donut and worked it silently out, over the labor of some fifteen minutes. At last he held the tiny packet, balanced on the flat of his knife. He turned and held it out to Drebber, who snatched it and retreated some twenty yards or so from the fading ring of firelight. Joseph wiped his brow; he had not realized how freely he'd been sweating—a practice that could prove fatal in a dry waste such as this. Keeping his footfalls as soft as he could, he followed Drebber away from the camp.

Already, Drebber was pulling at the paper with quivering fingers. His eyes were wild and fearful. With every crinkle the wax paper released, his eyes shot back to the sleeping form of Jefferson Hope, terrified that the telltale paper had betrayed him to the sleeping giant. Joseph could not help licking his lips as he peered over Drebber's shoulder at the stolen treasure. Fold by fold, the paper yielded, until at last the naked form of Lucy lay before them, bathed in moonlight. She was half crushed and all stale. Nevertheless, the sight of this forbidden delicacy drew a gasp of awe from the two men.

"Half," Joseph dared to whisper. "I want half."

Drebber's eyes flashed with fury and greed, but only for an instant. *Wait... yes. Yes. Let him eat.* It was the taste of donut Drebber craved, not the quantity. Far better to have a confederate. Should this crime rouse the fury of Jefferson Hope, he would rather it was a two-against-one argument. Here in the wasteland, a man was his own law. Strangerson wasn't much of a man, but half a donut was a small price for an ally, here where they all slept so vulnerable, beneath the wild sky. Let him eat.

Eat it, Joseph Strangerson, and whatever fate it brings on me, you will share, as sure as we shared Lucy.

Enoch Drebber voiced none of this; his eyes drifted to the knife in Strangerson's hand. It was not the instrument of a man, being pearl-handled and delicate of blade, and

Drebber had no fear of it, unarmed though he was. His mind traveled different paths.

"You split. I choose."

Joseph bent over the moon-drenched donut and, for a moment, his nerve failed him. He stopped, his blade trembling in the air above Lucy. Finally, conscious of what Drebber must think of him, he leaned in to do the deed. Strange, but as the blade slid into Lucy's soft flesh, he felt the hand of fate close on him. Othello must have felt it at Desdemona's last gasp. Hannibal, as he watched the Roman lines close at Zama. What had he done? Such a simple thing, but so permanent. No mortal hand had the power to mend that cleft; the closer side of the donut had been cut right through. Even if he were to put it back, Hope would know what he had done. There was but one way now: forward. The second cut was easier. He made one half noticeably larger, as if claiming the smaller share would lessen his blame.

With a muffled laugh of triumph, Drebber pounced upon the larger half and ran with it still further into the darkness. Strangerson picked up his half and followed. The two of them ate, already laughing, already reminiscing about their crime, not one minute past. To one another, they painted it as boyish mischief, a simple prank. For a few moments this lie comforted them, as their white teeth tore the flesh of Lucy. Yet moments fly fast in that desolate and open land; there is nothing to hold them in—no rocks, no trees, no buildings to stop them drifting away into the vastness. There, amongst the crumbs, the sky began to press down on the two men. They sat in silence for almost half an hour. Their joy faded. The deed remained.

"Let's leave him," Drebber said.

"We can't!" said Joseph, louder than he meant to. "A man can't live alone in a place like this! It's murder."

"It ain't! Ain't!" insisted Drebber, wide-eyed and shaking. "Look, we all come into this thing, free to leave whenever we chose. We ain't abandoning him. It's only… you leave the group and I leave the group, just at the same time. Tomorrow, you and me, we'll form a new group, but tonight we're just quittin'. That's all."

Joseph shook his head. "It ain't right."

"We don't need him!" Drebber said. "He's got us all the way out here, that's what we wanted him for. He don't know a thing about prospectin' and that's a fact. Look, Joseph, look: California's just over them hills. We kin make it!"

"I can't. I just… I can't."

Drebber rocked back on his heels. Strangerson disgusted him sometimes, the weakness of him. Though they were supposed equals in this venture, though Joseph in fact possessed the knowledge of geology they both hoped would make them rich, Drebber knew himself to be the master. He decided to show it.

"Fine," he said. "Better this way. You tell him… when he wakes up, you tell him I ate it. Tell him I took it all. Mebbe he won't look too close at those pretty little slits down the side of the box. Mebbe he won't know you had a hand in it. Mebbe he won't notice your tremble or how you hide your eyes from him, all the long years you work together. Mebbe not. Me, I'm strikin' out on my own."

"No. Enoch, no," Joseph mewled, but Drebber moved off to gather his gear, silently as he could. In the end, Joseph gave in—just as always. Jefferson Hope was a sound sleeper and the two made off that night without waking him. They left him little, only two canteens of water, and those half empty. They took all three horses and the pack mule, as it was Drebber who had paid for them. Strangerson left the knife; he didn't want it any more, never wanted to look on it. As the two rode off, dreading every clop of every hoof, Joseph Strangerson looked back at the sleeping bulk of Jefferson Hope. He tried to imagine what that form would look like with no meat upon it. Flesh could not bide in a desert such as this. No, this was the land of dry and bleaching bones. Without water or hooves, Strangerson knew, the desert would destroy Hope. The shifting dust would cover their crime. The open sky would never tell.

Let the desert have him.

12

A MAN COULD NOT HAVE SURVIVED, BUT JEFFERSON Hope was no longer a man. Love died. Reason died. All the better graces of humankind dried up and perished in him. Though hunger dogged him and thirst was his constant companion, he took no joy in food or water. Hate sustained him. He staggered about the desert, by day and by night, howling for vengeance with Lucy's empty wrapper clutched in his fist. The beast was all that remained in him. The reaver. Wendigo, the Indians called it.

Yet he who lives for revenge must find his prey. Madness is blinding; one may not steer by it. Only reason can make a clear path. Thus—not because it was welcome, but because it was needed—thought began to return to him. Jefferson Hope could not say how long he had wandered those wastes, living on scorpion meat and his own tears. It must have been months, maybe years, yet he knew he must leave the cradle of his madness. His destiny lay in the goldfields of California, though that metal did not shine for him now.

The mountains could not stop him. He crossed to

California. There he encountered his first test. Drebber and Strangerson, no fools, had elected to change their names. Nobody knew them here and they abandoned their tarnished identities in favor of a fresh start. Hope had no easy time garnering information. His grief had transformed him totally; he had lost command of the language of man, forgotten the taste of donut.

Had Drebber and Strangerson hidden in the wild, Hope could have tracked them like a wolf, but men hide amongst men, not trees. Even as the local prospectors and tribes began to whisper of the wild man, Hope began—word by agonizing word—to teach himself to speak again. He never did get it quite right, in those days. Though he always tried to pass himself off as a fellow human, when he did get a tidbit of information, it was never civility that afforded it to him, but fear.

That first winter after his return to the world of men, he had a breakthrough. He came across a trio of dejected prospectors, on the brink of abandoning their claim. They'd purchased it some months before from a duo from back east. One of the pair had been a geologist, they said, who had been in the territory not two weeks before discovering the vein that made his fortune. He and his partner had worked the claim for some months until, flush with money and tired of their labors, they resolved to head to one of the major cities and set themselves up as outfitters, to profit from the sweat of other hopefuls. These new owners were hot with rage, for having purchased the profitable claim with the last of their monies, they found it had been quite played out. They had no stomach for revenge themselves, but happily told Jefferson Hope that the pair had headed up to 'Frisco in early autumn, under the names Jenoch Strebber and Oseph Dangerson.

It was a hard and heavy winter that year; many an old squaw, huddled in her tepee, found it to be her last. Yet Jefferson Hope had no care of cold. He did not stop to rest. He no longer slept, except for when exhaustion took its hold and he fell where he stood. Foot by foot, step by step, he made his way north. The earth rejoiced at spring as Jefferson Hope reached his destination, but the man himself took no more comfort from the season of rebirth than he had in the season of death.

It was in San Francisco that Hope made his first attempts on the lives of his quarry. At first he had trouble nearing them, since they were respectable businessmen with the trappings of money and he was a ravening wild man in three-year-old rags. Only in the rough-hewn docks district was he accepted, so that was where he lodged. He took on work as a dockhand, slowly gaining money for a haircut and respectable clothes. He met his first true friend since the Lucy disaster (and as it turned out, the last one he ever had). It was the self-proclaimed ruler of the United States, Emperor Norton I. Norton allowed Hope to lodge with him for a time, and taught him the streets and customs of San Francisco.

Once able to blend with the general population, Hope began to hunt again. Drebber and Strangerson were easy to locate—they had opened their own outfitter's shop—but difficult to slay. Jefferson Hope's first attempts were artful, but met with no success. A load of lumber, being hoisted to build a new roof, fell and nearly crushed Strangerson, who leapt away at the last moment. Examination of the main hoist rope revealed that it had been cut (how alarmed Strangerson would have been to know it was his own pearl-handled knife that did the deed). Drebber found a bootlace woven in amongst his linguine one day and lucky for him that he had—it was rumored that bootlaces were indigestible and caused sickness or death in anybody unfortunate enough to ingest one.

In early June 1873, Drebber was very nearly the victim of a strange incident in which a gorilla appeared at the highest point of Lombard Street and began rolling barrels down at the unfortunate people below. Drebber only managed to preserve himself by leaping over the barrels as they rolled towards him. Two days later, the Union Square Theater reported one of their ape costumes missing and Enoch Drebber began to doubt the random nature of these occurrences.

The final proof came on August 2, when Hope—frustrated at his failed attempts—decided to simply shoot Strangerson down in the street. He bought a derringer from a dockside pawnshop and intercepted Joseph as he walked to work. Hope called Strangerson by name; he wanted his foe to know who it was that killed him and why he must die. Strangerson later recalled the moment when those terrible, angry eyes resolved into a once-familiar face and Jefferson Hope entered his life once more (though he had never disappeared from Strangerson's guilt-induced night terrors). Hope raised his pistol to fire, but at that very moment, Strangerson was rescued by what appeared to be a small outdoor dining area, packed with grinning patrons, which sped up the hill behind him. Strangerson leapt onto this passing monstrosity and made good his escape on what turned out to be the city's first cable car—the Clay Street Hill Railroad—on its maiden voyage. Hope fired, but the derringer, like most of its make, carried only two shots and was inaccurate at a range of more than three feet.

Once again, Drebber and Strangerson fled in the night. Leaving their inferiors to sell their shop and settle affairs, they abandoned their homes at about three that next morning to board the first steamer to Seattle. It didn't take Hope long to figure out where they had gone and he followed, hot on their heels. By the time he reached that northern town, he was once again short of funds and was compelled to take work as a timber-feller in the hills above the city. Drebber and Strangerson now went armed and took care with their persons, never walking alone, always sitting with their backs to the wall and their eyes on the door in every public establishment they entered. Still, Hope's attempts grew ever more bold until they were forced to flee Seattle as well.

So began the merry chase that stretched on for another eight years. From Seattle they fled to Cleveland, from there to Detroit, thence to Pittsburgh, Austin and finally New York. If only they had thought to settle in St. Louis, they would have been safe, for Jefferson Hope would have died of grief if ever he had happened past Hall and Sons' Bakery. In each city where they landed, Hope pursued menial labor while Drebber and Strangerson sought to expand their trade in the little time they had before their pursuing phantom materialized again and forced their departure.

Finally, they left the United States, thinking Hope would lack both the funds and the heart to follow them to unfamiliar lands. They first tried their luck in St. Petersburg, after hearing that the burgeoning Russian empire wished to modernize and open trade with the West. Unfortunately for the two pastry thieves, they spoke no Russian and ran headlong into that country's entrenched conservative values. Outsiders were not welcome. They were there less than a year, struggling to begin a successful trading company, before Hope found them. They could hardly have been more conspicuous. Strangerson, especially, was glad to shake the dust of the place from his boots and flee to Copenhagen.

From Copenhagen to Paris. From Paris to Barcelona. From Barcelona to Berlin. Here predator and prey parted ways. Drebber and Strangerson fled to Rome. Hope to London. Years of study had taught him well the habits of his quarry—Hope realized Drebber and Strangerson had a predilection for capitals. He also knew they were nearing the end of their patience with the language barrier. London, then. When the pair fled Berlin, Hope ignored their destination. Instead, he installed himself in London and found work as a cabbie. They would come, he knew. They would land here and when they did, this time he would already be on his feet, with a job, the funds to pursue them and knowledge of the terrain. London's streets are a study in madness, or perhaps randomness, or perhaps the threshold between the two. Nevertheless, with diligence, Jefferson Hope learned the streets well enough. His job took him often to the docks, to train stations, to hotels, and in each of these he asked after his prey. When they came, he would know.

PART III

ONCE MORE FROM THE JOURNAL OF
DR. JOHN WATSON, AND ISN'T THAT A RELIEF?

13

THE DRIVE TO SCOTLAND YARD WAS A LONG ONE AT THE best of times. In the middle of the afternoon, through streets bustling with traffic, trade and about six thousand "flower girls" showing off their "wares" it took even longer. Thus, Jefferson Hope finished his tale ere we arrived.

"As soon as I found they had landed in London, I began to shadow them," he told us. "I started spending most days and nights near Charpontier's boarding house. But they took care, as they always did, not to travel alone. That last fateful night, I followed their cab to Euston Station and watched 'em make for the trains. I don't mind telling you, I was desperate. I couldn't have them escape me again, for the pressure in my head and heart had grown so intense that I thought I might explode early."

At this point, I was forced to intrude myself upon the story and ask, "Now, precisely why are you convinced that you are going to explode?"

"Russian Gypsy wise woman," he remarked, as if it were a perfectly common avenue of medical advice. "Even before St. Petersburg, I felt the pressure growing. I knew I had to catch 'em. She's the one who told me I was likely to bleed profusely at exciting moments in my life story, due to my unnaturally high blood pressure. She seemed real sorry when she told me I'd explode after everything was all resolved, but I didn't mind much. I just want to have justice and be done with it. I don't reckon a man ought to outlive his own story on any count, do you, Doctor?"

Preposterous as it all sounded, you should have heard his chest. He gave me permission to examine him and I was astounded by what I found. His skin was hot and throbbed with an unaccountably powerful and uneven pulse. Though my medical training encompassed no such possibility, I found myself shying to the opposite end of the cab, lest his heart and brain burst in my lap.

"Anyways, they missed the train," Hope continued, "and they argued. Leaving my horse, I snuck through the crowd, close enough to hear 'em. Strangerson wanted to go on to another private hotel he knew—Halliday's—I guess they wasn't welcome back where they come from. Still, Drebber said he had business back at Charpontier's. Drebber weren't too nice to his friend that day, being already rotten with drink. He treated everyone pretty bad, I guess. Strangerson took one cab, Drebber another. I followed Drebber. I guess I hated him more. He went back to Charpontier's but didn't stay long. In no time at all, he comes running back out onto the street with a young man at his heels, waving a stick and threat'ning to beat him to death. Well I pulled up my cab to the curb to save him. Funny, but in that moment I wasn't thinking to kill him, only that I couldn't let nobody else do it, or I'd lose my chance forever. Wasn't 'til we were alone in my cab that I realized I finally had him. He hadn't recognized me. He was jolly as you like; kept taking swigs out of that flask of his and telling me about some pretty girl he'd just been courtin'. He said he was tired out and ordered me to take him some place to sleep."

"I drove him round to 3 Lauriston Gardens, what I knew to be vacant. He followed me in, friendly as you like, and complained of the darkness. I lit a candle, held it before my face and said, 'You know me, Drebber! Who am I?'"

"He musta thought we were playin' a game, for he guessed Abraham Lincoln, but when I showed him Lucy's wrapper, he knew what was comin'. He tried to push past me, but in that moment I had the strength to best a rhino. He tried begging, promised me money, but nothing, nothing was going to stay my hand. I'd come so far... I showed him the pills. I told him, "Now Drebber, you choose. One of 'em is deadly poison; the other ain't. You choose one now an' eat it. I'll eat th' other and we'll see if there's any justice in this world or not!' I weren't afraid, for I could feel Lucy with me, smell her sweet dough. Either she would be avenged, or I would join her in the boundless ever-after. Mewlin' like a baby cat, Drebber chose one and we ate. Then I seen his face tighten up and I knew he'd chose the bad pill. In that moment, I knew myself an instrument of justice. Can't tell you how good that felt. For a number of years up 'til then, I was afraid I might just be crazy. Felt so good to watch him die. It was only a fraction of the misery he'd caused me an' Lucy, but it still felt good. I stuffed the wrapper in his mouth and left. I didn't even realize I'd been bleedin' 'til then."

"No, no, no," I protested. "You carried that paper across ten years and two continents. Not a day after the murder, you risked capture to retrieve that wrapper from my very hand. Do you expect me to believe you just decided to leave it with Drebber's corpse?"

"Thought I wanted to," he shrugged. "I wanted to make him eat it, wanted it to be the last thing he ever tasted. Only, when I got back to the cab, I felt she was gone. I was alone, you know? First time since Nevada. Even in my madness, I had her there. I could smell her. My Lucy. I had to go back, but that damned cop had already come. I didn't know what to do, 'til I saw the ad in the paper. I pulled a dress off a clothesline and... heh, heh... I sure fooled you, Doctor!"

I saw no sense in arguing with the man. "You sure did," I said.

"Good thing, too," he added amiably, "or I'da had ta slice you up!"

I fell silent. He continued, "Once I had Lucy's ghost back, I drove round to Halliday's and began sneakin' round. I saw Strangerson up there, reading by his window. I went and found a ladder and climbed up to see him. I gave him the same choice I gave Drebber, but he weren't having none of it. He come at me and I let him have it. I meant to poison him, but I weren't sad to see him fall to

148

the same knife he took to my Lucy. I left Lucy's ghost in his mouth too, for I thought I wouldn't need it no more, then I went outside to explode."

"Only you didn't," I pointed out, in passive-aggressive defense of actual medicine.

"I shoulda figured—getting caught and explainin' myself—story wasn't over 'til I did that."

I shook my head again and reflected, "So... you followed these men for ten years; taught yourself the trades of dock work, lumberjacking, portering, cab-driving; taught yourself Russian, Spanish, German, French and Danish?"

"Guess I did," Hope said.

"That may be the most trouble any human has ever taken over the matter of a crumpet with a hole in it," I said.

"The perfect revenge," Holmes mused.

"Yeah..." Hope agreed, "only..."

"Only what?" asked Holmes.

"Now that I get to thinkin' on it, I shoulda done Strangerson first," Mr. Hope said, shaking his head sadly. "Shoulda killed him with that knife, cut him in half, poisoned half his body and told Drebber, 'I split, so you choose!' I'da eaten whatever half of the body he didn't, of course. I'da poisoned the smaller half. Drebber would have taken the smaller half."

Horror-struck, I said nothing.

"That would have been masterful," said Holmes.

Hope only nodded and said, "I know it. So... what about that gun? How'd you shoot my cab in half with one pistol shot?"

"It wasn't the gun that did the damage, Mr. Hope. I only had Watson fire it for appearances. That way, any neighbors who beheld the action would see what you did: a pistol, apparently loaded with a potent explosive cartridge. That is not the truth, but what else could one assume?"

"What's the truth then?"

Oddly, it was not Jefferson Hope but me that Warlock fixed with his otherworldly green gaze. He sighed. "Moriarty said I should be discovered if I took this case. I realize now, he was speaking of you, Watson. Strange... I have grown accustomed to denying everything. But one of you gentlemen is not long for this world and the other is too close and too observant to be fooled. I wonder, have either of you ever noticed the brimstone thread?"

"What's that?" asked Hope.

"Think of the world as a sheet of cloth, woven on the master loom. There are thousands of threads that make it up, each coming and going in patterns. As you travel through life, you happen upon various threads. There is one for poverty, one for plenty. There is a thread for love, two for lust, several for disappointment, one for balsa wood and, of course, the brimstone thread."

Holmes paused until Jefferson Hope said, "I still don't think you've answered my question."

"The brimstone thread is an echo. There are powerful things that exist outside our own, comfortable reality. They would like to be here; they are constantly searching for a way in. Thus, they are ever willing to do favors for people in this reality. After all, is one ever truly absent from a place that has felt one's influence? Do a favor for a millionaire some time and, whenever you remind them of it, you are sure to find yourself treated to a nice meal, if not a new house. They can never be entirely free of their obligation to you. With guilt, I must admit that I am a person whom these outside entities perpetually attend, all clambering to do me favors. I try to avoid accepting them, for with each deed they do for me, they are closer to this world. The brimstone thread shows itself more and more within the cloth. You must have noticed."

"I think I have." Mr. Hope nodded, a faraway look in his eye. "I think I was stuck on that thread for a while. I almost feel a part of it."

"It wouldn't surprise me," Holmes mumbled, but his eyes were on me, not Mr. Hope. When I said nothing, he chided, "Oh come now, Watson. You must have seen it! Why do the zealots of every religion behave in the same way? Whatever their native faith might teach, they always turn hate, violence and intolerance against the innocent! Regardless of the god they turn from, why is it always the same one they turn *to*? Why is any number, raised to the power of zero, equal to one? It doesn't make sense! It seems otherworldly because it is, but it is so well entrenched in our reality that we can no longer understand our own world without resorting to it. *That* is the brimstone thread! I know you have seen it, Watson, and I know you to be keen of mind and gifted with great powers of observation. I have hidden the existence of the outer realms from the simpletons who lodged with me previously, but you… Having caught one glimpse, one tattered edge of the thread, a man like you has the capacity to make a scientific analysis of it—a study in brimstone—which I would be powerless to stop, except by killing you or ruining your intellect."

"You wouldn't!" I retorted.

"No, I wouldn't! Really, Watson, you are a danger to me—exposure to the unsympathetic world being my keenest fear. But you have no idea what a relief it is not to be lodging with some drooling imbecile who grows slowly more and more frightened of me with each passing day until he finally makes his escape. Why, you even seem to be my better at this crime-solving business."

"Preposterous," I declared.

"Fact," insisted Holmes.

"I know how it can be settled," said Jefferson Hope. "Which one of you caught me?"

"He did!" said Holmes and I together.

"I did not," I told Hope. "He used his powers."

"I wouldn't!" Holmes protested. "Every time I allow one of those things to do me a favor, I sell them another piece of this world. I betray the entire race of man. I would never use my powers for anything so trivial as the capture of a single murderer!"

"Ah, so it was my pistol that blew up the coach?" I countered.

"Well… that hardly counts. That was Azazel smiting something. He loves to smite. Hardly a favor… Better to say, I did *him* a favor by giving him something to smite."

"QED: you used your powers," I said.

"Really, Watson, don't be foolish. It was you who figured out that Mr. Hope here would be a London cab driver with an American accent. All I did was to send the Baker Street Irregulars out looking for such a man. As it happens, there was only one."

Mr. Hope nodded his approval and congratulations. I sat stunned. *Stunned.* It really hadn't occurred to me before that moment, but I had done it—I had solved the crime. I was so enchanted with the power of Grogsson, the terror of Lestrade, and the mystery of Holmes that I had come to view myself as quite powerless but… in the end…

I sat speechless the rest of the way to Scotland Yard, whilst Holmes and Hope chatted about demons, pistols, the finer points of cutting men in half, et cetera.

That is about the end of the matter, except to relate one final event which, I will admit, caused me some sadness. It seems that cardio-cranial narrative-sensitive exploditis *is* a real condition. The story of his life having run its course, his revenge complete, his capture having illuminated his strange history, Jefferson Hope's head and heart burst that very night, as he slept in his jail cell. What surprised me most was the sheer power of the explosion. He was hardly more than a husk when they found him. The force was such that it tore the window and door from the stone walls of his cell. There was blood everywhere. Detective Inspector Vladislav Lestrade insisted on handling the investigation *personally*.

14

HOLMES WAS OUT, AS HAD BECOME HIS HABIT. IT WAS A habit I gave him, though quite by accident. In passing one day, I had shown him a penny dreadful that one of the nurses gave me to read during my recovery after my fever. I showed it to him only to recall the woman's kindness, but Holmes seized it and devoured it with scholarly zeal. For two days thereafter he paced and fretted, wondering why there was so little "real literature" left in the world. When I informed him that the profusion of penny dreadfuls on the streets of London had reached near-epidemic proportions, he seized his coat and ran forth to buy up every one he could find. After reading this initial batch, he developed a regular patrol—visiting every cheap bookseller he could find, waking them at all hours to demand new novels.

I was glad to have a moment alone. I was deep in my thoughts—some happy, some not, and all of them uncertain. I sat at the dining table, playing with a lead soldier I had purchased the day my ship left port—supposedly for India. His uniform and kit were the perfect mirror of my own, done in a clever hand, down to the minutest detail.

In recent days, the thing had become a source of some dismay for me. His face was stern, his bearing soldierly, his uniform so straight and perfect that I felt the little leaden man had the better of me. I should have been more like him, by all accounts. It boggled me to think how different my life might have been if I had been listening when Murray shouted "duck". If not for that bullet and that fever, who would I have become? Would I have extricated myself from thrice-cursed Afghanistan and made my way to Bombay? Would the daily practice of war have hardened me into the stiff-upper-lipped British medical officer my late father had so overtly hoped for?

Holmes stepped back in about half past ten and uttered what was becoming an ever more customary greeting for him. "This author, Watson! This Mary Bryce! She is some sort of sprite or fairy, you may count on it! I tell you, Eldar blood is in her veins, else how does she write them so exact?"

I had no heart to talk of fairies. "Holmes, I have something for you," I said.

"Oh? And what is that?"

I held up a single sovereign. "The rent."

I suppose I might have been taking my leave of him, settling our account like a gentleman before I went. Yet, I was not and he knew it. With a proper crow of triumph, he sprang across the room, swept the coin into his hands and cried, "Happy day, Watson! Gads, could this morning be better? A proper masterpiece concerning fairies, a Varney Vampire book that will anger Lestrade something wonderful, and now you have decided to stay? Ah! I am glad!"

"As am I," I assured him.

"Well then," he said, pulling out the chair opposite me and settling into it with a wide grin, "why don't you look it?"

I sighed heavily. "As you probably realize, Holmes, I have developed a taste for these adventures you claim are so commonplace to you."

"How could you not, Watson? The thrill of the chase, eh?"

"Indeed. Yet it is unsettling to me. I don't expect you to understand, Holmes, but I was supposed to be very different than I am and… well… I understand what it was I *should* have become, but not what I *have* become. Do you see? I understand medicine. You and all your 'peculiar' friends I do not understand at all. In fact, you make me realize that the world—which I thought I knew so well—is a wider, wilder, scarier place than I had thought. I can't figure out where I stand. Who am I? *What* are you? And how is this situation even to be maintained, for in spite of the lure of it all, I don't see how all this intrigue earns us a single penny."

Holmes's mouth spread into a sympathetic grin. He reached over to give my wrist a reassuring shake and said, "Perhaps I may help. You are John Watson: a man of worth, possessed of a sharp mind and a true heart. As for the last two points…"

He swept the lead soldier from the table and regarded it for a moment. His features turned suddenly whimsical and sad. He cupped the soldier between his hands so I could not see it and continued, "Have you ever heard of the alchemists, Watson? Suppose one of those poor fellows had succeeded. Picture the unlucky fool who finally learned to turn base metal into gold, only to find that in the same moment, he had turned his own, golden self into... something base."

He uncapped his hands and I gave a little cry of surprise, for from them issued a gout of sulfurous smoke and a surprising quantity of blood. I recoiled. I saw no wound upon his hands and his face registered no pain. Instead, he stood up resolutely and gave me a wan smile. "Welcome to the fight, Watson. We're all very glad to have you on our side."

He rose, leaving me to gawk and stare. There, in the middle of the table, dewed in blood and reeking of brimstone, stood my little soldier—once of simple dross, now gleaming gold.

THE ADVENTURE
OF THE RESIDENT SACRIFICE

JUST AFTER LUNCHEON, ON A QUIET TUESDAY AFTERNOON, I said, "No, Holmes; Robert E. Lee was not a demon."

Holmes stared at me, mouth agape.

"That is what you were thinking, is it not? Well, it is incorrect; he was a gifted general—that is all."

"But, Watson," Holmes gasped, "I said nothing! Nothing! *You have read my mind!*"

"I did no such thing."

"But you did! For that indeed was my last thought!"

I sighed, folded the front section of *The Times* into my lap and said, "Holmes, you know better than that. Simple observation has revealed your thoughts to me and—if you are going to persist in explaining away your demonic insights as detective work—I think you had better take the trouble to learn how to correctly observe and deduce."

"Do you expect me to believe your little parlor trick affords insight into another man's inner thoughts?" Holmes scoffed. "To that, I say a loud, abrupt 'pshaw.'"

"Holmes…"

"Pshaw!"

"Holmes! Let me detail my observations for you; perhaps you will begin to understand. First, I noticed you reading the featured article in my military history magazine, in which Lord Huffington sings the praises of General Lee's martial prowess."

Holmes nodded that this much was correct.

"You then ran to the bookshelf and picked up a volume of poetry by Stephen Crane, the newspaper correspondent who turned to apocalyptic poetry when he was sent to report on the war. It may be the darkest verse the hand of man has ever put to paper and I wish you wouldn't read it, for I fear it gives you ideas."

"It does, Watson. Oh, it does."

"After you had read enough poems to turn your mind from generalship to demonics, you suddenly gasped and stared in amazement at the portrait of Robert E. Lee which hangs above our bookshelf—for reasons I still do not understand."

"His was the picture that came in the frame when I purchased it, Watson."

"Ah—mystery solved. After staring for some time with your mouth hanging wide, you ran to the desk and began sketching another version of the same portrait, wherein the general has horns, fangs, a tail and slitted snake eyes. You then gave a cry of triumph and threw down your pencil as if you had proven a great truth, at which point I chose to inform you that Robert E. Lee was not a demon. Now do you see how observation led me to that deduction?"

"But it looks just like him!"

"Of course it does—you *drew it* to look just like him. This does not prove—"

The ringing of our bell cut me off.

"Yes?" I asked.

From behind our closed front door, Mrs. Hudson's voice said, "A gentleman to see Mr. Holmes." Judging by her breathy tone, I imagined it must be an attractive gentleman indeed—perhaps worthy of inclusion in one of her smutty novels.

"Enter," said I.

Warlock gave me an angry glance and flew back to his desk. He flung a book over his devilish sketch, still certain he had discovered a secret that must be guarded from the eyes of the common man. The door swung open to reveal Mrs. Hudson hanging from our guest's left arm in a half-swoon. She might have fallen in love on the strength of his facial hair alone, for our visitor wore a dashing moustache, such as one might find in the circus or on certain cavalry officers. He held himself with a feminine reserve and a demure, almost subservient air, yet his upper body bulged with musculature. As he stepped forward, I noted he had the trace of a limp and that his left foot turned in slightly.

"Mr. Percy Trevelyan," Mrs. Hudson announced, dreamily.

"At your service," our guest added, then asked me, "You are Mr. Warlock Holmes?"

I indicated my companion with a wave and sat back to watch.

"Yes, I am Warlock Holmes," said he, rising to shake Trevelyan's hand. "How may I be of service?"

"It is a matter of some delicacy..." Trevelyan said, then held his silence until Mrs. Hudson realized that he was waiting for her to leave. She favored Mr. Trevelyan with a gaze that promised... well... everything, then fired a hateful sneer at Holmes and me, and departed.

"Ah... that's better," said Holmes. "Now, tell me all."

"Well, I am the founder of Trevelyan's Aerial Ballet..."

"And a dancer," Holmes declared. "I perceived it at once."

"Trapeze, I think you'll find," I said. "Observe his calloused hands, muscular upper body and the club foot which would surely preclude a career as a dancer."

"Oh... Damn..." mumbled Holmes.

I saw from Trevelyan's glance that I had wounded him somewhat, but he agreed, "It is just as your... colleague... says. I'm sorry, you must be..."

"Dr. John Watson, at your service."

"Oh, well, I am very pleased to meet you," Trevelyan said, then, in a lower voice added, "Very glad to find you here, indeed."

I did not like his inference. I had observed the marks of—shall we say—a *gentleman's gentleman* about Mr. Trevelyan. I supposed he assumed himself to be in like company, and thought my relationship with Holmes was a romantic one.

"Holmes and I are merely fellow lodgers; it helps to share expenses," I explained.

"Even for a doctor?" Trevelyan asked, raising a mischievous eyebrow.

"Well… I… Yes, for *this* doctor. I am not currently in practice, so…"

"Ah!" said Trevelyan, raising a finger. "I am here to ask Mr. Holmes's advice over just such an arrangement."

"I think a different arrangement," I said, but he ignored me and continued.

"Last spring I was approached by a gentleman after one of my shows, name of Blessington."

I cringed, hoping the story was not to be too lurid.

"He found me at Le Café Majestique, taking dessert with a few of my admirers, still in my costume. He walked straight up to us, declared an interest in trapeze and offered to pay for the entire table if he might be allowed to join. Well, we were delighted and admitted him at once. Yet he proved to be so crude, I found myself amazed that a mind like that could have any interest in the arts at all. As the evening wore on and people began to excuse themselves, it became clear that he was waiting to be the last man at the table with me. When he had me alone, he made a very strange proposition."

I shifted uneasily in my chair, which drew a look of annoyance from Trevelyan. Holmes was yet to give any indication that he understood the situation our guest was describing.

"Blessington told me he wished to become a patron of the arts, but knew nobody in London's creative circles. That very night, point blank, he offered to support me. He promised me room, board, spending money and financial support for my trapeze show. All I had to do was come live with him and offer a share of my profits."

Here Holmes brightened and asked, "I say, do you make a lot of money at trapeze?"

"No. I don't. Nobody does."

"I imagine that did not concern Mr. Blessington," said I.

"It did not. I chided him for his forwardness, but told him I might be interested. He offered to show me the place that very night and I will confess, I agreed. Imagine my surprise when he had me installed in a separate room from his own."

"Why should that surprise you?" Holmes asked.

Trevelyan gave Holmes a sly look. I attempted to explain, "Well, Holmes, Mr. Trevelyan enjoys the company of other men…"

"As do I," Holmes agreed.

"No… I mean, instead of women."

"Well, that is understandable," said Holmes. "Much as I would like to say I am beloved of the ladies, I find I never know quite what to say to them. So, I suppose, I must also state that I find myself more comfortable in the company of men."

I sighed and said, "You misunderstand. Mr. Trevelyan is a *confirmed bachelor*."

Holmes threw up his hands. "Well? If anybody asked you or me to confirm our marital status, would we not have to proclaim ourselves bachelors also?"

"Holmes, when a gentleman agrees to move into another gentleman's house and allows that man to pay his way through life—"

Here Holmes interrupted to say, "Just as you and I do…"

"No, Holmes. This is a different arrangement entirely."

"It sounds exactly the same."

Finally, Trevelyan nodded to me that he would take over. He leaned close to Holmes and whispered a few words in his ear.

"Oh," Holmes said. "Yes, that is different. I have heard of such things, of course. But Mr. Blessington was not offering such an arrangement?"

"No!" said Trevelyan in exasperation. "Once he had me installed and dependent, he ignored me entirely. Still does. We rarely speak more than a few words to one another. I have the whole top floor to myself; he keeps the lower one. In payment, I give him four-fifths of my box-office takings whenever I mount a show."

"Eighty percent?" I coughed.

But Trevelyan waved me down. "It is a pittance! What is eighty percent of nothing, Doctor? He's squandered a fortune on me, yet he never complains of the loss. The only way I can upset him is by staying out too late. He is insistent that I spend every night in my rooms. He seems to want me there during all hours of darkness."

"Curious," mumbled Holmes. I agreed.

"This arrangement held until yesterday evening. Earlier this week, an actress friend of mine brought me a card. It bore

the name of Gerard Me'doreux—a confederate of the great
father of trapeze, Jules Léotard. She told me that Monsieur
Me'doreux wished to meet with me and might consent
to instruct me on a few of Léotard's techniques. Well, I
was ecstatic! I agreed to meet him at my house, yesterday
evening. Blessington spends his early evenings at his club,
so I knew we would not disturb him. Monsieur Me'doreux
arrived in the company of another gentleman—quite the
specimen. He was nearly fifty I should think, but muscular,
very short and with reddish hair. Monsieur Me'doreux
introduced him as a colleague, but said that his companion—
unlike myself—was unworthy to learn the secrets of the
Great Léotard. He made the man wait in the hall while
we spoke.

"If I hoped he would open the floodgates of knowledge,
I was much mistaken. Monsieur Me'doreux first insisted
that I tell him all I know of trapeze in order that he waste
no time instructing me in that which I already understood.
We spoke for almost an hour but all I had from him were
questions—it was *I* who shared my knowledge. Just as
it seemed he might be ready to favor me with his own
wisdom, his companion burst in upon us and announced
that it was time to go, as Monsieur Me'doreux had theater
commitments later that evening. He bustled the old man
out without another word.

"I was frustrated by the meeting and still hopeful that
I might arrange another, when Blessington came home. I
heard his footsteps in the hall and then a few moments
later, a great cry. In a twinkling, he was up the stairs and

crashed through my door, demanding to know if I had been in his rooms."

"You hadn't, of course," I interjected, "but you must now realize that the old gentleman was merely keeping you busy while his accomplice rifled Blessington's rooms."

"I fear that is so," said Trevelyan.

"In which case, the old man probably had no knowledge of trapeze to impart. That is why he endeavored to keep you speaking of what *you* knew; as soon as he was forced to demonstrate knowledge, his sham would have been revealed."

"Likely," sighed Trevelyan. "Alas, for I heartily crave contact with the master of my art and his secrets."

"Just as I crave a heart attack, on the part of Mrs. Hudson," said I. "Yet here we both sit, disappointed. Tell me, did you recount any of this encounter to Blessington?"

"No. I merely said I had not been in his rooms, at which he grew pale and agitated. I think he was up very late. When I awoke this morning, I crept out, hoping to shield myself from further interrogation. I returned just before lunch, to find him erecting a barricade across the top of the stairs. I had no idea what to do! I could not account for his strange behavior and he refused to answer my questions. One of my friends suggested you, Mr. Holmes, as a man who understands the bizarre better than he understands the commonplace."

I had to laugh at that, but Trevelyan ignored me and asked, "What do you think, Mr. Holmes? Can you make any sense of the matter?"

"Hmm… let me see…" Holmes said and tapped his lips thoughtfully with his finger for a few seconds before deciding, "No. I can't. How about you, Watson?"

I had a few notions, but most of the story was a mystery still, so I asked, "Did Blessington tell you nothing? He gave no further clue?"

"Well… I did hear him talking to himself last night. He was pacing back and forth in his bedroom below me and I several times heard him swear, 'He shall not have it, by God, Moran shall not have it.'"

In a trice, Holmes was on his feet.

"Watson, get your coat!"

Upon our arrival at Trevelyan's residence, Holmes stepped cautiously from the cab, observing the street in both directions before approaching the door. Trevelyan and I followed, uncertain. We were just behind Holmes and a little off to his left when he reached the door and knocked. No sooner had his hand touched wood than a series of loud reports rang out from behind the door. Shattered wood erupted towards us as a series of holes traced itself across both the door and adjacent wall. Dust and flying splinters filled the air. I can hardly describe the familiarity and horror a battle-wounded soldier feels when he realizes he is once again coming under enemy fire. I must have cried out. Holmes calmly stepped to one side, a look of irritation on his face. Trevelyan froze—the wrong instinct, but one I could well understand, for I had

A STUDY IN BRIMSTONE

done so myself at the Battle of Maiwand. Turning from the door, I flung myself upon Trevelyan and pulled him down into the gutter.

"Holmes! Get down!" I cried, but he disregarded me and stood his ground, just to one side of the door.

"Calm yourself, Watson," he said. "He's nowhere near me. The shots are all off to my left."

So they were, but not by more than two feet. One round struck the top hinge from the door, then the cascade of bullets began to travel in Holmes's direction. Warlock huffed his annoyance and took a few steps to his right as the stream of bullets came closer, tracing a line of destruction. A round or two must have struck the latch, for there was a shower of brass and iron lock parts.

At last the firing ceased. The door sagged on its one damaged hinge, then slowly fell outwards into the street. From within, I heard a voice call, "Don't come any closer! I have a gun!"

"So it would appear," Holmes shouted back. "I don't suppose you would stop firing it long enough to speak with my friends and me?"

"Who is that? Moran?"

"My name is Warlock Holmes; I am here with Mr. Trevelyan."

"What does he want?"

"To return to his quarters without being blown to scraps," said Holmes.

Raising my head, I could just see past the ruined door, into the hallway and up the stairs to a curious fort. It was

171

constructed as if by a child on a rainy afternoon. Several cushions had been propped up with empty suitcases, becoming makeshift walls. Half of them were draped with blankets, to form a cozy little hiding place. If the armor afforded by this emplacement was sparse, it was more than recompensed for by its armament. A six-barrel Gatling gun protruded from between two cushions, venting smoke.

An instant later, a fat, flushed face—which I assumed belonged to Blessington—appeared over a cushion. "No! You can't come in! It's my fort!"

"Blessington," Holmes remonstrated, "I *am* coming up there."

"No."

"I may be your last chance to set this right, Blessington."

"I don't care! Go away!"

"I am going to count to three and then I am coming in."

"I won't let you!"

"One…" Holmes said slowly. As he spoke, he gestured for me to get to safety.

I propped myself up out of the mud somewhat and said, "Holmes, you mustn't." With one hand I indicated first Trevelyan and then the rest of the world—meaning that the former should not see Holmes perform any unnatural feats and the latter should not be overrun with demons. I think he understood—vague as my warning was—but he tutted away my protests and again gestured for me to get clear.

"Two…"

"Damn him," I cursed, then grabbed Trevelyan by the sleeve and dragged him to safety further down the street.

"Three," said Holmes and stepped in through the door. Blessington opened fire; I heard three more shots ring out, then a strangled scream and a series of thuds, as if someone were kicking the walls inside the house. A lone sofa cushion bounced down the stairs, out the ruined door and into the street.

"Come on," I told Trevelyan. "Let's go see what he's done in there."

There were two possible outcomes and I wasn't sure I liked either of them. Either Blessington had triumphed and I was about to behold Holmes's earthly remains, or Holmes had triumphed and I was about to behold… well, it might be anything. I hoped it wouldn't be too bad—that I wouldn't find the upstairs crawling with chittering imps or every wall dripping with shreds of Blessington.

When I peeped around the remains of the doorway, I beheld Holmes, standing on the landing at the top of the stairs, looking down at Blessington's bulk. All seemed well enough, until I crested the stairs and got a proper look at Blessington. He lay athwart the wreckage of his pillow fort, flat on his back with his limbs contorted. His eyes were open wide and rolled back and forth in a paroxysm of fear. From his mouth issued tendrils of black, oily smoke. These spilled down upon the floor and splayed outwards, moving with an undulating regularity. So cohesive were the strands that it looked as if an octopus made of smoke had just set up home in Blessington's mouth and was now feeling about the floor with all its tentacles, searching for the wallet it had dropped on its way in. Just as disturbing was the impression that Blessington was pinned to the floor by a great weight situated at the back of his mouth. His limbs would convulse and strain from time to time, yanking his torso this way and that. Yet, try as he might, he could not make the back of his head budge from its spot.

"By God!" cried Trevelyan, from the stairs behind me. "What has happened to him?"

Holmes whirled around and, in wide-eyed guilty stammers, explained, "Oh! Um... He was... He fell down, you see..."

I raised a finger, stepped in front of Holmes and told Trevelyan, "Holmes has employed the ancient art of *kara-tei*, a sacred fighting style from far Japan."

"Yes, but that's... that's just kicking and punching, isn't it?" Trevelyan asked.

"It is," I said.

"Then where did all that smoke come from?"

"You have seen Blessington take a cigarette from time to time, have you not?" I asked. "Holmes struck him in such a way as to release all the residual smoke that was trapped within him, after all those years of tobacco. It should be quite cleansing for him."

"Remarkable!" said Trevelyan.

"Thank you," Holmes said, with a sigh of relief.

"And here we have a chance to practice some deduction," I continued. "Now, Mr. Trevelyan, did you not tell us you keep the upstairs rooms, while Blessington here has the lower floor?"

"I did," Trevelyan said.

"Then why do you think he has constructed the barricade across Mr. Trevelyan's door, Holmes, and not his own?"

Holmes shrugged, "It might have just been a better place to build a fort."

"It might," I conceded, "but perhaps there is a more logical deduction. Perhaps he has stashed something precious in Trevelyan's quarters. Mr. Trevelyan, would you come with me please? I should like to search your rooms. If you find anything that does not belong to you— or anything that does, but which is out of place—you must point it out to me immediately."

He agreed with an earnest nod. Holmes and I tossed aside the cushions and stepped through, but there was nothing to find. Trevelyan kept his quarters neat and had decorated them with circus and trapeze paraphernalia. The best of his pieces was an ingenious clockwork tableau. Only wind the key, press the lever on the front and the whole thing came to life. As the clockwork ringmaster raised his hat, the cannon behind him elevated and fired a thrashing clown towards a solid brick wall. Just before he hit, a man on a trapeze swooped down, caught him by the hands and swung him to safety. I found the story highly unlikely, yet I could not help but marvel at the hundreds of minute brass gears and levers that turned a simple swing of a pendulum into such perfect mimicry of life.

My fascination with this clockwork wonder notwithstanding, we found nothing of interest in Trevelyan's rooms. He was able to answer for every item, down to each plate and spoon—nor did he think that anything had been disturbed. Lost for further inspiration, I suggested, "Shall we journey downstairs, gentlemen, and see what Blessington was so keen to protect?"

"He keeps a great deal of money in the house," Trevelyan suggested. "I thought that must be the source of his fear."

"Is it well hidden?" I asked.

"Not at all. He keeps a cashbox on his desk."

"Well secured?"

"No. Not even locked."

"Strange," I pondered. "Given the amount of time you spent with our Monsieur Me'doreux, I would have thought his accomplice must have discovered such an obvious haul. If so, they would already have taken it, wouldn't they? Blessington would be furious at the loss, but what would be left for him to protect? Either this cashbox was overlooked, or the thief was after something else."

"I'm sure I don't know what." Trevelyan shrugged.

"Well, show us the box, to begin with," I said. "Perhaps we shall find another treasure."

In the hall we passed Blessington, still pinned to the floor, gasping for help.

"He'll be all right," Holmes said, then gave Blessington a little kick and reminded him, "I did warn you, if you recall."

Blessington's rooms were... what shall I say... like a kingly hovel. At first I thought the thief had ransacked the place, yet I soon realized that no man but Blessington had wrought this destruction. The mess was too personal and too established. Dirty clothes lay in every corner, the wreckage of meals in every nook. Yet—even in this filthy den—the man's wealth was evident. I kicked aside a discarded dinner jacket; its extreme size testified that it did belong to Blessington, but only when it was in the air did I realize it was one of Savile Row's finest, fit for any duke. Hanging from a doorknob nearby was the shirt to match it and in the cuffs were a pair of platinum links, emblazoned with a pure gold monogram: H.M. The workmanship was extraordinary and the cost must have been vast. Clearly Blessington was accustomed to the finer things, but not to treating them finely. For a moment I despaired of ever finding a clue amidst the clutter, until Trevelyan said, "Ah! There's his cashbox."

Holmes gave a sudden gasp and stood frozen in the doorway to Blessington's study. Peering round him, I beheld the plainest wooden box I think I have ever seen. It was constructed of some kind of dark, well-worn wood. It had hinges of heavy bronze and a latch of the same. Apart from that, it was all but featureless. I could not name the artistic style it was constructed in, nor even guess at the country of origin. All I could say for certain was that it was old—very old indeed. I tried to push past Holmes to examine it, but he thrust me back, crying, "Do not touch it, Watson!"

"What is it?" I asked, but he ignored me and turned instead to Mr. Trevelyan.

"Have you ever seen Blessington open that box?"

"Many times."

"What does it contain?"

"Well… money, obviously."

"Nothing more?" Holmes demanded.

"Not that I have seen."

Holmes edged into the room, eyeing the box with deep distrust. Taking up a silver fountain pen, he inched closer to the box and gingerly pried back the latch. Then, with his eyes squeezed almost shut, he tipped the lid up, ever so slightly.

Nothing happened.

Holmes breathed a thankful sigh and casually flipped the lid open the rest of the way. I could just see a disorganized wad of one- and five-pound notes, which rested on an equally disorganized wad of ten- and twenty-pound notes.

"Only money," Holmes laughed, then snatched up the box and swept past Trevelyan and me into the hall and up the stairs. When he reached the top landing, he crouched over the recumbent bulk of Mr. Blessington and reached inside the fallen man's mouth. Holmes plucked out an object that looked like a fuzzy, coal-colored cotton ball—from which the tendrils of dark smoke emitted—and flicked it into a nearby corner.

"Where is the other box?" Holmes demanded.

Freed from his smoky bonds, Blessington hauled

himself into a sitting position and shuffled backwards, coughing and wheezing, until his back bumped against the far wall. Holmes had no consideration for the man's recent plight, but urged, "The other box, Blessington! It's a matter of some urgency, as I think you must realize."

Yet, when our rotund host found his voice again, it was only to say, "No other box."

"You mean to say you have never owned another box? Just like this one?"

"No. Never. Why should a man want more than one cashbox?"

"For that matter, why should a man keep so much money in one, then leave it unlocked and unguarded? There's a perfectly good bank just round the corner," said Holmes.

"Ha!" Blessington scoffed. "Never trust a bank, Mr. Holmes! No, I shall never trust a bank!"

"You, of all people, wouldn't, would you? I will ask you one more time, Mr. Blessington, and then I am leaving: where is the other box?"

"There is no oth—"

"The truth! Speak the truth to me, Blessington, or I cannot help you!"

Yet, he did not. "Get out! Get out of my house!" he shouted at Holmes, then turned on Trevelyan and howled, "And you— you mincing fairy—get back in your rooms, do you hear? You get back in there and don't you dare leave before I say!"

Holmes shook his head, stood up and turned to

Trevelyan, saying, "Don't. That is very poor advice. In fact, I think you had better only set foot in there once more. Go and gather those things that are most precious to you—only as much as you can carry. Make haste. You are moving out."

"Today?" asked Trevelyan.

"This instant."

"But... but what shall I do? I have nowhere to go."

"We shall just have to make sure you possess the means to render such concerns moot," Holmes shrugged. He flipped open Blessington's cashbox, extended it towards Trevelyan and said, "How much do you think you will need? Keep in mind that it should be enough to start anew—somewhere far from here, if you are wise."

"Stop that, you!" Blessington shouted.

Holmes turned back to him with disgust and said, "Unless it is the truth about the other box that is crossing your lips, I do not wish to hear more from you."

"You can't give away another man's property!"

"This is not your property," Holmes countered, then turned to us and said, "He stole it. So don't feel bad, Mr. Trevelyan. Take what you need and forget this place."

"To start anew..." Trevelyan reflected.

"In comfortable style," said Holmes.

"Well that might take... perhaps... five hundred pounds, don't you think?"

Five hundred pounds, indeed! I don't know how much Jules Léotard earned in his storied career on the trapeze, but I will wager it was less than that kingly sum. Holmes just smiled and said, "It's best to be sure, though, don't you think?"

"So… seven, then?" Trevelyan asked, hopefully.

"That sounds apt," Holmes agreed. Blessington gave a cry of protest, but was silenced by a harsh look from Holmes.

"Now go to your rooms," Holmes ordered Trevelyan, as soon as the latter had selected his handful of banknotes, "and gather what is precious to you. Watson and I will wait. Take a few minutes only, this place is not safe."

"I shan't need much," Trevelyan said. "Why keep those old rags now?"

"Why, indeed?" said Holmes.

Trevelyan disappeared into his quarters and I hissed to Holmes, "I can stand it no more! What in the world is that box?"

"This box? Merely a portal."

"To what?"

"Another box."

"Don't be vague, Holmes," I said. "If you keep secrets from me, how can I be expected to deduce the truth?"

Holmes softened somewhat, but said, "I will not speak of it in front of Blessington. He may yet have some chance to work mischief before you and I are prepared to deal with the second box. We must return on the morrow, girt for battle. All I will tell you now is that you have heard of this item before, or at least its first unfortunate owner."

"Have I?"

"Pandora. As with all myths, the story has diverted

from the truth, but the cautionary core—that a terrible beast lives within a simple box—is correct."

That was enough to quiet me. Trevelyan returned, dragging a laden trunk. As I assisted him down the stairs, Holmes turned to Blessington, who still sat on the landing clutching a pillow across his breast and staring past us at the front door with an expression all of fear, devoid of hope.

"Last chance," Holmes said. "Tell me the truth and I may yet save you. Cling to your promises, your lies and your misbegotten treasure and they shall devour you."

Blessington said nothing. Holmes shrugged. "I thought as much. Well, I wish you luck of it. Perhaps we shall meet again." Holmes chucked the cashbox and remaining bills into Blessington's lap and turned for the door.

We hailed two cabs. Trevelyan drove away in the first, still in awe of his newfound fortune. Once we were settled in the second, Holmes asked, "What do you make of Blessington?"

"To begin with, Blessington is not his true name," said I.

Holmes sat up in surprise and fixed me with a look of admiration. "I say! Well done, Watson. How did you know?"

"I noticed a pair of cufflinks in his rooms. They were monogrammed 'H.M.'"

"Well, that solves one little mystery, then," said Holmes. "He must be Henry Moffat."

The name struck me as familiar, but though I wracked my memory, I could not say why. Holmes watched me puzzle a moment, then prompted, "I think you must have heard of the Worthingdon Bank Gang."

"Ah! The Worthingdon Imploders! Yes, it was in all the papers. I recall the trial: They caught the gang, hanged the leader, sent the rest to jail. The one who informed on them got a shorter sentence—that would be Henry Moffat, I assume. If I recall, Scotland Yard never did find out how the gang smashed open the bank vaults, did they?"

"I think I know, Watson," Holmes mused. "They used ancient and terrible magics. The box we saw today, as I told you, is a portal to another box. Whatever is placed in one box can be withdrawn from the other, no matter how far away the boxes may be. The contents effectively exist in two places. There is one notable exception: in the dangerous box—the true Pandora's box—there lives a terrible beast. It can only enter and exit through the true box."

"What has this to do with bank robbery?" I asked.

"It is quite elementary. Suppose Blessington—or one of his confederates—is in possession of both boxes. He goes to a bank and deposits the true box. It sits in the vault, dormant and harmless, until one night the owner of the boxes pricks his finger and drops some blood into the second box. Remember that whatever is present in one is also in the other—so now the beast has had a taste of blood. Hungry for a complete sacrifice, the monster abandons its home in the first box and seeks prey. At night, there is nobody in the bank—maybe a night watchman, but he would be outside the vault. That is important, for the beast would have to go to get him and everything it touched on the way would corrode."

"I remember it from the papers," I said. "At each bank they hit the vault doors had rusted away and the walls had crumbled to dust."

"After eating the night watchman—or whoever else it could find—the beast probably slunk back to its home, happy and docile as a well-fed cat. Then the robbers needed only to walk into the ruined vault and stuff any surviving monies into the dangerous box, knowing they could be removed from the safe box at any convenient moment. A few days later, the owner could go withdraw the dangerous box from the wreckage of the bank and deposit it in the next one they had decided to rob."

I shook my head and said, "Such things are foreign to my understanding, Holmes. Yet if it works as you say, it is an ingenious method."

"Moriarty was clever," said Holmes.

The statement piqued my interest, for I knew Moriarty only as the demonic voice that issued from Holmes from time to time. His prognostications had always proved true—and highly useful—yet I knew Holmes to harbor extreme distaste for him. I chose my next words delicately. "How does Moriarty enter into this, Holmes? Who exactly is he?"

"Nobody now," said Holmes. "He is gone forever."

I knew that to be untrue, but I held my tongue until Holmes added, "He used to be a criminal mastermind. Oh he was a spider, Watson, ever at the center of a vast, invisible web. He never got his hands dirty and his name was unknown to most of his victims. Yet make no mistake, he was responsible for almost every crime of a magical nature committed on this continent—much of America and Asia too, I think. Through these crimes, he amassed a collection of magical artifacts unmatched by any other man in history. And how did he use them? For further crime. He armed his gangs with an arcane arsenal sufficient to render his men unstoppable and their methods inscrutable to the common investigator."

"How do you know all this?" I asked.

"I knew Moriarty. I knew him very well," Holmes said. "In fact, I have seen the boxes before. I knew them to be a prized possession of Moriarty's, though I failed to guess the true nature of the thing that lived therein. My first inkling came when Trevelyan mentioned that Blessington was trying to protect the box from a man named Moran. Sebastian Moran was a trusted lieutenant of Moriarty's—a most dangerous fellow in his own right, I might add. Once I learned Moran was involved, saw the box, saw Blessington's wealth and heard his low regard for banks, I surmised the rest."

"Well that is it, Holmes! That is deduction! Well done!" I cried. "But exactly what is it, Holmes? The thing that lives in the box, I mean."

"Time."

I think I must have sat agape for a moment, until Holmes took pity on me and leaned forward to disclose one of the greatest secrets of this world.

"I have told you before that our realm is a virtual paradise to the beings of other realities. That is not to say we have no demons of our own. The greater ones are so dominant that they are perceived by mortal men not as monsters, but as fundamental qualities of reality. They are gone beyond entities; they are physics.

"Time exists in every realm I know of, but in many of them it is not a poison. In other realms, age is more likely to improve a thing than to wear it down—thus very ancient things are amongst the most powerful. Here, every man and bird and rock and tree must know that time will eventually corrode and destroy it. That is what lives in the box: the ability—or no, let us say, the onus—of time to destroy all things. Let me tell you: if outside entities understood exactly how deadly time is in our realm, they might be less eager to join us."

I gave a low whistle and asked, "If that is so… if that is our nemesis, how are we to combat the killing power of time?"

"That is the question of the day, isn't it?"

Holmes returned his gaze to the world outside the carriage window. He had a particular love of windows and seemed always fascinated with what lay beyond them. He could stare for hours at the world presented by the pane, wondering if the things he saw were true or only a projection upon the glass, offered to deceive him.

I hardly saw Holmes for the rest of the day. Upon our return to 221B Baker Street, he flew from the cab, up the steps and into his room. There, he busied himself with a number of his books and his strange alchemical laboratory. He spent the remainder of the afternoon tink-tink-tinking at tiny scraps of metal with a minute hammer, staring down at them from time to time with that magnifying glass of his. Gradually, the metal scraps and the bubbling beakers of foul-smelling fluid he occasionally dipped them into became too much for his tiny desk to accommodate. At this point, he emerged from his room and begged the use of the sitting room, enjoining me to find some outside entertainment for the evening.

I made Holmes a steaming pile of toast and a pot of soup, then wiled the evening away at a local second-run theater. I returned home at just about ten to find Holmes still puttering. He looked worn, but rebuffed my attempts to get him to rest. I myself went to bed less than half an hour later. I did not see him again until the dead of night. As I lay in slumber, a shadow fell across my face and the sudden change in light induced me to wakefulness. There was Holmes, leaning gleefully over my bed.

"Watson, I've a gift for you!" Warlock piped up, then immediately his expression fell to one of deepest dismay and he cursed, "No! Damn! I can't say that, can I?"

I rolled over and stared at him, blinking the sleep from my eyes. "What are you talking about, Holmes? What gift? What time is it?"

"Gift? There is no gift. Damn! You see? Now I can't give it to you. I've promised you a gift and it wouldn't work if this was the gift, would it? Ownership is damnably important in magical matters."

"I have no idea what you are speaking of. I ask again: what time is it?"

"Two or so…"

Holmes had roused me from almost the exact middle of my slumber, to announce that he had chosen this moment to give me something, or not to. The revelation was not a welcome one. I think I yelled. Holmes merely raised a finger and said, "Just a moment, please; I shall be back presently."

He leapt through my doorway and into the sitting room. He returned, not fifteen seconds later, with his shirtsleeves flapping freely about and declared, "There! As I said: a gift. For you."

In my hand, he deposited a pair of cheap tin cufflinks.

"Why have you given me your cufflinks, Holmes?"

"No. They are *your* cufflinks. I got them for you."

"Then why are they inscribed with an H?"

"Ah… well… because your middle name is Heimdal!"

"True, Holmes, but this is something I prefer to conceal—an undertaking which would not be aided by having to explain it over and over to everyone I met, from this day on, as evidence that I am not wearing another man's cufflinks."

"You have much to learn about gratitude, Watson," Holmes huffed.

"Again, I ask: why have you given me your cufflinks?"

"Look, the important thing is that I have. I promised you a gift—now I have delivered one." He beamed at his own cleverness and reached into his pocket. "It must therefore be a completely separate transaction when I mention that I have made you something. Oh! Damn! Well that won't work either, will it? If I have made it for you, that's as good as giving it to you, isn't it?"

"I am going back to sleep, Holmes."

"No you aren't. Wait a moment, I'll figure this out."

With that, he scurried into the pantry. I could hear him banging about in there, occasionally calling, "You aren't asleep, are you? Really, don't make me fetch the accordion, John—you know I will."

In less than five minutes, he returned, announcing, "There, I have made you something: this plate of toast."

"I don't want it."

"Watson, don't be difficult. Take it. Eat some—at least one bite—it is a matter of some importance."

With a sigh, I reached over and snatched a slice of unbuttered toast from the plate he offered and bit into it with exactly no eagerness at all.

"There," he said, over my dry, reluctant crunching. "That's better. Now, as a separate matter—for we must admit that both previous issues have been brought to conclusion—I would like to inform you that I have made this."

From his pocket, he drew a sort of amulet—an irregular yellow disc, hanging from an ornate chain.

"It is *not for you*," he continued. "It is mine and mine alone. The magical protections bound within this amulet were granted to me and my possessions, not to any other man. Therefore, I do not give you permission to touch it, much less wear it always. But I do admit that it would be greatly beneficial to you if you did. It may even protect you from the foremost evils of this world, though such punishment would wear it out quickly. And now, I will leave it undefended, in your room."

"You needn't bother," I snorted. "I have no desire to wear such a thing."

"Damn it, Watson, yes you do!"

"It looks horrid! What is it anyway?"

"The rent," he replied, raising his eyebrows as if he had just done a hideously clever thing. "So—though it is from you—it is a thing you owed to me, which makes it very much mine. Remember: I am not giving this to you; you gave it to me. Such matters can be of great magical importance."

"Why is it all yellow and lumpy?"

The dangling abomination was indeed roughly the same shape and size as a one sovereign coin, but was encased in a rubbery coating that hid its true nature entirely. So hideous was the medallion that it took me a moment to recognize the beauty and intricate workmanship on the chain. Warlock had not deigned to answer my question, so I asked another. "I say, that is a singular chain. What is it made of?"

"Ah," he said, "that was no small trick. Some links are copper, some are bronze, some iron. I had a devil of a time shaping such fine pieces, much less getting them to fit together."

"You made this?" I marveled, staring at the links. They were minute, irregular shapes, joined together with such cunning that I am sure I could not describe the process, even if I understood it. Three shapes were repeated, over and over, in the three metals. They were familiar to me, but I could not say from where. A book, I realized. I had seen them in a book, somewhere. On numerous occasions. A medical book?

"Good lord, Holmes, are those… ear bones?"

"Well spotted, Watson! The hammer, the anvil and the stirrup—the tiny, calceous marvels that allow hearing!"

"But why?"

"It has often been said, Watson, that the ear is the gateway to the soul."

"The eye."

"What?"

"The eye, Holmes. The eye is the gateway to the soul."

"Egads, Watson, don't be disgusting! Anyway, it is the ear, I assure you. Whenever magics must be bound to a particular individual, the bond is always strongest if they are bound to the ear. Or hair. Or ear hair."

"The ear? Well then… Oh God… Holmes! This is earwax! You have coated the sovereign I gave you in earwax?"

"Of course I did."

"And you expect me to wear it? You wish me to clothe myself in another man's earwax?"

"Well," said Holmes, with a shrug, "not *another* man's…"

"By God! Do you mean to tell me that you are holding in your hand a sovereign coated in roughly two tablespoons of my own earwax?"

"Just so."

*"It has often been said, Watson, that the ear
is the gateway to the soul."*

"Well, you are lying," said I, "or you are jesting with me. There is no possibility I ever had that much wax in my ears."

"Not all at once," Holmes conceded, "but you must realize that I was concerned for you before you even took up residence here. I must take some care to shelter all my living companions from harm. Thus, I began my harvest on the night you moved in."

"You've been stealing my earwax?"

"*Stealing* is not a term worthy of a gentleman…"

"Since the day we met?"

"If you have been feeling a bit… dry… you now know the cause."

"Damn it, Holmes!"

He gave me a hurt look and sat at the foot of my bed. "Watson, please understand: we are hunting dangerous prey. I have no idea where the true box may be hidden, but I know the thing inside has become used to regular human sacrifice. It might sally forth at any time it considers itself slighted or hungry or even bored. It would surely devour the first man it finds. I am not sure I could defend myself from such a beast and I know that I could not defend you. I only wish for you to be as safe as possible, Watson."

My thoughts were sleepy and troubled. I did not know whether to yell at Holmes or thank him. As I struggled to decide, Holmes's words closed a link for me. I made a sudden connection.

"I know where the box is."

"How?"

"Think, Holmes: Blessington had no interest in Trevelyan as a lover, did he?"

"He doesn't seem to have."

"Then why did he want him? Why would he open his home to another man, support him and keep him?"

"I don't follow," said Holmes.

"The box!" I cried. "If Blessington—or Moffat, or whatever his name is—if he knew the beast might erupt at any moment and slay the first man it found, wouldn't he take care not to *be that man*? That's why he wanted Trevelyan always to spend his evenings at home! He wished Trevelyan's bed to be always occupied. That's why his Gatling emplacement was set across Trevelyan's door and not his own! Don't you see? The box is built into the underside of Trevelyan's bed! Blessington kept him not as a lover, but a sort of resident sacrifice, always on hand in case the beast got hungry!"

"By Jove, I think you've got it!" Warlock cried. "Come, Watson, let us go put a stop to it!"

"Right now?"

"How could you sleep at a moment like this?"

"But… it's cold outside. How would we ever find a cab at this hour?"

"Tosh! It is less than an hour's walk."

"Holmes…"

"We are engaged in a race, Watson! If Moran is indeed seeking to reclaim that box, I am loath to surrender even a minute to him. If he finds it before we do, the box will disappear into Moriarty's criminal empire and who can say how many innocents will be sacrificed to it, ere we have another chance to get our hands on it?"

I grumbled, of course, but he was right. Besides, I was firmly awake by that time and faced only an empty, sleepless night if I stayed. Though I bundled myself up tightly, the cold crept in at every seam as we walked the streets betwixt Baker Street and Trevelyan's. My muffler continuously slipped down, revealing my nose—moist from my breath—to the mercy of the cold. I sniffled and snorted piteously as we approached our goal.

Holmes's urge to hurry proved prophetic. As we rounded the corner onto Moffat's street, we beheld a trio of shapes emerging from the bullet-riddled ruins of his door.

"Stay close by me, Watson," said Holmes, stepping out into the middle of the street. Through the patchy clouds, enough moonlight shone down that the intruders could not help but notice him. He threw open his overcoat and let it flap about his shanks as he advanced slowly down the street. This Holmes did to show himself unarmed but his steely gaze declared that he had no need of pistol or blade. He himself was the weapon. I scurried from the shadows behind him, wary of danger and longing for the warm bed I had left behind.

The first of the three figures instantly beheld Holmes and turned his steps to intercept our own. Behind him, the others followed, though with less zeal. As he neared us, I got my first look at an adversary who would haunt several of my future adventures. His hair was chestnut, shot with gray at the temples; he wore it in a short, martial cut. Indeed, everything about the man was short and martial. Though he stood no more than five foot three, he had the bearing of a soldier. His gaze was cold and unwavering, devoid of all fear. He did not walk; he marched. Something in his stride gave the impression that you might shoot him two or three times in the chest and not arrest his progress. I couldn't recommend shooting him a fourth time—he might be very cross with you indeed. He wore a gray bowler at what would have been a rakish tilt, if it were not for the fact that rakishness, happiness, hope and humor all withered away within a twenty-yard radius of the man. As he drew up before us, Warlock announced him: "Sebastian Moran."

"Warlock Holmes," Moran replied. A shudder passed through his two companions and they exchanged glances. They must have recognized Holmes's name, I realized. They must have feared it. One of Moran's companions was commonplace in the extreme—an old man with a bushy white beard. Over one shoulder he carried a short stepladder and in the other hand, a box of tools. Judging by Trevelyan's descriptions, I supposed this to have been the man who passed himself off as Monsieur Me'doreux, with Moran himself as the "unworthy" accomplice.

Moran's other companion was horrific. He was shorter even than Moran, a fact accentuated by his deformed spine, which hunched him forwards and well off to the right. His hair hung in greasy black strands and his skin—even in moonlight—gave the impression of a greenish tint. In his right hand, he held a dagger. His left hand walked nervous fingers up and down the blade. The knife was clean, but his right trouser leg was not. With horror, I noted the dark stripe where he had wiped the blade upon his trousers. I was sure it must be blood. He smiled at me—a goblin's grin.

Nodding his head towards Moran's empty grasp, Holmes noted, "I see you've failed to find the box, eh?"

"I do not answer to the unworthy vessel," Moran said, "but—" and this still to Holmes "—it is good to see *you*, Master."

Suddenly, Moran, his confederates and the street behind them lit with a green glow. Though I was behind him, I could tell that Holmes was the source of this illumination, so I knew the voice that would come next. A deep, slow laugh escaped Holmes's lips and in the creeping tone I had heard just three times before, Moriarty spoke, "*Faithful one, you please me.*"

"You are well, Master? You are sheltered?"

Moriarty did not answer; instead Holmes slumped forward, then staggered to one side. It was common for him to be weak when Moriarty departed, even for him to be rendered entirely insensible. Yet this time, Holmes did not fall all the way to the ground. Even as he stumbled, he slapped aside Moran's outstretched hands and declared, "I'm not sheltering him, Moran; I'm digesting him."

"Time shall choose a victor," said Moran, then turned his eye on me and asked, "And who is this new face?"

"Tell him nothing, Watson!" Warlock urged, struggling to reclaim his balance. "And for God's sake, John, don't let him learn your name!"

Moran smiled. I sighed and shook my head. Then, since it seemed I had nothing to lose by it, I extended my hand and said, "Dr. John Watson, at your service."

This surprised Moran, who stared at me as if trying to decide whether it was madness or boldness that lay behind the gesture. He crept slowly forward and took my hand in his. The grip was firm, but more remarkable was the steadiness of his hand. I had thought that only a surgeon could cultivate such absolute stability. Only later did it occur to me that a sniper might, as well. As we shook, he leaned in and stared unblinkingly into my eyes, taking the measure of me. After a time, he said, "You call yourself a doctor, but I think you are a brother of mine. Are you not a son of Mars, Dr. Watson?"

It took me a moment to fathom his meaning. Mars? The planet? No, the Roman god of war!

"Very astute," said I. "I was a soldier for a brief time."

"How many have you slain?"

I was taken aback. "Well… I prescribed morphine to a sunstroke victim once; that did the trick."

"You jest with me, but I perceive that this hand has sent many to the grave. Either it has, or one day shall."

I pulled back my hand and cried, "No, sir! It has not and it shall not! I am a doctor! I took an oath. Yes, I have seen battle, but I did not revel in it. I have no love of war!"

"That is ungentlemanly, sir, and unkind! *He* loves you!"

For just a moment, Moran's inexpressive façade cracked and he fixed me with the look most people would reserve for someone who had just called the queen a common street harlot. It took him only a moment to recover his composure. He stared coldly up at me and added, "Perhaps one day you and I shall meet upon the bloody field to see whom he favors more."

I stared at him a moment, then whispered, "You, I expect."

"I expect so, too," said Moran.

Turning to Warlock, I noted, "Really, Holmes, the quality of people you associate with leaves much to be desired."

Holmes snorted and said, "Who? Moran? Think nothing of him, Watson. I'd say he is merely a lapdog, but surely a dog would have been able to sniff out the box before now."

"No need to worry, Holmes, I expect the box shall soon make itself known," said Moran, turning to smile at the smaller of his two companions. The stunted man raised his dagger and tapped it twice against his own chest. I turned back towards Holmes to ask what the little creep meant, but found he had gone. Holmes was no longer by my side, but pelting down the street in the direction of Trevelyan's house. For lack of a better plan, I took to my heels as well. One cannot run with a walking stick, so I was forced to waddle after Holmes as best as my wounded and wasted frame allowed. I am sure my progress must have been more amusing to Moran than frightening. Over my shoulder, I could just hear him call, "Until next time, Doctor…"

My first instinct would have been to run up the stairs and search Trevelyan's rooms for the missing box, but as I entered by the shattered front door, I heard Warlock cry out from within Moffat's rooms downstairs. Bustling in after him, I beheld a horrible sight. I'd not had time to guess what purpose Moran had for the ladder and toolbox his elderly hireling carried. Now I saw his reason and— even as a doctor, accustomed to blood and viscera—it turned my stomach.

Moran and company had taken their time with Moffat. Four sturdy anchors had been affixed to the ceiling in the bedroom. From these hung iron chains; tangled within them was Moffat himself. He had been stripped to his undergarments and hung spread-eagled over his precious cashbox. He was soaked in blood. His face was pale. He had been stabbed in several places—on the inside of his thighs, the base of his neck, and the inside of his arms, just below the armpit. Though the wounds were small, they told a clear tale to my doctor's eye. Moran's little knifeman had nicked both Moffat's jugular veins as well as his femorals and axials. It must have taken him some time to bleed out—indeed, he may have still been alive— but the wounds were mortal. Compounding this cruelty, the cashbox had been opened and placed directly beneath Moffat. The chains were arranged such that he could pull himself to one side, while he had strength, causing the blood to drip beside the box, rather than into it. As most of the blood soaked the carpet, I could see that Moffat must have struggled as long as he could to see that no blood touched the tousled wads of banknotes within the box. Yet, as his blood had drained, the strength left him. He must have slumped into unconsciousness even as we entered, for the thin red stream that dripped from his vast belly had only just begun to paint its crimson upon the money. From the floor above us, there came a terrible rumble. The house creaked and squealed, as if all the boards of her frame had warped, pulling at the nails that bound them.

"Oh, damn!" Warlock cried. "Quick, Watson, the stairs!"

We rushed upstairs to Trevelyan's bedchamber. With a reluctant grimace, Holmes opened the door and peered inside.

How can I describe what I saw?

I am familiar with height, width and depth, but I think there must be four or five spatial dimensions, for the creature defied physics as I understood it. Its horrid appendages seemed disjointed, appearing in several different places at once, though through their movement I began to perceive how they must come together, into a whole. It had no color—or no color I could understand. Its shape was defined to me as the area I could not see—the space where human perception failed. It pulled itself up out of the center of Trevelyan's bed, which wasted and fell in upon itself, even as we watched.

Only when Holmes shut the door did I realize that I had been screaming. I clutched at the sides of my aching head and felt my pulse pound against my hands with terrible force.

"Oh dear," said Holmes. "It's even worse than I expected."

"Wha… what do we do?" I stammered.

"Hmm… That all depends upon you, I think. Watson, did you or did you not steal my protective amulet?"

My hand went to my chest. I flushed. Understand, I was not embarrassed that I had stolen the thing—Holmes had made it abundantly clear that such was his wish. No, I was merely ashamed to be wearing such a monstrosity; horrified by the feel of the ever-warming earwax of Holmes's horrid trinket against my skin. Though I said nothing, Holmes must have comprehended my expression, for he said, "Good! Now understand, Watson: that thing is looking for a human sacrifice. Moffat is gone. Trevelyan is gone. There's only one thing for it. Good luck."

With one hand, Holmes swept open the door. With the other, he thrust me inside. The wave of sickness that washed over me made it impossible even to protest. I heard the door slam shut behind me and turned to face my destroyer. One of the creature's unspeakable upper limb-things shot towards me and impaled my chest. It passed straight through me. I felt no pain; indeed I felt nothing touch me at all, for the beast and I did not share an equal number of dimensions.

Instead I saw a flash. No, I saw *the* flash: the fundamental, big, bright start to everything. All the matter that ever was or would be spun across an expanding cosmos in a luminous cloud. Gravity began to work upon it, drawing this sea of chaos into whirling spheres, which grew into stars and planets. Plasmas cooled to burning gas, then liquid and finally stone. Water rained down. Upon one such planet, slimy things began to crawl with legs upon the slimy sea. These creeping forms became ever larger and more distinct—fishes, insects, slugs and snails. They grew legs and traversed the cooling continents as plants sprang up all around. In an instant so small I could barely perceive it, man came. I saw the pyramids rise and the winds begin to corrode them. I saw great armies march, fight and fall. I saw my parents, younger than I had ever known them. I saw myself, but even to me, I was a thing of no value. What a small part I was, of the whole. What an insignificant jot was the span of my existence. It was already over, I realized. If ever I had truly been—if that tiny period of time was enough for anything to be said to exist at all—such a thing as might live in that inconsequential blink of time was of no account. I was gone as soon as I began.

Yet as this revelation struck me—even as I ceased to be—the tentacle that probed my chest happened across the amulet. There was a whoosh—a great rush as all of time fell in upon me, drawn into my chest and up into my body. Suddenly, everything but the room around me was gone. There were no more planets in my mind, no more stars. Something must have been holding me up in the air, for I fell almost from the ceiling down to the floor. My head crashed into the floorboards and my left ear flared with burning pain. I had a moment of panic, for in my time as all things, I had forgotten how to be only one thing. I had no recollection of how to be an animal and no longer knew how to breathe.

Old habits began to recall themselves to me and at last I drew a gulping breath. I curled up on the floor and stayed there, letting the air fall into my chest and out again, re-acclimating myself to the strange sensation of owning arms and legs. Behind me, a door creaked open. A head interrupted the light outside and poked in to intrude itself upon my bedroom realm.

"So..." said Holmes, "how did that go?"

We stayed in Trevelyan's room well into the day. As the sun slowly warmed the room around me, I became more and more myself again.

Holmes set Trevelyan's clockwork tableau before me. Over and again he wound it and I beheld the clown flung through the air to his sure demise, saved at the last second each time by the man on the flying trapeze. I marveled to see the tiny figures. They moved and existed in a way that so resembled free will, yet I knew the action and outcome every time it began. The little clown had no way to prevent his ordeal. The shining brass trapeze artist, no alternative but to save him. Did they believe themselves masters of their own choices? If so, they were deceived in that notion.

I cannot say why, but this was comforting to me.

"You might as well keep it," Holmes said. "Nobody owns it now."

Dumb, I nodded. After a time, I asked, "Is it gone? The thing in the box?"

To answer my question, Holmes drew two plain

wooden boxes from the folds of his overcoat. One was from the ruins of Trevelyan's bed, the other from Moffat's study downstairs. He flipped open both lids and showed me the contents.

"See? Nothing."

"So… what does that mean?" I asked. "Have we changed the world? Can time no longer waste us?"

"Oh, no!" Holmes scoffed. "The beast still lives upon this plane, Watson. We have merely bound it. Understand that the power of time to wither all is not anything the beast does on purpose, merely a side effect of its existence."

"Oh."

"So, it will still kill us all."

"I see."

"It just won't *lunge out* and kill us all."

"Well… that's something, I suppose."

"Against such a foe, Watson, yes it is. It is indeed. I think I'll leave the boxes here. Moran must be skulking close by, waiting for the house to fall in and reveal where the dangerous box was hidden. Let him have it. He'll find it disappointing, I think."

I rose and wandered about. The rooms were familiar to me, but they seemed a distant memory. Still, I began to recover enough of my senses to recall that I had things I wanted to accomplish, both great and small. I drifted downstairs and finished one of the smaller errands, ere I left.

Holmes was waiting for me upon the bullet-riddled front step.

"Ready to go home, Watson?"

"Holmes, did you know the amulet would save my life?" I asked. "Or did you mean to sacrifice me?"

He smiled. "I knew that either the amulet would save you, or you would be doomed anyway."

"I hate it."

"Well, you don't have to wear it anymore. I am sure that after such a strain it is useless now."

"Good." I dug down beneath my clothing and began pulling melted, re-fused chunks of earwax out of my chest hair. A charred and twisted sovereign fell from my shirt. Holmes swept it up and regarded it with a jolly smile. The chain I kept. I prize it still.

Holmes waited patiently as I divested myself of the ruins of his gift. After a time, I said, "Oh! Holmes, I got a present for you."

"Did you?"

"Yes. Here."

In his hand, I deposited a pair of platinum cufflinks, emblazoned with Holmes's initials in 24-carat gold.

"Wonderful, Watson! Wonderful! You shouldn't have," he proclaimed, tracing the W and H with his fingertip.

Though he had the means, Holmes was not in the habit of purchasing luxuries for himself. Still, he could appreciate fine things when they were presented to him. He seemed to like the cufflinks; I often saw him wearing them and occasionally smiling at them.

We stepped into the street and directed our steps homewards, to Baker Street. I don't know if it ever occurred to him to wonder what I had been doing in the house that day, while he waited on the front step. I laugh to think that, in all the time we spent together, he probably never realized how Henry Moffat's fine platinum cufflinks would appear if one wore them upside down.

THE CASE OF THE CARDBOARD... CASE

TO THE BRILLIANT MIND, THE TRUE ENEMY IS inactivity. At least, that's what I tell myself, because I like to pretend I'm an intellectual. And because I know how badly I cope with idleness. I still cringe when I recall how much I hated the pause that came between Holmes's and my first two adventures and our third.

Our Study in Brimstone took place over two days in early November. Just one week after that, we handled the Adventure of the Resident Sacrifice. I prided myself on how well my medical knowledge had prepared me to solve crimes and I was eager to prove my mettle on our next adventure. Yet the remainder of November passed without any call to action. December followed. Each telegram, each piece of post, each visitor to our door would—I prayed— reveal our next challenge, but each of them failed me. I hardly knew what to do with myself. I formed the habit of taking long walks about the city, if only to fill the time.

Returning from one such walkabout at around ten on New Year's morning, I found Holmes slouched in his armchair before the fire, honking away with his accordion and singing "Auld Lang Syne" at the top of his lungs. I waved a greeting and he nodded back, but any verbal exchange would have been lost in his cacophonous song.

Upon finishing the final verse, he paused. Tilting his head to one side, he listened intently for a few moments, then complained, "Nothing. Nothing! When will you answer, oh being from another world?"

"What being is that, Holmes?"

"Oddlingsygn. Last night and this morning, it seemed every reveler and passerby I saw was calling upon the same entity. All London is bent on summoning him, yet he will not appear! So strange…"

"Not strange, Holmes," I said. "That is not a name, it is a Scottish phrase."

"Oh, I think I know a demon's name when I hear one, Watson."

"'Auld Lang Syne' means 'for the sake of old times.'"

"Oh! A nostalgia demon—he must be potent indeed…"

"No, not a demon at all, I am telling you… Wait! What is this?"

My eye had fallen across a white envelope that lay upon the side table beside Holmes's armchair.

"Oh, a letter," said he.

"From whom?"

"Well, I don't know! Honestly, Watson, would you put aside the chase for a reluctant demon just to read an everyday letter?"

"Yes."

"Well, do so then. I have other matters to attend."

He launched back into the first verse of his supposed summoning ritual. I stepped to the table, unfolded the letter and read. I must have made quite a face, for when he observed my expression, Holmes at last lay aside his accordion and asked, "What does it say, Watson?"

The message was short. It read:

```
To the esteemed consulting detective
Warlock Holmes and his colleague
Dr. John Watson:


Help
—Lestrade
```

When I read it to him, Warlock sucked air through clenched teeth and declared, "Ouch. Sounds like a bad one. What say you, Watson? Ready for an adventure?"

"I don't know, do I?" I replied. "He gives us no hint of what we might expect." At the bottom of the letter, Lestrade had included an address, but nowhere was there any indication of what was wrong or how we should prepare ourselves.

In the delay between adventures, my frustration with Vladislav Lestrade had only grown. At first I had sought to raise his spirits whenever I caught him moping. Holmes had given me to understand that this was a useless gesture, as Lestrade was an annihilist. At first I thought he meant a nihilist: a person who believed in nothing. But no, he was an annihilist: a person who believed there *should be* nothing.

Thus, anything that was, is, would be, or might possibly be offended the little Romanian, by dint of its very existence. Every man, woman and child, every object and every idea was a slap in the face to Vladislav Lestrade, who was convinced that the only way to avoid tragedy and suffering was simply not to exist. He many times commented that, if only he had the ability, he would cheerfully annihilate himself, me, and all of creation. Without commenting on the philosophical validity of this position, let me just say: Vladislav Lestrade did not have many friends.

"Of course he hasn't given us a clue," Holmes beamed. "The little fiend is playing on my curiosity, as well as my duty to help my comrades. Let us chide him for it when we get there."

So—in only the time it took for us to gather our hats, coats, gloves and Holmes's shoes—we found ourselves bouncing along in a hansom, bound on a new adventure. The address was not in an area of London I often frequented, but the streets were familiar to me and became more so as we drew nearer our destination. As we made our final turn, I realized why.

"Wait! This is Grogsson's street! Are we going to Grogsson's house?"

Very nearly. In fact, our destination was just next door. As we approached, I could see Inspector Lestrade pacing the pavement in front of the house. I knew he must be perturbed indeed to suffer daylight just to wait for us. Holmes must have thought so too, for the moment the hansom pulled to a stop, he sprang from the cab calling,

"Lestrade, what is the matter?"

Lestrade made no answer, except to tilt his head and raise his eyebrows as if to say, "It's bad." He turned and walked inside, leaving Holmes and me to follow.

The first piece of bad news greeted us with a smile. In the hall stood a smirking man/boy. I call him such, because his face looked to be no older than twelve. In spite of his seeming youth, he wore a badge that declared him to be a detective inspector of Scotland Yard—of equal rank to Grogsson and Lestrade.

"This is Inspector Lanner," said Lestrade. I winced. On his many visits over the past few weeks, I had heard Lestrade complain of him often. Of all the things Lestrade hoped would cease to exist, he rather hoped Inspector Lanner would go first. Though Lanner had solved less than half the number of cases that Lestrade had solved in the last year, and less than a third as many as Grogsson, he was considered a rising star at Scotland Yard. He therefore enjoyed the support of his peers and superiors when he had declared he would at last discover the true nature of the two supernatural detectives. It seems Grogsson and Lestrade's success bred more resentment than esteem.

"Ah! Holmes!" Lanner said as we marched in. "I am *so* glad you could be here to see this."

"And what is it you intend to show me?"

"Your little group is going to shrink today, Holmes. One of your freakish cadre is bound for jail, perhaps the gallows. Come see what that oaf Grogsson has left for Miss Susan Cushing."

He led us into the sitting room. On a sofa sat a young lady in her late twenties. She was haggard and pale, her eyes flushed from a morning of crying, but I caught my breath when I saw her nonetheless. She was strikingly pretty, yet it was not her beauty alone that caught my attention—it was her kindness. She wore it in her eyes. Understanding began to dawn upon me. I knew Grogsson to be a lonely fellow and easily fascinated by any person who possessed grace or beauty. Yet beyond that, if Miss Cushing displayed any kindness to him, she must be the only lady who ever did so. This would be invitation enough for Grogsson to hope that she might one day look beyond his monstrous form and begin to care for him. She also lived just next door and was likely seen by him every day and… In an instant I understood that he must be wretchedly in love with her.

"Gentlemen, this is Miss Susan Cushing," Lanner announced, "and *this* is what she found on her doorstep this morning."

On the table in front of the lady lay a package, clumsily wrapped in brown paper. It had been tied with tarred string, bent into a knot so convoluted and crude that she had been forced to forgo untying it and simply snip the string with scissors. Writing was just visible on the inside of the paper, but as the box hid most of the characters, I could not decipher it. Within the paper lay a battered cardboard case—the kind used to hold inexpensive cigars. Within that case, on a bed of coarse salt, lay two disembodied human ears. Two left ears.

"A token of his esteem, no doubt," Lanner declared. "Like the cat who brings a mouse to the foot of your bed, Grogsson has surrendered his trophies."

Holmes's features sank. Lestrade gave an almost imperceptible nod to indicate that he concurred with Lanner's interpretation of events. With a deep sigh, Holmes asked, "Where is Grogsson?"

"Fled," Lanner smiled. "He is not so great a fool as to stay. Miss Cushing confronted him this morning and he ran off. Hasn't been seen since. It won't take us long to find him, I think. There are few places in this city where a beast like that can hide."

"I think our friend will soon be returned to us. Lanner has issued a warrant for his arrest," said Lestrade. "Either the police will find Grogsson and arrest him, or they will find him and he will slay as many as he can, before they bring him down. However it goes, Holmes, I think things are not looking good for Torg."

Holmes, brightening to the role of great detective—a role in which I had been tirelessly instructing him—declared, "We shall see, Vladislav, we shall see. Appearances can often deceive, but careful observation will reveal the underlying truth. Isn't that right, Watson?"

"It is."

"And I said it correctly?"

I clapped my hand over my brow; he'd been doing so well. With a deep sigh, I said, "Yes, just as we rehearsed."

Lanner laughed. "Your charade is unraveling, Holmes. Soon the light of truth shall shine upon you and your confederates; we shall know who you really are."

"Perhaps, Lanner," Lestrade growled, "but in the meantime, Holmes and I will investigate. Holmes, won't you come upstairs and help me examine the rest of the house?"

"What do we expect to find up there?" asked Holmes. Lanner's expression led me to believe he was wondering the same. Vladislav gave Holmes a pointed look and Holmes quickly amended his statement, "The truth! The undisclosed truth—that is what! To the stairs, gentlemen!"

I excused myself, with a bow towards Miss Cushing and an angry glance at Lanner. By the time I reached the top of the stairs, Holmes and Lestrade were already deep in conference.

"What do you suppose, Vladislav? Can he be bribed?"

"I don't know. Lanner hates us, Holmes; he has for some time. If he will accept money to overlook this little incident, I'm sure it would be a tidy sum."

"Ah... well... To allow Grogsson to come home, though... that's worth a lot to us, isn't it?"

Lestrade nodded and I will admit I was touched by the camaraderie they showed for their fallen brother. I had to remind myself that—in all likelihood—Grogsson had just killed or maimed two men.

"Yet I fear the situation has moved beyond the point where bribery is an option," Lestrade sighed. "Though the warrant lacks a second signature, forces have been dispatched to arrest Grogsson. The hunt has begun. If Lanner were suddenly to call it off, he would lose face.

Surely the chief inspector would want to know why he had mobilized such a large portion of the force then changed his mind."

"Well then…" Holmes suggested in a conspiratorial whisper, "perhaps we must consult my friend Azazel, concerning what should be done with Inspector Lanner, eh?"

"Holmes!" I whisper-yelled. "You can't kill him! You can't murder an inspector of Scotland Yard!"

"Oh, I'm fairly sure I could manage it, Watson. And anyway, I *know* Azazel could. Gads, he'd be practically gagging to."

"Holmes, I forbid it!"

Lestrade laid a calming hand on Holmes's arm and said, "What would it accomplish, Warlock? It might put you and me under threat for Lanner's murder and it would do nothing to clear Grogsson's name. Even if Lanner were gone, the rest of Scotland Yard would still hunt Torg down."

"True," Holmes conceded and the fiendish green glare that had just begun to kindle in his eyes died out. "What do you propose, then?"

"I think our friend is finally done for," Lestrade sighed. "Either we try to talk Grogsson into surrendering peaceably, or we help him flee the country."

"But where would he go?" said Holmes. "His home is here! He knows no other language, no other land, no other custom… How could we expect him to establish himself in a strange country?"

I gave a derisive harrumph and Lestrade shook his

head, saying, "I thought perhaps some place savage? Siberia? Australia?"

At this point, I was forced to interject. "Gentlemen, a moment, please. It seems to me there is no specific evidence against Torg. Lanner is happy to assume Grogsson's guilt, but do we presume to damn our friend on such circumstantial scraps?"

Holmes and Lestrade both rolled their eyes at me.

"Doctor, please, don't be naïve," Lestrade complained.

"He's right, Watson," Warlock said. "I've known Grogsson a long time and… well… tearing off men's ears and presenting them as a token of his valor to a pretty girl… I can hardly think of a more Grogsson-like act. I suspect we already know the truth of what happened."

"We don't need the truth! We don't even *want* the truth," I told him, scarce believing the words that poured from my own lips. "All we need is doubt."

"I *have* no doubt," Lestrade said with a sullen shrug.

"Then I shall go find you some," I huffed. "You two are welcome to sulk up here; I am going downstairs to save Grogsson!"

I turned on my heel and blustered down the stairs. In truth, I had not taken my third step before I began to suspect I would be unable to back my promise with deeds. Nevertheless, I was determined not to abandon the chase until I had to. I set my jaw and strode back into the sitting room. Lanner greeted me with a satisfied sneer and suggested, "The investigation upstairs fails to yield fruit?"

"Patience, Inspector. As I am merely an amateur and you are handily outperformed by Lestrade, it seems premature to doubt his methods, don't you think?"

He frowned.

Turning my attention to Miss Cushing, I felt an immediate swell of sympathy. It was strange, but I often felt towards victims of crime as I felt towards my patients. I had that same urge to correct what ailed them and now I found myself using much the same bedside manner. I noticed there was nothing on the table before her save the gruesome package.

"Miss Cushing, I am so sorry for your trouble," I said. "I wonder if I might make so bold as to offer you a cup of your own tea?"

"Oh!" she said, with a sudden start. "Oh, I hadn't thought... Forgive me, you must be... I shall make a pot straight away!"

"Nonsense!" I cried, clasping her hands and guiding her back down to the sofa. "I am sure I can manage it. You've had a hard enough morning, I warrant. I doubt this cad has stopped his gloating long enough to lend you a single kind word, has he?"

Miss Cushing was too much the gentlewoman to answer such a question, but Lanner spluttered in protest, "I say! How dare you? She is in no danger, Doctor, as a medical man such as yourself must know."

"That does not mean she is devoid of feeling, Inspector! How long have you left her sitting here, with nothing before her but that grisly box? For shame! Let me clear this away, won't you, Miss Cushing? I'm sure you've seen enough of it."

"Oh, I have," she agreed.

I closed the box and bundled it back into its paper wrapper, even pulling the string back over it, much as it must have lain when it was tied. I winced when I beheld the rough words scrawled on the outside of the wrapper.

2 Mis S Cushing

The handwriting was crude, large and almost certainly Torg's. I despaired at this, but refused to abandon all hope. I began my campaign by discrediting Lanner.

"How well do you know Grogsson, Miss Cushing?"

"Not too well," she said. "He seems shy. Yet he's always been kind."

"Do you know his occupation?"

"I do not."

"It may surprise you to learn—as it certainly surprised me—that he, like Lanner there, is a detective inspector of Scotland Yard."

She gave a gasp that made me laugh, in spite of myself.

"Hard to believe, isn't it?" I said. She nodded and smiled at the silliness of it.

"Would it surprise you to know then, that he is much better at the job than Lanner is? Last year he solved more cases than Lanner did. By a factor of three, if I recall."

Lanner seemed rather annoyed that I knew that particular statistic; he protested, "That is untrue!"

"The numbers don't lie," I reminded him.

"But they do! He always uses that consultant, Holmes!"

"Whereas all Inspector Lanner uses," I told Miss Cushing, "is his own bent wit. That is why he has been too pleased over Torg's seeming crime to consider your feelings. I apologize that this petty workplace rivalry has worsened an already terrible day for you. This is the kitchen?"

I strode out, leaving Lanner to craft a slew of impotent apologies. I was heartened by Susan Cushing's coolness towards him. Despite the box of ears, it seemed Miss Cushing still found Torg's company preferable to Lanner's. Despite the box of ears.

Upon reaching the kitchen, I threw the case of ears down upon the table and busied myself finding the kettle and a box of matches. Once the fire in the stove was lit, I turned my attention to the horrible package. Unwrapping the box, I smoothed the paper out across the table and examined the writing I had seen on the inside of the wrapping. The piece of paper had been torn from a larger whole, so most of the writing was missing. What was left of it consisted of two headings: "Traverser" and "Nantucket". Under each of these was a list of names, followed by a simple figure, for example: E. Potter—£1 6s 9d—Dancer 10:1. I took it to be a betting sheet. As I knew only sailors to use tarred string, I supposed this entry must mean that Mr. E. Potter, from the sailing ship *Traverser*, had placed one pound, six shillings and ninepence on "Dancer" to win some sort of contest.

With a whistle, I realized how stilted the odds were in favor of this Dancer. Bets for two such contests were scrawled on the inside of the paper. In the first, a one-hundred-pound bet on Dancer would pay back only the original bet, plus ten extra pounds. A one-hundred-pound bet on his competitor—a man named O'Keefe—would yield nine hundred pounds. In the second contest, the odds were even longer, seeing only a three-pound payback on Dancer and three thousand on his competitor, Hanson. Given the nature of the trophies within the box, combined with the fact that the competitors had men's names, rather than animals', I took the betting sheet to reflect the sums that had been issued for an illegal boxing match. The docks were famous for them. I supposed Dancer to be a mocking soubriquet for Grogsson; somebody must have found out about his fondness for ballet.

Nearly every bet was against Grogsson. Here was evidence that human nature can always overrule human intellect. Though I myself could not imagine laying money against him in a contest of strength, I could understand why so many of the sailors had. After a few drinks, where is the lure in winning a three per cent payout? Wouldn't it be more tempting to chase the luscious payout to be had if Grogsson actually lost? The chief nemesis of reason is hope.

Though the betting sheet did not record the winner of either contest, the two severed ears testified that perhaps things had not gone well for Mr. Hanson and Mr. O'Keefe. It seemed Grogsson must have won both fights and taken the ears as trophies. With so many bets placed against Dancer, whoever was running this fight must have been making a positive fortune on Grogsson.

I shook my head sadly. The water for the tea had not yet boiled and here was proof of my friend's guilt. If one needed further evidence, one need only examine the ears themselves. They had not been severed cleanly, as by a sharp blade or skilled hand. They had been yanked—just *yanked*—from their victims with such extremity of force that I found myself wincing.

Was there nothing here to save my friend?

As I stepped back into the hall, I practically bumped into a picture-laden curio cabinet. Miss Cushing had not one but two such assemblies in her hallway, bedecked in photographs of absent friends and family. I think she must have been a lonely person, indeed, to have kept two such shrines to her isolation. My eye fell across a photograph of three ladies dressed in holiday frocks. The oldest was perhaps twenty-five, the youngest still in her teens. The family resemblance was palpable. I called out, "Miss Cushing? Do you live here by yourself?"

"I do," she called back. "Mama has passed on. My sisters used to live here, but they are both wed now."

"Is this the three of you?" I asked, leaning into the sitting room and waving the picture.

She blushed and answered, "Yes. Sarah is the eldest, Mary in the middle, and I am the child."

Sarah? The sister's name was Sarah? It was my first, faint glimmer of hope. I fished for more.

"Look at you!" I said. "You are all so beautiful... all so carefree."

"Yes. Those were happier times."

"Oh? What happened?" The kettle was boiling now, so I headed back to the kitchen and dropped the steeping ball into the teapot, then poured the water in atop it.

"You don't care to hear it," Miss Cushing said. "It is of no matter to the case. Family drama, you know."

At this, I leaned through the doorway again to shake a finger at my host, declaring, "Nothing is unimportant, Miss Cushing! The truth can hide in any detail. Tell me all! Oh… and where might I find the sugar?"

"In the left-most cabinet, on the top shelf," she said, then added, "It's just that my sisters and I fought. Mary wed Dr. Armstrong, who I… rather thought… might have had eyes for me."

After a little scrabbling I found a picture of the middle sister and her groom. To my surprise, I recognized him. I'd attended one of his lectures once. He'd presented himself as a perfect quack.

"I was a foolish girl," Susan chided herself. "Then Sarah married that Jim Browner. Oh, we all told her not to, but Sarah was always the willful one."

I located a picture of Sarah Cushing, standing next to a gruff-looking man in a battered peacoat. My chest swelled with sudden hope. I leaned into the sitting room again to ask, "Is this him?"

"It is."

"He looks like a sailor."

"Sometimes a sailor, often a porter or a deckhand," she said. "Usually onboard ship, and it's better for everybody when he is."

"Not the best husband?" I hazarded.

"Well, look at him! He's a brute!"

"How your sister must suffer..."

"Oh! She is far from blameless, let me assure you! The way she carries on! The moment Jim is on board a ship—the very *moment* his watchful eye is removed—oh it is scandalous, the way she behaves!"

This was something! This was good! With raw material such as this, I was sure I could craft a narrative where someone else—anyone else—was guilty. My hands shook as I picked up the teapot and called out, "So, the marriage is troubled?"

"Ha! At the very least!" she scoffed.

"Has she ever left him?"

"She's been back here a few times, but they always make up. Then they're off again, to some port or other. I have no idea where they are now. I only see her when she needs a place to stay."

I carried the tea tray into the sitting room and set it on the table before her. "How do you take your tea?" I asked.

"Sugar, please. One lump. And a dash of milk."

"Just as I do. Inspector?"

"Black. Two sugars," he groused.

I delivered the teacups with quaking hands; only one line of questioning remained to me and on it rested Grogsson's fate. I waited until Susan had enjoyed a few sips of her tea, then said, "I must ask, Miss Cushing... Lanner here says the package was found on your doorstep. Do you have any certain knowledge that Mr. Grogsson delivered it, or are you merely assuming so?"

She thought about that for a moment, then answered, "Well… I suppose he never confirmed it had come from him, but he did not deny it."

"Strange," said I.

"He didn't have much of a chance, you see. I… Oh, this is awkward, Dr. Watson, very awkward. But I supposed he might be *courting* me with them. It sounds grotesque, I know, but that is what I supposed. When I found what lay within the package, I ran next door and confronted him. I told him that such thoughts were disgusting and that he was a monster and then he left, almost without a word."

Here she stopped and stared guiltily at her teacup for a moment, as if she had a secret and was wondering whether to tell it. I knew that in these moments silence is the greatest prompt. I waited.

"I think he may have been… crying," she muttered.

I smiled. "Miss Cushing, on the second day I knew Grogsson, I saw him shot twice in the chest, point blank. He shed not a single tear. Do you suppose you did what the pistol could not?"

She stared down a moment more. Finally, she whispered, "Yes."

"As do I, Miss Cushing. As do I."

I placed my cup and saucer on the table and rose to leave, adding, "Yet do not fret, my dear. A lady has a right to rebuff any suitor she will—we would live in a savage land indeed if that were not the case. England would be reviled the world over as a living hell for her entire female population and the only bright aspect that I can think of would be this: I would be married to a duchess. Well, I think I'd better check on Holmes and Lestrade. Thank you for the tea."

I found the two of them just outside the door; they had removed Miss Cushing's upstairs shower rod and sharpened one end. I sighed.

"Out of the way, Watson!" Holmes declared. "It must look like an accident! It must appear as if Lanner has carelessly slipped and impaled himself while showering!"

"In the living room? Fully clothed, in front of a witness?" I hissed. "Holmes, nobody will ever believe such an act to be accidental."

"No, they won't," Lestrade agreed, with a snarl, "but I just need to *stab that little bastard, right in the face.*"

"No!" Holmes insisted. "Straight through the heart; I thought we agreed."

"Face."

"Heart!"

Holmes and Lestrade stood staring angrily at one another for a moment, until Holmes at last blinked and suggested, "Throat?"

"I suppose... Yes," Lestrade decided. "Because you have always been kind to me, I will settle for stabbing him through the throat."

"We have a gentlemen's accord," Holmes said, starting for the sitting room.

I leapt betwixt them and the door and declared, "Wait! We have had a dark day, surely, but I think I can see some light. You might not know it, Holmes, but you have just solved this case. Come, let me tell you what you've figured out…"

When we entered the sitting room a few moments later, Lanner was holding forth on how the arrest would go and how he would be sure to keep Miss Cushing safe from any further advances by her brutish neighbor. He smiled when he saw us and called out, "Welcome back, gentlemen. If you are quite done upstairs, I wonder if I might borrow Inspector Lestrade for a moment. I need a second detective's signature on this arrest warrant, you see, and I thought he might at last be willing to do his duty."

"I might," Lestrade said, "but Holmes has formed his own theory…"

"He always does," I added, clapping Holmes on the back.

"We thought you might like to hear it," Lestrade finished, then he and I propelled Holmes forward into the sitting room.

Miss Cushing stared expectantly up at him. Lanner gave a derisive snort. Holmes licked his lips nervously. We really had given him too many lines and far too much coaching to expect him to remember it all. Nevertheless, he began. "Miss Cushing, I will thank you to surrender that package to Inspector Lestrade; it does not belong to you."

"It will be entered into evidence when the time is right," Lanner protested. "Until then, you have no right to demand it."

"I do," Warlock said. "It should never have come into her possession. It was not intended for her."

"It is *addressed* to her, you buffoon."

"Excuse me, it is not! It is addressed to Miss S. Cushing. What you failed to notice, Lanner—probably because you failed to inquire—is that she might not be the only Miss S. Cushing in residence."

"But she is."

"But she *might not be*. Her sister, Sarah Cushing, has been known to take up residence here on more than one occasion."

Lanner looked deeply annoyed by this, yet still managed his keenest insight of the day, stating, "Even so, Sarah Cushing is married and packages to her would be addressed to Mrs. Sarah *Browner*."

"And yet it would be correct to address her as Miss Cushing if her marriage had been dissolved, which, Miss Cushing—" and here Holmes addressed Miss *Susan* Cushing "—I believe it has been. I am sorry."

"I am not so sorry," Miss Susan scoffed, "not if you are correct."

"I am," said Holmes. "The sender is in a unique position to know that the marriage is no more, just as he is privileged with the information that Sarah is likely to return here. You see, the sender is none other than Sarah's ex-husband, Jim Browner!"

"Ludicrous!" Lanner declared. "You know just as well as I do who is to blame for this crime! Don't pretend it is any other man!"

"Careful, Lanner," said Lestrade, in his iciest tone. "I know you very much wish for Grogsson to be found guilty of this crime; do you think your eagerness to see him hang has clouded your judgment?"

Lanner went red with fury and I saw my chance to play devil's advocate. "Go easy, Lestrade," I said. "I'm sure Inspector Lanner has ample reasons for suspecting Grogsson, else he would never have summoned half the force to his pursuit." I then turned to Lanner and asked, "What are they?"

"Hmm?"

"Your reasons for suspecting Grogsson—what are they?"

"Well... he as much admitted it! He fled!"

"Ah, I see," I said, raising a finger. "You think he might have fled because he felt guilt?"

"Obviously."

"So he might," I conceded. "Yet, we have no compelling evidence that he is guilty. On the other hand, he may have fled because the object of his affections rebuffed him— said he was a monster and that she would never love him. Might that have caused him to flee? Because we know for certain that such an exchange did occur, don't we? What do you think, Lanner—would the Grogsson you know have stood gamely by and allowed somebody to see him cry, or would he have fled?"

Lanner's face, so recently flushed, began to lose its color. Upon his features I began to read two words: *what if.* What if he were wrong? What if personal vendetta had just led him to mobilize four dozen constables in pursuit of their own innocent superior?

"Yes, but... she told me he had done it," he said, leveling an accusatory finger at Miss Cushing.

"And I can certainly see how she might think so," I said with an understanding nod to her.

"Yet it is not her job to know such things." Lestrade grinned. "It is *yours*, Inspector. If you are lucky, it may still be yours tomorrow."

"No," Lanner insisted. "No. There is no evidence that this phantom of yours—this Jim Browner—is in any way connected with—"

Warlock did not let him finish. He loomed forward and pointed a long, bony finger towards the kitchen. "Tell me, Lanner, what is that parcel tied up with?"

"String!"

"What kind of string?"

"I don't know! Just string!"

"*Tarred* string. Do you know why string is treated with tar?"

Lanner did not answer, so Holmes leaned in further and fixed him with a predatory smile—he could look terrible when he smiled like that. "To prevent salt air and salt water from corroding it. Now answer me this: do detective inspectors spend a great deal of time at sea?"

"...No."

"Do sailors?"

"...Of course."

"Is Grogsson a sailor?"

"You know he isn't."

"Is Jim Browner?"

Lanner was positively pale now. Warlock closed in upon him, grinning, practically shouting, "Sarah Browner had an army of lovers, everybody knows it! Jim Browner knows it! He caught her at it, don't you see? He left her, sent her back to her sister—or at least assumed she'd wind up here again. But he wasn't done yet! He found two of her lovers! Two of them! He did his deed! He worked his murders! He took the ears and he sent them to his wife, so that she could tell her next lover—tell him that the cost of touching her would be his life—that his would be the next ear in the box!"

"But... but no! The writing, on the package! It looks like Grogsson's hand! His spelling!" Lanner stammered. "Miss Cushing, is that your brother-in-law's handwriting?"

Miss Cushing, glad for an excuse to leave the fray, ran to the kitchen to examine it, calling back, "It doesn't look like his."

"I wonder, Miss Cushing," Holmes laughed, "have you ever seen his handwriting when he is drunk? When the fury is on him? When he is knee-deep in the gore of two men he has just murdered?"

"I... well... no, I haven't," she said, then a moment later asked, "What is all this written on the inside of the paper?"

"A betting sheet," said Holmes. "It is the record of sailors, betting on a fight. Do you see the names of the ships they were on?"

"Is that... is that *Nantucket* and the *Traverser*? Are those ships' names?"

"They are. Has Jim Browner ever served on one of those ships?"

"I don't know," came Miss Susan's doubtful voice from the kitchen. "He's been on so many ships…"

"I think he has," said Holmes. "And I know that Inspector Lanner here—being a skilled observer—will have noted that the wrapping paper is only one part, torn from a larger whole. He now suspects that, if I were to find that sheet, Browner's name would be on it. He knows that I will find that sheet…"

Since Susan was in the other room, Holmes allowed some of the terrible green fire into his gaze as he closed the gap between him and Lanner, adding, "…*because he knows me and he knows how strangely apt I am at finding such things!*"

The look on Lanner's face was most satisfactory and I think Lestrade and I did not mind that Holmes was betraying a hint of his true nature, until he slipped too far. Suddenly he rose from the ground to hover a few inches from the floor. All the shadows in the room bent in towards him and his deep voice boomed, "*FOR I AM THE SEER OF HIDDEN TRUTHS! THE FINDER OF LOST THINGS! AND MY NAME SHALL BE KNOWN ACROSS THE LAND FOR I AM COME TO—*"

But he did not finish, for Lestrade and I jumped onto the tails of his overcoat and pulled him back to earth. Lestrade hushed him and stroked his brow while I nervously proclaimed, "Yes… well… I think that's enough for now, don't you, Holmes? I suppose the only thing to do is to wait for them to bring Grogsson in. Unless, of course,

Lanner wishes to forswear his warrant…"

"He can't. He needs a second detective's signature to cancel the arrest," Lestrade smiled, "but I think I could sign my name to that."

Five minutes later we were in a carriage, bound away from the shaken Lanner and Miss S. Cushing.

"Phew. I am glad that's over with," said Holmes, dabbing his forehead with a handkerchief.

"It isn't," I said. "Most of the force won't know the warrant is cancelled. They may still find him. Even if he comes quietly, it won't take them long to realize he's guilty."

"Wait!" cried Holmes. "He is? After all those facts… After making me recite that venomous rebuttal, Grogsson actually did do it?"

"By God, Holmes," I shouted, "were you not in that house? How could you go there and not realize? Yes! He is guilty!"

Lestrade shook his head and muttered, "So guilty."

"We must find him," I said. "We must coach him before he speaks to the police. Remember: Grogsson never lies."

"I think, perhaps, we can persuade him to remain silent, though," Lestrade suggested.

"That is my hope," said I.

"Yes, but where will we go?" Holmes asked. "He isn't at home. He might be anywhere."

"He might," I admitted, "but at least we have a starting point. He left a clue."

My gaze fell upon the grisly package, which bounced on the seat beside Holmes. Our first stop was St. Katharine Docks. The light was already fading, so we sped from berth to berth, asking after the *Nantucket* and *Traverser*. We had no sign of them, until at last the wizened old dock-master told us, "Not here, sirs, but I know the *Traverser* was due in at Tilbury... oh... two, three days ago."

I was dismayed. The journey to Tilbury was more than twenty miles. There were no trains until the morning, so we were forced to hire a coach.

By the time we reached our goal, the night was well on—and it was a cold and biting one. Lestrade did not mind at all; he was quite at home in the frigid dark. Holmes pulled his overcoat tight around him and began to hum snatches of random tunes. From time to time, a wisp of stinking smoke would escape his collar. I realized he must have called upon the fires of some distant hell dimension to warm the lining of his coat, which infuriated me. I hated it when he did that. For my part, I shook with cold.

I led my two companions on a quick search of the neighborhood, until I found what I was looking for. Dockside doctors keep their signs always alight, they must rise and tend the sick and stricken whose ship might dock at any hour. Espying one such sign, I pounded upon the door until the sleepy-eyed doctor opened it.

"Last night you tended two sailors—Hanson and O'Keefe—they'd had their ears torn off."

The surprised look in the doctor's eye told me he knew of no such cases, but the second doctor we found proved to know more. I could tell because, upon hearing my description, he slammed his door shut, declaring, "I don't know a thing about that! It's none of my business! Go away!"

"Dockside fights are illegal," I reminded him, through the closed door. "A man could lose his practice if it came to light he'd been patching up the brawlers."

After a moment of silence, a voice behind the door asked, "What do you want?"

"Where is Dancer?" I asked. "Where is tonight's fight?"

We could hear him scratching about behind the door for a few seconds, then a scrap of paper slipped out through his letterbox. We had an address—a squalid little warehouse two streets down from the waterfront.

By the time we arrived I was breathless and so cold I could not feel my feet. Each gasp sent the burning frost deeper into my lungs so it came as a magnificent relief when the warehouse doors parted to allow us entry to a steaming, sweating crowd of sailors, clustered around a makeshift ring. Pallets and boxes had been stacked along the walls of the warehouse, leaving the center of the space bare. Lanterns hung from every post and beam to light the scene. There, in the center of the ring—quite alone—stood Grogsson. He was stripped to the waist and his fists were wrapped in tattered bandages, stained with dried blood of the previous night's competitors. He had been crying. He still was, a little, but his red and puffy face was contorted with rage as well as pain.

"McCullogh will not fight!" cried a barker from the side of the ring. He wore a garish jacket and a green bowler. "McCullogh will not fight! Who will step inside the ring? Who will face the Dancer?"

It didn't appear that many were eager for that particular honor.

"Gwwwaaaah! Gwwwwwwargh! Cowards!" Grogsson bellowed. If he was trying to convince anybody to take the risk, he was doing a poor job of it. The crowd began to mutter and sway, but none stepped forward.

"Any weapon!" Grogsson offered.

"Do you hear that, friends?" the ringmaster called. "Any weapon you like! The Dancer will face you with only his fists! The house will pay ten-to-one odds against the Dancer, and the challenger will receive a quarter share of all bets rendered, win or lose! You must like those numbers, eh? Who will fight? Who's good with a knife? Who's good with a pistol? Have you got a rifle, friend? Have you got a cannon? Step forward!"

Nobody did.

Grogsson screamed his frustration and threw his fists against his chest and his own, swollen eyes, "Three men! Any weapon!"

"Three men!" the ringmaster cried. "Three, armed however they will, at five-to-one odds! For centuries now, England has huddled behind her wooden walls, kept safe by ships and sailors! Are there not three men left? Are there not three sailors in all England to answer this call?"

Apparently, there were not.

"Perhaps things had not gone well for Mr. Hanson."

"You can win!" Grogsson howled, lashing out with a fist against one of the beams that held the warehouse's roof. I heard it crack. The entire building shook with the blow and the two hundred or so sailors within ducked and scuttled, fearing the roof might come down around their ears. I heard shingles clatter to the ground outside.

"Torg will let you win!" Grogsson promised, but still the crowd was too terrified to face him.

I knew better. Or, I knew Grogsson. He held honor as the most sacred virtue—far more important than life itself. I knew he was not lying. Was he seeking to be punished for his misdeeds? Was he seeking death? I began to push my way through the crowd.

"Torg!" I cried. "Torg!"

But he did not look up. I had to climb inside the ring—right inside with him—before he spied me. A cheer went up from the assembled crowd and the ringmaster declared, "Here's a... um... likely lad!"

Money was already flying from finger to palm when I called out, "No! No bets! No fight! Torg! Torg, please! You have to come with me."

"Watson man?" he asked, peeping up at me.

"Torg, come home."

This suggestion cast him once more into grief-fueled fury. He smote the ground and bellowed, "Torg has no home! Torg can never go home!"

"No. It's all right, Torg. It's all right. Scotland Yard is not hunting you anymore."

He wrinkled his brow at me, as if that was a very queer

thing to say, and I realized he had no idea the Yard had ever been seeking him.

"Come on. Let's go home."

"No. Can't. She will see me, Watson. She called me 'Ogre.'"

From the side of the ring, I heard Lestrade coax, "Torg, listen to Watson."

"Can't go home," Grogsson insisted.

"Come to my house then," I urged him. He paused to consider that.

"Oh, I don't know…" said Holmes. "By happy chance, there are three of us. Holmes, Lestrade, Watson. We could just fight him."

Grogsson cut loose with a wracking sob, but there was laughter behind it.

"Come stay with Holmes and me," I said.

Grogsson cast his eyes down, stood still for a moment and finally gave a resigned nod. The four of us made our way out into the cold.

"How does our friend fair?" Warlock asked me as I strode into our sitting room. February was proving just as miserable as it ever does in the great, gray city, and I had just finished the long walk back from Grogsson's.

"Not well," I answered, yet I will confess my own spirits were high. Whatever Grogsson might be feeling, my month of misery was over. He was now installed in his own house once again, and I no longer had a giant moping in my sitting room, eating all my crumpets.

"Yes, but you do think he will recover, don't you?"

I shrugged. "I am not so sure, Holmes. I think our friend may have suffered some permanent damage. I had to close every curtain on the west side of his house, lest he look out the window and spy her."

"Well," Holmes sighed, "we did the best we could."

"Did we? Honestly, I think he might have preferred exile to Siberia."

"You jest, Watson."

"Not at all. Think about it Holmes: there is no law there but brute force. There are no societal mores to violate, no beauties to break his heart. He'd have all the tundra wolves he could punch and to top it all, the Russians are *famous* for ballet."

I did jest, but there was some truth to my words. I have never, since that day, been to Grogsson's home and found his west-facing windows uncovered. He cannot look upon Susan Cushing—the shame and the hurt are too much for him to bear.

In later years I found out that the phrase "I faced the Dancer" was a common dockside boast. I have never heard of any that claimed to have beaten him, only that they climbed into that ring, faced him and survived. Of course, most of the sailors who make that boast are lying. They do not understand the depth of that claim. But I do. Because I did. I climbed into that ring. I faced the Dancer.

And I pitied him.

THE ADVENTURE OF THE YELLOW BASTARD

AS I SIT TO PLACE THE HISTORY OF MY ADVENTURES with Warlock Holmes on paper, it necessarily follows that I must pause to reflect upon my actions. I am generally proud of them. Yet, when the light of retrospection shines down upon any man's past, it is bound to cast one or two unsightly shadows. This is one such case.

Ever since the conclusion of our first mystery, I had labored under the resolution to teach Holmes the process of deduction. He had used it—but not well—to explain away his demonic insights on the first day I met him. I had since seen him make the same attempt to other fellows. Though Holmes had a good facility for lying, he had never bothered to learn the tricks of observation, inference and deduction that he claimed mastery of. Therefore, several men had seen through his lies and this caused Holmes to fear his true nature might one day be discovered by the wider world—an event likely to be followed by torch-waving, pitchfork-brandishing lynch-mobbery such as would be remembered for all ages. Thus, I took every opportunity to demonstrate observation and inference to him. I may have taken it too far, on occasion.

I remember, we had just returned from Regent's Park to find Mrs. Hudson standing outside the door to our rooms, brandishing a battered tobacco pipe at us and complaining, "He wouldn't stay! I told him wait an' he said he would an' then a second later, he up and walks out again, leaving this still smoking on the side table. Almost burned me curtains, he did."

"Who did?" I asked.

"Man with the pipe," she said, eyeing me as if I were an imbecilic child.

"That is not helpful, Mrs. Hudson."

"Go easy, Watson," said Holmes. "You can hardly have expected more, eh?"

"You don't think so?" With a huff, I snatched the pipe from our stunted landlady and turned it over once or twice in my hands, examining it.

"The man who owns this pipe is left-handed, just as you are, Holmes. He has a strong grip and good teeth; he is not wealthy, but comfortable enough not to have to worry about extra expenses. He is a man who prizes old comforts, but not enough to take care to preserve them."

"I can do better than that," Holmes scoffed. "Hand it to me."

As he stepped forward to take the pipe, his coat began billowing about his frame in a manner that foretold a fairly impressive demonic consultation was about to begin. I placed a hand against his chest, held the pipe away from him and said, "I do not doubt, Holmes, that you could find a way to tell me the man's name, his hair color, his favorite tie and what he ate for dinner last Wednesday. That is not the point. The point is to learn as much as you can from the clues presented to you."

"That is the hard way," he complained. "Besides which, I can do better."

"You can't! I won't let you. Listen, Holmes... See how the pipe is singed down its right side? No simple match does that; he likely lights it from a burner or—since that is liable to sear the hand—a gas lamp."

"So?"

"See how the burns are all on one side? That means he must have held it on the other. Observe how my hand covers them if I use my right. He must therefore regularly hold this pipe with his left. He has gnawed all down the amber of the stem; to leave such marks, he must possess a strong bite and good teeth."

"I don't care about such things, Watson."

"Well you ought to, or you will be caught!"

"Caught at what?" asked Mrs. Hudson.

"Nothing!" Holmes and I said together. Mrs. Hudson frowned even harder and made her way out. At least she had a good sense of when she was intruding—a pity it did not stop her doing so whenever the chance presented.

I tried a different tack. "Here, Holmes, hold the pipe in your left hand and see if you can tell me why I suppose the owner has a strong grip."

He gave a huff to indicate that he was only doing so to humor me, then took the pipe from my hand. At first he seemed uninterested, but as he turned it from side to side, I could see his curiosity getting the better of him.

"Your thumb is on it, right now," I prompted.

"Yes… It's this silver band, I suppose. It seems a touch jagged and irregular. What is it?"

"Well done, Holmes! It is a repair. With only the strength of his thumb, our man has accidentally snapped off the stem of his pipe, then had it repaired with silver. Such a repair would cost more than the pipe had originally. Also, it would take more time than simply purchasing a new pipe, but he was willing to go to the expense and also to stand the wait. Why? Because he loves old, familiar things."

"But not enough to keep him from thrusting them into gas lamps."

"Precisely, Holmes! By Jove, we shall make a detective of you yet!" I clapped him on the shoulder and he beamed proudly at me, but our reverie was cut short. Before either of us could utter another word, a tall man in his late thirties or early forties came up the stairs and swept past us. He marched into our sitting room, flung himself upon one of the armchairs by the fire, heaved a sigh of annoyance and began patting down his pockets.

"Who is that?" inquired Holmes. "What is he doing?"

"I don't know," I said, "but I would suppose he is searching for his lost pipe."

Holmes and I followed our strange visitor into our chambers. I held his pipe out towards him and asked, "Were you looking for this, sir?"

"I was!" he said, at first delighted. Then his expression

returned to one of annoyance and he asked, "How did you get it? Who are you?"

"I am Dr. John Watson and this is Warlock Holmes. *We live here.*"

"Capital! You are just the fellows I came to see! I must... Hang on a moment... Did I knock?"

"You did not."

Our guest threw his hands up and cried, "Ah! I am sorry, gentlemen, heartily sorry. The truth is I am so put out that I cannot concentrate. I hardly know where I am and I'll be dashed if I know what to do with myself."

"Perhaps we can help, Mr. Munro," I offered.

"Yes, I... By God! How did you know my name?"

"It is written inside the brim of your hat, which is turned towards us." I fixed Holmes with a look that said he ought to remember this trick and endeavor to repeat it whenever possible.

"Ah. Yes, so it is," said our guest, with a nervous laugh, "Mr. Grant Munro. Pleased to make your acquaintance."

"Likewise," said I.

"I came because I have seen Mr. Holmes's name in the paper. I will confess: I previously made sport of you, sir. But my wife seems to think you one of only a few in London who possesses a true understanding of the world at large."

"She sounds like a wonderful lady." Holmes beamed. He joined Munro by the fire, sinking into the remaining armchair. I took a seat on the sofa.

"She is. And—as it is she whom I wish to consult you

about—I chose to follow her advice and seek your help above all others."

"I shall do my utmost to justify her confidence in me," said Holmes. "Now, tell all. What has upset you so?"

"My wife! Now, I understand that the fashion is for a man to care for his wife but also maintain a certain aloofness. Ask most men and they will tell you they love their wives, but they will also speak of how they are henpecked. They may accuse women of pettiness or smile at the failings of what they call 'the weaker sex,' but I will not. I love my wife, gentlemen, and I tell you that I never did anything to deserve so fine a companion. She dotes upon me! She sees to my every whim and care. She cooks my meals, brings my tea and slippers, she rubs my shoulders when I am distraught and listens to my every gripe, though I know my problems are often petty. All the while, she treats me as if I am the best, most noble creature that ever walked the earth. Well, I protest that I am not, but *she* very well may be. We have known one another three years now and spent them each declaring the other to be our better. We live in a state of mutual worship."

"It sounds like the ideal match." I smiled. "Why, if man could design himself the perfect companion, it sounds as if your wife would be the result."

"It does," said Holmes, though some thought made him crease his brow as he said it.

"But now she has become distant," Munro wailed. "Something which I do not understand has come between us and… Oh God! What shall I do? I cannot bear the thought of losing her, gentlemen. I do not understand what has happened and I do not know what to do and I dread the consequences!"

"Calm yourself, Mr. Munro," I urged. "You must tell us exactly what has upset you so. When did it begin?"

"Well, the first thing—the first strange thing I can think of—occurred about six weeks ago. She came to me and asked if she might have some money. She asked if she might have a hundred pounds."

"What for?" I wondered.

"That is what I wanted to know," said Munro. "Understand, that if she had wished to purchase the world's most expensive biscuit, I should not have protested. The money is hers by right. She was a widow when we met, just recently arrived from America. She'd been left well-monied by her previous husband and when we wed, she insisted on transferring all this wealth to me. It and all she owned belonged to me, just as *she* belonged to me, she said. Of course I protested that it was not her money that had captured my interest. She said she knew it was not, but that I must take it anyway, for I was master now."

I shook my head and declared, "I have read of such things in cheap romances, but I never thought a real flesh-and-blood woman might do such a thing. What do you think, Holmes?"

He was lost in thought, distant and worried. "I do not suppose a real woman would, Watson."

"But the important thing," Munro continued, "is that she didn't tell me *why* she needed one hundred pounds. We had never kept secrets before. I tried to put it out of my mind, but over the following weeks the thought would return and vex me. What could she be keeping from me? But then, the day before yesterday, I had another shock that almost chased it from my mind. My home is in Norbury. On our lane is a little cottage, which had been vacant since we moved in, but which had just begun to show signs of life. As I passed the cottage that night, I cast my eyes up at it, wondering who my new neighbors might be and when I should call upon them. Just then I saw... the thing..."

Here he stopped and wrung his hands for a few moments. With no trace of judgment or humor, Holmes asked, "What kind of thing?"

"Silly. So silly to say... It was only a face—a man's face, I think—but there was something about it, Mr. Holmes. It seemed... false somehow. It was rigid and... well, I cannot describe just what was wrong with it, but as I beheld it I had the feeling that it had come for me from a long, long way away and I would never be free of it. Well, I ran right home to tell Effie all about it—"

"F.E.?" Holmes interjected.

"Yes. My wife—Effie."

"You married a Final Edition? Cad! Sorcerer! Anthromancer! Get away from him, Watson!"

At this, Holmes rolled out of his armchair, crashing to the floor. His left hand groped towards the fireplace until it chanced across the coal scuttle, which Holmes snatched up and flung at our guest, scattering bouncing pieces of coal across half the sitting room.

"Holmes!"

"I... I don't understand!" cried Munro. "Have I said something wrong? Effie is only a name—my wife's name!"

"Not a particularly uncommon one, I think you'll find," I added, raising a warning eyebrow.

Holmes would not be soothed. "But think of the creature he describes, Watson! She is totally devoted to her mate! Devoid of free will, she dedicates all her effort, all she owns and *all she is* to her husband, without reserve. You yourself doubted that a real woman would do such a thing, Watson. You are right! You asked whether—given the chance to design their ideal mate—men would not create exactly such a creature. Don't you see? They did!"

"Holmes is possessed of a magnificent imagination," I told Munro.

"Anthromancers," Holmes continued, contorting his hands into disgusted claws, "lonely malefactors—twisted creators of the saddest creatures that live. No woman would touch such a dark practitioner, Watson, so they turned their forbidden arts to the creation of one that would! The first generation was easy to spot; they had rubber skin. The Nexus Twos were halting automatons with immobile smiles they had no power to change. The Nexus Fours were simple pleasure models, but the Sixes were an impressive achievement. Just before their cabal broke up, the anthromancers produced a few Final Edition

Nexus Sixes, capable of giving them their deepest, most chilling desire—heirs."

"I apologize for my friend…"

"He is a wicked sorcerer, Watson!"

"But I am not!" Munro protested. "I am a simple hop merchant!"

"Hops?" Holmes roared. "What are those? Are they vile?"

"They are plants, sir, used in the brewing of beer."

"Huh… Is that all?" said Holmes, visibly confused. "Well… beer is slightly vile, I suppose. You are sure you're not a sorcerer?"

"Preposterous," said Munro.

"I could have sworn…" mumbled Holmes, returning to his chair.

Realizing the time was ripe for me to regain control, I said, "Regardless of my friend's wild theories, I am curious to know how Effie reacted to the news about this rigid face."

"She told me I was being silly and must not be worried by such things. Yet she was much disturbed by the news. She seemed near tears all through dinner, but I could not draw the cause of this anxiety from her. When we went to bed that night, she did not sleep. Eventually I nodded off, but I am sure Effie lay still awake. I was unsettled and slept lightly. I awoke around three in the morning, to find Effie just removing her cloak. She smelled of cold night air and I could tell in an instant she had been outside.

"'Wherever have you gone?' I asked her.

"'Only to take a walk along the lane,' said she, then paused and added, 'Grant, I may need more money.'

"Well, I was very interested to know why she had suddenly begun the habit of walking the lane at night and what had occurred there to convince her she needed funds. She would not tell me. She said she *could* not—that she was bound by promises that pre-dated the ones she had made to me and which she had no power to break. She enjoined me not to worry and said that, if I did as she said, our happiness need not be interrupted. Well, that set me in a highly worried state and I pleaded with her until the dawn to tell me what was happening. She would not be moved and so, as the sun began to rise, I climbed from our bed to begin my work day."

"You must have been exhausted," said Holmes.

"I was, but more than that, I was distracted. As I passed the cottage, I noticed lights in the downstairs window and a shadow upon the curtain. I had the feeling that whatever was bothering Effie might have to do with the new occupants. Since they were up, I resolved to meet them. I went up to the door and knocked. In a moment there was a bustling, then the door opened to reveal a… how shall I describe her… a tough old battleaxe of a woman. She looked to be in her mid-fifties, stern and with little time for interruptions, but what stood out about her were her injuries."

"Injuries?" said I.

"Yes. She had a tremendous bruise on her neck that ran down under her collar. One arm hung limp and seemingly useless. And her face! She had the most magnificently scratched face—as if she had just lost an argument with a jaguar. She stared at me, but said nothing.

"'Hello,' I said, 'I am your neighbor, Mr. Grant Munro. I just wanted to stop by and welcome you to the neighborhood. If there is anything you require while you are settling in—'

"But she cut me off! She said, 'We'll call if we need ya,' in the most horrible American drawl and shut the door, right in my face. As I trudged back down the path to the lane, I turned back and saw the man again at the upstairs window. I was closer this time, so I just made out a pencil-thin moustache and slick black hair, but again, it seemed rigid and immobile to me."

"Could you tell the age of this man?" I asked.

"No," said Munro. "I only remember dwelling on how unnaturally white and shining his skin seemed. He was at the window only a moment, then disappeared. I don't mind telling you, gentlemen: I was distraught. I did not go to work, but instead to the local inn, where I took a little food and an early draught. I sat and pondered what I should do. Soon it was almost lunchtime and I had no stratagem. I elected to simply head back and ask Effie what she knew of the cottage's occupants.

"I made my way back home, but when I got there, Effie was gone! The maid looked affrighted to see me. When I asked her where Effie was, she said her mistress was taking the air and would be back presently. She then got me settled in my chair with a warm cup of tea and asked me to wait. I found myself too anxious to comply, so I stood and began to pace. When I passed the window, what should I see but our maid, hastily running down the lane towards the cottage! I realized Effie must have gone there and set the maid to warn her if I returned home. I set out after her, but by the time I had my shoes and coat on, she had already reached the cottage. When I got there, I did not knock or wait for entry. I flung open the door and stepped inside, resolved to confront my wife, my maid, the scratched-up crone and the strange man in the upstairs room."

"Did you?" asked Holmes, leaning forward as the tale quickened. He was practically at the edge of his seat.

"No! There was nobody there! No one! I ran to the upstairs room and found it empty. It was in a terrible state and I could hardly believe anybody would be living there, but on the windowsill I found a photograph in a silver frame. It was a portrait of Effie, which I had commissioned only three months before!"

"Sorcery! Witchcraft!" cried Holmes.

"No, it isn't," I said. "Think, Holmes: if Effie does indeed have dealings with the strange new neighbors, might she not have taken the picture over herself?"

"Oh. I hadn't thought of that."

"Well, you should have. This fact is far from supernatural, but it does prove two things. First: Mr. Munro is right and his wife's recent disturbance is tied to the appearance of the new neighbors."

"Second?" asked Mr. Munro, eager for any relief of his anxiety.

"That whoever resides in the upstairs room knows Effie well enough to desire a picture of her. I have begun to form a theory, but I would like to hear the rest of Mr. Munro's tale before I speak of it. Pray, continue."

"Well, I suspected they must have escaped out the back door as I approached the front," said Munro, "so I ran out after them, towards the woods. As I neared, who should emerge but Effie herself.

"'Grant, you must not go in there,' said she. 'If you do, all our happiness is ruined. Please, just a little more time and more money and we can live untroubled.'

"I tried to push past her, but she blocked my path and threw me back. I tried again, but she threw me—bodily threw me—away from the woods. We were both in tears at that point and I stumbled clear. I did not know what to do, Mr. Holmes. I wandered. Eventually I found my way here. I have not seen my home or my wife since yesterday afternoon and I cannot guess as to their state."

"Guessing will not be necessary, Mr. Munro. The light of reason shall reveal all," I said. "Now, I wonder if you could tell me more about Effie's past. You said she was a widow when you met her?"

"Yes. She had a husband, back in America, and a daughter too, sadly. Sad, I say, because they both died of yellow fever."

"I see. And this husband, what do you know of him?"

"Well... his name was Hebron—Octavius Hebron."

"An unusual name," I noted.

"Perfect for an anthromancer…"

"Holmes, shut up. Please continue, Mr. Munro."

"Well… Effie always speaks well of him, but every time a conversation turns his way, she spends half her time making excuses for his behavior. It embarrasses me to speak ill of him, for I still enjoy the fruits of his investments, but I think he treated Effie quite badly and if I had the chance to meet him, I would like to bloody his nose."

"Have you ever seen proof of this husband?" I asked. "Either his life, his death or his marriage to Effie?"

"I have multiple stocks with his name and signature, a copy of the marriage certificate—by which right Effie claims the funds of his investments—as well as a birth certificate for their child and a death certificate for Hebron himself."

"And you believe these documents to be genuine?" I asked.

"Well, there is one discrepancy," said Munro, rubbing his chin. "Though Hebron's death certificate lists yellow fever as the cause, Effie says it is not correct. She once told me that that diagnosis was only arrived at because of the yellowed color of his body, but that he had actually died in childbirth."

"He?" I asked.

"Yes. He. Hebron."

"And what aspect of childbirth, Mr. Munro, do you suppose might be fatal to the father?"

Munro shrugged and said, "Well I don't know, do I?

You are the doctor. I know nothing of what goes on in the birthing room and—let me tell you—now that I know what became of Octavius Hebron, I am even less likely to wander into one to find out!"

"In that, you show your wisdom, sir," said I. "As a medical doctor, I can tell you that the birthing room is no place for a husband. Having the father present destroys marriages. He who can walk out of a birthing room with any shred of desire left for his wife is the same man who can walk out of a slaughterhouse hungry for a steak. Many of my medical contemporaries lament that Elizabeth Blackwell or any of her sex were ever granted a medical degree, but I am firmly of the opinion that we need more lady doctors, as fast as they can be trained. Let the schools be filled with them! Let them take over the job of birthing and let us male doctors wash our hands of it—and we would wash them thoroughly indeed. We would scrub and scrub. We would heave a collective sigh of relief heard round the world and thank our gods that the womenfolk were now left in sole possession of their own secrets—those sticky, stinking, screaming, bleeding, pushing, howling, juicy secrets which…"

I became aware of Holmes and Munro staring at me.

"Ahem… Well… I have digressed, gentlemen, but the fact is clear: as a medical doctor I can confidently state that no danger to the life of the father is posed by the act of childbirth. Octavius Hebron's cause of death is false. His death certificate is false. And I feel sufficiently sure to say his death itself is false. Mr. Munro, I believe him to be alive and seeking to reclaim his fortune from your wife."

"By God!" Munro shouted. "That would explain it all!"

"Would it?" said Holmes. "I just don't see it, Watson."

"Holmes, how can you not? We know from the photograph that the person in that cottage has a personal relationship with Effie. We know that Mr. Hebron's death certificate is patently false. Ah! A thought occurs! What if Octavius Hebron conferred his own name on a stillborn child? Thus, the child's death would result in a death certificate in Hebron's name! Let us also remember the sometimes-fatal condition of jaundice, which is common in newborns and results in a marked yellowing of the skin. Effie says she is bound to her mysterious antagonist by promises older than those she made to Mr. Munro, suggesting her previous vows of fidelity to a first husband. We know that she tried to throw money at this person in the hope that they would go away and she has hinted to Mr. Munro that she intends to do it again. This jibes well with the notion that her tormentor is indeed Octavius Hebron. Since she is in possession of his thousands, he is unlikely to settle for such a paltry sum as Effie first delivered. The situation obviously causes her some distress, as she has twice expressed that she wishes this episode resolved so that she and Mr. Munro may be happy together."

"And thank God for that," Mr. Munro interjected. "If the worst comes to pass, he can take his money and go. I don't care, so long as I keep Effie."

"You really are quite attached to her, aren't you?" asked Holmes with a sympathetic smile.

"I told you I was," said Munro, "and it will be a relief indeed if she still favors me. Oh, I hope it is exactly as you say, Dr. Watson. I shall return home at once and confront them both! Let me keep her love and I will chance whatever else may come!"

"Have a care, Mr. Munro," I advised, "my case is incomplete. Even if the situation is as I think, there are many questions still unanswered. Why did Hebron fake his death? Is there some hidden advantage he has gained by his obfuscation? What is his final goal? We assume it to be the recovery of his funds, but have no proof of it. No, if you are to confront him, I suggest you do not go alone into his den. Go in company. Go in force."

"What, shall I raise a militia?" Munro laughed.

"No need," said Holmes. "I can tell from his zeal that Watson is volunteering our services. Isn't that so, Watson?"

"There is a train for Norbury that leaves within the hour. I propose we board it, gentlemen, and see this mystery through to its conclusion!"

"Bravo!" cried Holmes.

I will now confess a certain lack of empathy, on my part: my eagerness to see the case through had nothing to do with Mr. and Mrs. Munro's happiness. I merely wished to teach Holmes a lesson. In the train we were all excited, but I had the especial glee of one who was about to prove a point. As we neared Norbury, Mr. Munro became ever more nervous. So did Holmes.

"I wonder if we have prepared as much as we ought," Holmes said.

"I have my pistol, if it comes to that," I reminded him.

"Yes, but if he is an anthromancer, he may have made one or two modifications to himself, which—"

"Holmes! Stop this nonsense! Here in a public place, in front of a man you have only just met, you spout the very hocus-pocus you fear people will associate with your name. Well if they do, you have only yourself to blame! You must learn the lesson of Ockham's razor: *entities must not be multiplied beyond necessity*. In other words, the simplest explanation is usually the correct one. This tale has no need of demons or hobgoblins to make it whole; it makes perfect sense without them."

This seemed to cause him discomfort. He shifted in his seat for a few moments with a knitted brow. After a while he said, "Well... you make a good case, Watson. And I will admit that I have learned much from you in only a short time. Perhaps my... peculiar history has rendered me incapable of understanding the mundane. Do you think it is a flaw in my perspective that leads me to imagine that wicked, supernatural phenomena underlie our daily strife?"

"Yes. I do think that."

"Oh."

As we neared the mysterious cottage, my mind was set, my heart was true and my resolve unshakeable. The same could not be said of my companions. Alighting from the trap we had hired, Munro and I spotted a woman sitting on the cottage front step, looking down the lane towards us.

"She is waiting for me!" he gasped, and suddenly he began to trail guiltily behind Warlock and me, occasionally muttering something like, "To have brought strangers... Whatever will she think?"

I strode straight up the lane with Warlock by my side. "Effie Munro?" I asked.

"Yes," she replied. She was a tall woman, lithe and athletic with nary a wrinkle upon her face nor trace of gray in her hair, despite the troubles that assailed her.

"Stand aside," I said. "On behalf of your husband, we mean to search this house until the truth is known to us."

"Intruders will not be tolerated," Effie Munro said in an even, factual tone.

This had a strange effect on Holmes: he left my side and slunk back to join Munro. Though my companions' will had failed, mine held. Approaching her, I declared, "I say again, stand aside!" I laid a gentle but forceful hand upon her shoulder to guide her out of my path to the door. Suddenly I had the sensation of one hand on my coat collar and another on my belt. Almost too fast for the eye to follow, her dainty foot kicked my right leg out from under me, then returned to reprise the deed against my left. I had no chance to fall. She yanked me bodily towards the very door I had sought to reach, but swung me back away from it in a wide arc and flung me off the front step, over the fence and into a cow pasture.

I remember my thoughts as I flew: surprise and dismay, but not for the reasons one might assume. It took only an instant to recognize that the amount of force that had just been applied to me was far in excess of that which is commanded by any normal woman (for that matter, any normal man and I think most gorillas). This I took in my stride. No, the thing that bothered me most was *being wrong*. I had been so methodical and—let me admit—I had thought myself awfully clever, until just a few milliseconds before. How was it that Holmes was right again? How was it that his flawed, ridiculous anti-logic should prove superior to my deductions?

This self-piteous line of reasoning lasted exactly as long as it takes an airborne Londoner to travel thirty feet or so into a muddy field. It was finally arrested by the ground, which also stopped my physical form with a bone-jarring crunch. I have never been so glad to find myself hurled into the mud. If the field had been rocky, I'm sure my spine would have been dashed to powder. I rolled over a few times and slid to a halt, accompanied by the sound of applause. This latter emanated from Warlock Holmes, who clapped like a six-year-old lad at the circus, shouting, "Oh! Marvelous! I had heard the Final Editions were impressive, but I hadn't realized…"

"Intruders will not be tolerated," F.E. Munro repeated.

"And what of me, Effie?" Grant Munro cried. "What of the husband you say you love so well? Will you fling me aside too?"

"Probably not," said Holmes. "She says she is still

bound by old loyalties, but when she promised herself to you, she was effectively transferring ownership. If you order her to stand aside, she may."

"Is that true, Effie? If I ordered you aside, what would you do?".

The automaton stood for a moment, then said, "My first husband once told me that to love unconditionally and obey unconditionally was the basis of a woman's nature—"

"Chauvinistic and untrue," Holmes noted. "But then, it *is* the basis of a romantically purposed homunculus' nature so... do continue."

"—so I knew how much I would love you—the day we met, I knew. What I never expected was to be loved in return. It is so nice, Grant. It's wonderful. I do not know how I would survive if I were forced to return to a life of loving without being loved in turn. I do not know how I should go on without you. Yet, if you walk through this door, I fear that will come to pass."

"What can be inside, Effie? What is it you feel is strong enough to break our bond?"

"I cannot tell you. Oh, Grant, go away! Please! Come live with me in our house down the lane. Let loose with some of the money from time to time and let me come here in the evenings for an hour or so. Do that and never think of the cottage—it is the only hope for us."

I think I gasped aloud. Such had been the last few months of my existence that I almost *expected* to see demons. But to see a grown woman ask her husband— straight to his face, ask him—for permission to give her body to her hated ex-husband once a night so that her new marriage might be uninterrupted... Well, that is a thing I thought never to see.

Yet the impropriety of the thing seemed not to matter to Grant Munro—at least not as much as the fact that a secret would still lie between him and his beloved. "No!" he cried. "Stand aside, Effie! I will discover this secret and I will love you in spite of it!"

"Oh, if only that could be true."

"You cannot hide such a thing from me! Let me pass, I say!"

Effie hung her head, which began to bob with arrhythmic jerks. She stepped to one side. "Go then," she said. "It has been good being loved by you, Grant. So good..."

With tears in his eyes, Grant Munro stepped past his wife into the cottage. Holmes moved to follow, but stopped ere he crossed the threshold to ask, "Just to be clear, F.E., what should happen if Watson or I try to go inside?"

"Intruders will be tolerated," she whispered.

"Capital. Come along, Watson."

My first impression of the cottage was that it was so still, so lacking in the fundamental heat and movement of life, it must be uninhabited. I saw no sign of the much-abused American woman, nor of the mysterious pale man, but Grant Munro knew better. With fierce resolve he mounted the steps, moving inexorably towards the room at the top of the stairs and the strange face that had haunted him so. I had not yet caught up to him when he reached out and turned the doorknob, so I could not see what lay inside, but I heard the terrible shriek that issued forth from the room. Grant Munro recoiled in terror. Bounding to the top of the stairs, Holmes and I at once looked in to behold F.E.'s secret.

The beast stood barely more than three feet tall. It had a more or less human form, though it was bulbous and possessed of elbows and knees that seemed to flex in both directions. Its skin was bright yellow. It hissed at us, revealing a maw of irregular fangs. It turned and bolted for the windowsill, where it kept its secret identity: a battered Guy Fawkes mask with white skin, black lacquered hair and a pencil-thin moustache. This it thrust on, to cover the shame of its monstrous face, then turned back towards us, seemingly unsure whether it was wisest to hide or to attack.

From behind me came a voice that was at once calm, yet despairing. I had not heard F.E. climb the stairs behind me, not until she announced, "Gentlemen, this is my daughter."

"Ohhhhhhhhhhhhhh!" said Holmes, amiably. "Now I get it! So, Octavius Hebron really did die in childbirth."

"He was not the only one," F.E. confirmed. "For years I believed I was the only one in the room to have survived. But my midwife, unbeknownst to me, was a witch. She used her skills to preserve not only her life, but also the life of my child, who was raised in a coven these past three years. Only recently did they manage to track me down to England and deliver the news that my daughter yet lived.

Midwife Eleanor—whom you met, Grant—promised to bring her if I paid their fare across the ocean, which I did. I installed them here, hoping to be near enough to split my affections between the two people I owed them to—my daughter and my husband—knowing that if the two ever met, I should lose all. Now Eleanor is fled, my secret is revealed and… it's all coming down, Grant. All is ruined!"

As she spoke, Grant Munro's gaze drifted between her and the hissing yellow beast that crouched in the corner. I can hardly describe the stress that played across his face. He blinked. He sweated. When F.E. was done he said, "Well…" He looked at Holmes and then at me, but we had no answer for him—a fact we both decided to communicate with helpless shrugs.

"Well," he said again and suddenly his voice was filled with a shaken confidence. He stood to his full height, straightened his shirt, and walked towards the hideous half-breed three-year-old.

"It seems you and I are at an impasse," he told it. "The love between a mother and child is nature's closest bond. By such measures, you have a stronger claim on Effie's affections than I. Yet, despite that right, I can tell you that I adore her far too much to surrender her to you. I refuse to let you steal my wife from me. I can think of only one course of action."

He paused to straighten his already straightened shirt, held out his arms and said, "I am your father. My name is Grant."

Warlock smiled. F.E. burst into tears. The child

huddled in the corner, unsure of what to do. It would not approach Munro until he held one hand back towards the doorway and beckoned F.E. to join them. Once its mother was present, the child had no further fear. The three of them embraced.

"What do you call her, Effie? What is her name?"

"She has none. Her father was to have named her, but..."

"Well, I am her father now and I think..." Grant Munro smiled down at the yellowed girl. "I think we shall call her Amber."

A tap on my shoulder compelled me to turn my attention to Holmes, who softly said, "Our work is done."

I nodded and turned back towards the stairs.

Outside, raindrops were falling. A glance skyward told of more and heavier soon to follow.

"Our carriage is gone. It must be at least an hour's walk back to the train station," I complained.

"Look on the bright side, Watson," said Holmes, "perhaps the rain will wash some of that mud off you."

I would have laughed, but he was not joking in the least. I pulled my half-crushed bowler down low, turned my muddied collar up against the rain and set off into the gathering downpour. Warlock followed.

Halfway down the path, I muttered, "You were right, Holmes."

"Yes... well... never mind that, though."

"That is kind of you," said I. "And yet... if ever I should become overzealous, or place too much confidence in the power of my reason, I hope you will lean close and whisper 'Norbury' in my ear. I would be indebted to you, Holmes."

We walked in silence and in rain.

THE ADVENTURE OF THE _ECKLED _AND

"EYE-OH, WADSAH!" CALLED WARLOCK FROM THE SOFA. I stopped, hat still in my hand. My eyes narrowed. I presumed him to mean "Hi-ho, Watson!"—a greeting he often employed when his mood was good. Yet his mood was terrible. In fact, I was just returning from wandering about the city all day in the express attempt to avoid being caught up in his sulk. It now being over a month since our last case, Warlock was bored, inconsolable and insufferable.

My hand moved slowly as I placed my hat on its hook and ventured a tentative, "Hullo, Warlock. I must say, you seem to be in good spirits this evening."

"Mmmmmmmmmmmmmmmm," he agreed.

"What might be the cause of this sudden reversal?"

"I toog mah medisuh."

"Medicine?"

"Yah. Medisuh," he said jovially. He gave me a silly smile and sank back onto the sofa with a relaxation so profound that he seemed almost boneless. His head lolled forward just beyond the arm of the sofa, then suddenly fell. His brow smashed down onto our side table with a sickening thunk, but this drew no protest except for a grunt of self-recrimination, followed by a childish giggle.

Let me tell you: there are few surer ways of attracting a doctor's interest. I sprang across the room to learn what medicine Holmes had dosed himself with. On the table next to his head stood a wooden goblet. A few sips of silvery liquid remained in the bottom, with fatty white chunks floating lazily in it. The odor it gave forth burned the nose, but had a familiar scent—almost like almonds.

Since there was no apparent source of this medicine in the sitting room, I ran to the door of Holmes's bedroom and peered inside. On the desk where he kept his alchemical kit lay a paper parcel from our local dispensary. The largest jar of mercury I have ever seen lay open and half empty in the middle, surrounded by a vial of cyanide, an open packet of strychnine, and a half-used cake of Mrs. Hudson's cleaning lye.

"Holmes!" I cried. "What have you done? You'll be dead in minutes!"

"Nah," he scoffed.

"Why, Holmes? Why did you do it?"

"Wadsah, calm dow. Ih has no effeh ohh me."

"No effect?"

"No effeh."

"If that is so, lift your head off the table!"

He gave a few feeble flops. His arms and legs seemed not to respond to his will in the least, but his torso could still bend back and forth. He looked like a salmon that had been caught and flung in the bottom of a boat. Holmes endeavored three or four of these contortions, managing only to raise his head a half inch or so from the table, before letting it plonk down once again, beside his deadly goblet.

"Meh..." he said, "I don'd wand do righ now."

I stood, helplessly racking my mind for a way to save him. Lye I could deal with, though even if life was preserved, terrible and lasting damage was a certainty. Mercury is a comparatively slow killer, but even if I could void it from his belly, some quantity must already have been absorbed into his tissues and could never be purged. Even if he survived the day, madness, blindness, organ failure and death might follow. I could give him tannic acid for the strychnine, yet there was little hope in that. But cyanide? The body absorbed it so quickly that death was certain within minutes and little could be done.

As I panicked, my eye was drawn to the deadly silver semi-circles his goblet had left upon the surface of our side table. They looked to me like four crescent moons: unfeeling, unforgiving and unstoppable. One might as well try to halt the nightly waxing or waning of the moon above as to save the man that had partaken of those four crescents' deadly brew.

But wait...

Four?

Even if Holmes had spilled some of his terrible "medicine" down the side of his glass on his first drink, he would have then had to put down the goblet and pick it up four more times to have left those marks. Probably, there was a fifth hiding below the base of the glass. Lye is even more notable for its level of pain than for its efficacy. How could he have sat blithely sipping on it for long enough to leave *four marks*?

"Holmes… When did you drink this?"

"Lungetibe."

Lunchtime? A glance at the clock on the mantelpiece confirmed that it was now past eight. Even given Holmes's liberal interpretation of when it might be proper to take the midday meal, six hours must have passed since his first drink.

Well… four hours, anyway.

"Are you telling me you've been sipping on this poison for half the day?"

"Yah, buh dond worry, Wadsah. Id has no effeh," he said. He gave me a broad, friendly smile and lapsed into unconsciousness. His pulse was weak, his breathing shallow and interrupted by strychnine spasms and periods of apnea which lasted sometimes four or five minutes. I can hardly describe the mixture of hopefulness and helplessness I felt as I sat by him that night, wishing that all the medical knowledge I had spent so long mastering would prove false.

It did.

I do not recall dropping off to sleep, but I must have done shortly before dawn. I had no sense that I'd slept at all, only the sensation of jarring back to wakefulness when I heard Holmes say, "Watson, get the door, won't you? I am indisposed."

"Huh? Warlock? You're alive?"

"So very alive! I tell you, Watson, I am renewed; I am rejuvenated."

"Are you?" I asked, carefully appraising his physique. "Because you seem to be still unable to move your limbs."

"Pish-tosh! Such pursuits are overrated. I tell you: I am relieved at last. None of the little buggers are whispering to me this morning. Not even Moriarty; I can't hear him at all."

"Is that why you drank poison?"

"Of course! Don't you remember me telling you I had a penchant for poisons, on the day we met?"

"Well yes, but you didn't mention that you intended to poison *yourself*!"

"I haven't. What I have done is poisoned the thousand demons who clamor for my attention at all hours of every day. Yes, sir, I have clobbered them all into comas and I intend to enjoy each instant while they are knocked out. I myself am quite unaffected by such mortal draughts."

"So you keep saying…"

"Look here, are you going to be argumentative all morning, or are you going to answer the door?"

"What—" I started to ask, but was interrupted by a rapping at the door and Mrs. Hudson's shrill voice calling, "Didn't want to knock you gentlemen up, but she insisted. Wouldn't go away, would she?"

"I am sorry, I'm sure," said a second lady's voice, "but the matter cannot wait. And besides, it is nearly ten o'clock."

The response of any well-bred Englishman to the

realization that he has left visitors standing unattended on his doorstep is one of pure horror. I leapt across the room and swung the door wide. I was beginning to form some word of welcome or apology or both, but before I had quite decided on the phrase to use, Mrs. Hudson got a look at me and said, "Oh dear, Dr. Watson."

I was still in my shirtsleeves from the night before. My collar had come undone and I found a patch of slick, sticky drool stretching from my shoulder, all the way down to the waist of my trousers. As for those trousers, I must have unfastened them at some point in the evening, for they were loose and headed down towards my ankles at a rapid rate. With a gasp, I caught them and pulled them back into place. For a moment I had the horrid realization that this must have been an occurrence straight out of one of Mrs. Hudson's shameful novels. I was mortified to have stumbled into such a position, sure that she would gain indecent delight from having caught me so. Yet, her expression betrayed no intimate desires whatsoever. In fact, her raised eyebrow seemed only to say, "Meh... I've seen better."

"*Oh dear*," she said again.

"Yes... Good morning... I... I fear we are not prepared to receive visitors," I stammered. "Do come in, though. Do."

Mrs. Hudson did not come in. Instead, she indicated her companion with a jerk of her thumb, announced, "Miss Helen Stoner", and shuffled off down the stairs.

I could think of no way to explain my situation, so I

only said, "Welcome, Miss Stoner; please come in. May I offer you some tea?"

"How generous," said she. "I would love a cup."

It struck me as odd that she seemed in earnest when she called the offer generous. In this, the era of Victoria, a cup of tea is not a kindness when hosting; it is a necessity. I am not sure which would be more shocking: to enter a stranger's home and discover their house had no floor or to enter and not be offered tea. I deduced that our guest was a person unused to kindness or even civility.

Her appearance did not disappoint that assessment. Though she was yet within her early twenties, her hair was shot through with gray and she wore a worried air. She dressed in the style of the country gentry, but there was a threadbare quality to her clothes. Her dress was dark and dour—suited more to an elderly spinster than a young one, I thought. She had a fair face and—given her age and station—she might have been quite the tempting marriage prospect, were it not for the overall haggard and harried look of her.

"Miss Stoner, I am Dr. John Watson. The gentleman on the sofa is my friend and colleague, Mr. Warlock Holmes."

"Ah! It is him I came to see."

"I thought as much; I shall attend to the tea. May I first take your coat?"

"Thank you."

I settled our guest in one of the armchairs across from Holmes. He smiled at her and said, "Good morning, Miss Stoner, I hope you won't mind if I don't get up."

"Of course."

"I absolutely could, though, if I wanted to."

"Er… yes, Mr. Holmes, I am sure that must be the case."

"I'll be a few moments with the tea," I said. "Miss Stoner, why don't you tell Holmes what is wrong."

She shook her head and averted her gaze to her hands, which lay upon her lap, each fretting with the lace of the other's cuff. "I am not sure anything is wrong," she said. "Yet, I am in fear for my very life."

"Hmmm… mysterious already," said Holmes. "Do tell us all."

"Well… I live with my stepfather in Surrey. Until two years ago, my sister lived with us, but she is gone now."

"Gone?" asked Holmes.

"Dead. Murdered, I fear. And—oh, it is silly—but I have it in my mind that I am next. Julia was my twin, you see. Sisters are always close and twins, they say, are even closer. Julia and I shared the further bond of growing up together without a father."

"What happened to him?" asked Holmes.

"He died when we were only two. We grew up with my mother. We were comfortable enough; Mama had some family money and my father's army pension. When we were eight, she married Dr. Grimesby Roylott—that's my stepfather. God forgive me, but I do not know what she saw in the man."

I suspended my tea-making long enough to ask, "He has a temper, I presume?"

"Oh, have you heard of him? Yes, his rages are famous throughout Surrey. They joke of him in the taverns, I know it! Only when he is not there, I am sure. When he is present, none would dare to laugh. Dr. Roylott is... Well, I will not speak ill of him, but I hate to think of what he would do if he knew I had come here today."

There was something particularly dark about the way she said it and I had to ask, "This is off the topic, I know, Miss Stoner, but has your family ever been troubled by scurvy, rickets or polio?"

"No, nothing like that."

"Neither your mother, your sister nor... yourself?"

"Certainly not."

"Ah well, I apologize for the interruption. How did your mother get along with Dr. Roylott?"

Miss Stoner barked out an angry laugh and said, "Seven years ago she was killed in a railway accident and let me tell you, Dr. Watson, it must have come as a great relief to her. I cannot account for her attraction to the man, or why she would want to go live in his dreadful little house. Now she is gone, just like Papa is gone. And Julia is gone and... Oh, why should I even try to preserve myself? We're all going, don't you see? Chance is picking us off one by one and maybe the living are not so fortunate as the dead..."

She was entirely hysterical at this point. Abandoning my tea, I rushed to her side and took her hand. "There, there, Miss Stoner," I said. "All is well. You have come to Holmes and me now; we will put things to rights, you will see."

"Yes," she agreed. "Yes, of course. I wonder… is there a place where I might…"

"Just this way, Miss Stoner," I said, taking her by the arm and leading her to the bathroom. "Take your time. Holmes and I are perfectly comfortable out here."

I ought to have left her and gone back to the sitting room. Indeed, I gave her every impression as the door closed that I was doing just that, but as soon as the latch clicked, I hastened back to it, as quietly as I could.

"What are you doing?" whispered Holmes.

Unwilling to make a noise, I carefully mouthed "listening" so Holmes might read my lips.

He nodded his understanding, then screwed up his face and a moment later said, "Watson, I'm surprised at you. Listening at the door while a lady uses the lavatory—it just isn't like you."

"Holmes! Damn it! I—" I rushed back into the sitting room "—I am not listening to hear her use the lavatory! That is… No! She is hysterical and she is wearing a whalebone corset! Did you see her? She can barely breathe in that thing. I am listening for the sound of her falling to the floor."

"The floor?"

"Yes. You may be unaware of this, Holmes, but proper English ladies will often ask for a quiet place to compose themselves. Once installed, the constriction of their undergarments often causes them to faint."

"I did not know that."

"Well, it would be of little concern, but if she happens

to fall in a posture that makes breathing even more difficult, that whalebone corset may prove to be the end of her."

"Ha! That is a silly way to die, don't you think?" laughed Holmes.

"Is it? Then why do you suppose it is so very popular?"

I strained to hear if our guest was still on her feet, but presently she ran some water in the basin and I knew her to still be conscious. Warlock gestured me over to him to make a confession.

"I don't even know why she's here, Watson."

"She needs help, can't you see?"

"But *our* help?" said Warlock. "I told you of the brimstone thread once, do you remember? How it moves through the tapestry of life, crossing one strand, then the next?"

"Yes, yes."

"Like cloth, reality moves in distinct patterns, Watson. As such, threads that cross the brimstone must bear some proximity to one another. I myself... how shall I say... I run parallel to the brimstone thread and right along it. Thus, the people who come to me for help usually do so because they—like me—have encountered the brimstone thread more than once. Their problems tend to be ones that can only be addressed by those who have become accustomed to the mystic and the weird."

"What is your point, Holmes?"

"As yet, Miss Stoner has given no indication that her troubles are... unusual. There seems to be no particular reason she has been brought to me as opposed to, say,

Scotland Yard. Should we ask her to leave?"

"Certainly not! Did you see her left arm, Holmes?"

"She's wearing a long-sleeved dress."

"Yes, and even so, it is clear that her left forearm curves notably away from her body. Did you observe her shoes?"

"Erm… they're black?"

"Immaterial. What is important is that the soles are of differing thicknesses. One of her legs is shorter than the other, yet she claims to have suffered none of the bone-deforming illnesses that haunt our age."

"So?"

"So, at some point, her left arm has been broken and she received no medical care for it. Likewise, her left leg—I am guessing her left femur at the distal epiphyseal plate—was broken in her youth, severely enough that it never grew to its proper length. From the little she's told us so far, I have to presume that this stepfather of hers is to blame. The man is a monster, Holmes!"

"Ah. Well, she'd better stay, then."

"Quite," said I and walked back towards our bathroom door to check on our guest. I had taken no more than two steps before I recalled to whom I had been speaking and turned back to say, "Not a *proper* monster."

"No?" said Holmes; he looked disappointed.

"It is only a figure of speech. I mean that I presume him to be a normal man whose behavior is abominable. I say this to you now, because I don't want you to sulk if it turns out he isn't a minotaur or something."

Holmes gave me a sour look, but nodded his agreement.

Soon, the click of the bathroom lock gave me to believe our guest was returning. She stepped back into the sitting room, calmer and more collected than she had been.

"I'm sorry," said she. "I'm not even sure why I came here."

"I know! Neither am I," said Holmes. "It's funny, isn't it?"

"Perhaps I should just return home to Stoke Moran and forget this—"

She didn't finish. I'm sure if he could have made it to his feet, Holmes would have been on them. He shouted, "Stoke *what*?"

"Moran?" I said.

"Yes. Stoke Moran. That is our home. It was one of the great houses of Surrey once, but now it's gone to wrack and ruin."

"And one may presume the house is named for the family that established it?" I asked.

"It is," Miss Stoner said. "The Roylott side of the family has had it for a generation or two, but the house was traditionally held by the Morans."

"*That's* why she's here," Warlock declared. "I knew there must be a reason."

"Do you know if any of these relatives might be named Sebastian Moran?" I asked.

"A few, I think. Sebastian is a common name, out our way."

"May one also presume that Dr. Roylott is far from the only member of the family with a sour reputation?"

"One may indeed," Miss Stoner agreed, "though I think few of the locals would put it so delicately. The Morans have been hated for generations."

"If your stepfather is anything like the Moran I know, he is a formidable gentleman indeed," said Warlock.

"Perhaps. I've never met any of them, apart from Dr. Roylott," Miss Stoner said, shrugging.

"Pray, let it continue to be so," I muttered. "But let us return to your unfinished tale, Miss Stoner. You have not yet spoken of the reason behind your fear. Why do you suppose yourself to be in mortal danger?"

"The timing of my sister's death... and the strangeness of it. You see, she had just become engaged when she died. I thought my stepfather's famous temper would have been woken, for the existence of what little remains of Stoke Moran is reliant upon my sister's and my inheritance. So long as we live with Dr. Roylott, he is steward of those funds. In the event of marriage, the inheritance would, of course, have followed Julia and her groom."

"Yet Dr. Roylott was not troubled by her engagement?" I asked.

"No. In fact, he took pains to make himself cordial to both Julia and her fiancé. We half fancied he had undertaken a campaign to ingratiate himself to them and was intending to cajole from them the funds he needed to maintain the house. Julia and I were speaking of it on the night she died..."

Here Miss Stoner paused to collect herself, for the tears had come again. Presently she told us, "We were in my bedroom. The night was early; the sun had only just set. She complained about her own room. It was stuffy, she said. The window could not open far because of the bars and the vent brought no comfort—no fresh air but only the stench of Dr. Roylott's cigars and his horrid animals."

"Animals?" I asked.

"Yes. Roylott had his practice in India."

"So did I, almost."

"He was forced to leave it when—in an altercation over some stolen silverware—he beat his native butler to death."

"You know, Watson," Warlock noted, "he does sound an awful lot like Sebastian Moran."

Miss Stoner continued, "When he came back, he brought a monkey, a cheetah and a box of trained cobras. The snakes are confined to his room, but the monkey and the cheetah have their freedom to wander the grounds, so Julia and I had bars upon our windows and we locked our doors at night. Julia made such complaint of her room that night that I offered to share my bed with her, as we used to when we were little. She said no, she would sleep in her own bed and stop being silly. But she asked me if I ever heard noises coming from my vent, sometimes."

"Do you?" I interjected.

"Naught but wind and rain, as you would expect. Yet Julia said she often heard a rasping, a sort of metallic bang and the sound of soft chanting, deep in the darkest hours of night. I thought it only fancy, but it seemed to disturb her. Well, finally she took her leave of me and went back to her room. I don't know what time it was—it must have been some time after nine, maybe ten in the evening. I only saw her one more time after that. At two o'clock she came back."

"To your room?"

"Yes. I was awoken by the rattle of my doorknob and a scratching on my door. At first I was afraid it was the monkey, but in the confused noises, I recognized Julia's voice."

"What did she say?"

"Nothing that could be understood. She sounded frantic, at first. But by the time I had risen and opened the door, she seemed quite calm. She stood in my doorway, staring straight ahead, tilting on her heels as if dizzy or drunk. She didn't even look at me. Then she said, 'The _eckled _and,' and then... and then..."

"What happened, Miss Stoner?"

"Her eyes—they shrank."

"*Shrank?*"

"Yes, back inside her head, like two rotten grapes. Then all her skin fell off."

"What?"

"Yes, all upon the rug in a great heap. She was only muscle and bone. She stood there for a moment, trying to say something—it sounded like 'the _eckled _and' again— and then her muscles fell away and her skeleton collapsed down on the whole pile of it all. That was the end of her. That is how she died."

"Disgusting!" Warlock declared, though his tone of admiration was unmistakable.

"And, gentlemen, I fear I shall end the same way,"

Miss Stoner continued, "for now—through fortune I scarce dared to hope for—my neighbor Mr. Greymalkin has asked my hand. The wording of Mother's will is such that if I do wed, not only my share of the inheritance will follow me, but Julia's share as well. Without those monies to support them, Stoke Moran and Dr. Roylott must fall into abject poverty. Yet he did not protest. My stepfather only offered his congratulations and immediately began work on Stoke Moran."

"What sort of work?" I asked.

"Stone work of some sort. I'm not sure the exact nature of it, but it has made my room uninhabitable. Dr. Roylott insists I stay in Julia's chamber, that very chamber where she was stricken to death—or so I suppose. Oh, I didn't want to go of course, but Dr. Roylott is... possessed of a most convincing character and I must admit that I spent last night sleeping in my dead twin's bed."

Even more palpable than my sympathy for Helen Stoner was the swell of hatred I felt for Grimesby Roylott. If any chance remained that I might forgive him, Miss Stoner removed it when she burst into fresh tears and said, "And what should I hear last night, in the depths of darkness? I heard the metallic rasp! I heard the banging! I heard the chants! Oh, I could not stay, gentlemen! I fled to the pantry and hid until first light, then made my way here. But I am to return, don't you see? He expects me to sleep there tonight! I don't know if I can face it again! What should I do? Oh, what should I do?"

Holmes digested the question for a few moments then

said in slow, thoughtful tones, "Well... I can't put my finger on exactly why, but... I don't know... it just seems inadvisable to sleep there. What do you think, Watson?"

"Holmes! Of course she shall not sleep there! She will not play meekly into this villain's hands! Shame on you for considering it! No, Miss Stoner, here is what I propose: you go back to Stoke Moran and pretend that nothing unusual has occurred. This afternoon Holmes and I will..."

But my eye fell across the immovable carcass of my friend and I amended my statement to, "Well... at least one of us will come there to examine the room and formulate a strategy to save you from this mischief."

"Hear, hear!" Holmes proclaimed.

"Could you? Oh, could you?" Miss Stoner cried, alight with new hope. "We have not discussed payment yet and my stepfather controls the finances, but once I am wed..."

"Let us just consider it an early wedding gift, shall we?" I said. "Expect me by train this afternoon. I presume the house is set back from the road?"

She nodded. "There is a long drive up to the house. Do watch out for the cheetah. And the monkey."

I gulped. "Try to watch the main road to intercept me and keep my arrival a secret from Dr. Roylott. I shall see you in a few hours, Miss Stoner. Until then, be of good cheer; this world yet contains justice and the hearts of men are not so hard as to turn away from a lady in need. You will be safe, I swear it."

I ushered her out, bid her farewell and went back upstairs to dress for the country and check my pistol.

I had just set about clearing away our teacups when Mrs. Hudson's voice rang out from the floor below us, screaming in protest. A moment later, I heard heavy steps on the stairs then our front door fell in with a sudden crash. The hinges bent and failed; the lock splintered the doorframe as it was forced into our sitting room. In the doorway stood an angry, red-faced giant of a man with Mrs. Hudson dangling from his left sleeve, still trying to arrest his rampage. I was sure her collection of illicit novels must have offered no end of tips on how to wrestle men to the ground. Also certain was that she had been eagerly awaiting the chance to put these ideas into practice. She didn't look pleased with the way things were going, however. Our monstrous guest paid no heed whatsoever to the struggling septuagenarian clinging to his arm.

"Warlock Holmes!" the trespasser cried. "Which of you is Warlock Holmes?"

Warlock began to screech out terrified, high-pitched wails, contorting his body as violently as he could in an attempt either to stand or simply to wiggle under the sofa. I stood my ground and assessed the invader.

His shoulders were impossibly broad. Compared to his vast torso, his legs were small and bowed outwards from the strain of supporting so heavy a load. He wore a red frock coat, a pale yellow scarf and a top hat. His right eye clutched a monocle with such force I thought the glass would shatter. He had cultivated a magnificent ginger moustache, the tips of which quivered as he raged. The overall effect was one of a furious, steroid-riddled circus ringmaster. Yet, the family resemblance was obvious—he was certainly related to Sebastian Moran. In fact, I think if Moran and Grogsson could somehow be made to have a child together, the resultant monstrosity would exactly resemble Dr. Grimesby Roylott.

"What a quaint method of knocking our country cousins have," I said. "No wonder they find themselves impoverished. They must spend a fortune on doors."

"What are you doing?" Holmes squeaked.

In truth, I was baiting Dr. Roylott. He was a frightening specimen and I might have lacked the courage, if it were not for the fact that I had my hand resting on the handle of my service revolver. Some men find courage in a bottle, but I keep mine in my coat pocket.

"Where is my stepdaughter?" Roylott roared. "I know she has been here! Has she been here? Has she?"

"How should I know? We have not been properly introduced," I said.

"Don't play the fool with me! Where is she? She's no business with you and you've no business with her, do you hear?"

I smirked and noted, "Look at that silly little top hat, Holmes. Don't you hate it when country folk put on airs?"

"Don't antagonize him, Watson!"

Yet Roylott was not antagonized; he was thrilled. Though most people shy from conflict, Grimesby Roylott seemed to draw a fierce glee from it. Striding into our sitting room, he looked around for a moment, then walked to the hearth. He drew our poker from its stand. At first

I thought he meant to use it as a weapon, but instead he placed one hand at either end and twisted the iron rod into a perfect circle. Holmes squealed. Not content with this show of force, Roylott thrust the center of the new-made ring into his mouth and bit down until the two halves separated and fell, clanging, to the floor. He smiled at us, then turned to spit the section of iron rod that remained in his mouth into the fire and said, "If you come to Stoke Moran... If you come to my house—"

"I shall certainly endeavor to treat your possessions with more respect than you have shown mine," I interjected.

"—you will not escape alive. We in my family do not tolerate interlopers. Is that clear?" He shook his fist at me. It was a monstrously large thing, with bulging veins and knotted knuckles. His hide was spattered with grotesque freckles from which grew tufts of curling red hair.

"Quite clear," said I. "Now, is there something we may help you with, or will that be all?"

He turned on his heel, threw Mrs. Hudson onto our dinner table and strode out through the door. A moment later, we heard the door to Baker Street bang open and I knew he had gone. Mrs. Hudson was not injured (at least, not as much as I secretly hoped she might be), but Holmes seemed quite unhinged.

"Holmes! Cease that screaming, if you please. You're giving me a headache."

"I don't like him, Watson!"

"Neither do I."

"You cannot go to Stoke Moran," Holmes insisted.

"Not alone. He'll kill you, Watson. Can't you see? He isn't... He's not normal."

I wanted to protest that all would be well, but the severed halves of our poker argued that Holmes might indeed have a point. If I were caught alone by Roylott, without witnesses and unprotected in his house, what hope would I have?

"Still... I must go," I decided.

"Perhaps we will discuss it further when Mrs. Hudson has gone," Holmes suggested.

A moment later, he suggested again, louder this time, "*When Mrs. Hudson has gone!*"

She gave him a bitter glance, brushed a few pieces of rubble off her dressing gown, then mumbled something rude about the quality of our guests as it compared with the state of her doors and tottered out.

"Really, Watson, you mustn't go alone," Holmes insisted. "I don't know what sort of medicine he has been studying, but he has the marks of a man who has made one or two mystical modifications to himself. Such treatments often result in less than beneficial effects to the psyche. If you wish for a second opinion, go to Charing Cross Hospital and consult with my friend Dr. Jekyll on the matter. He can tell you."

"No. I believe you, Holmes. Yet, what choice is there? Miss Stoner will be in immediate danger in only a few hours and you are in no state to accompany me. There's no way we'll have you fit for an adventure in the time we have."

He thought for a moment, then said, "But... try, won't

you? You're a doctor, after all."

I attempted to explain that there was no known procedure for rehabilitating victims of this sort of poisoning, since none had previously survived it. Yet Holmes would not listen and insisted that I endeavor to cure him. I began by flexing the affected limbs (so... all of them). He had no strength and no voluntary control. It was too late for ipecac, so I gave him great quantities of water to flush the toxins from his tissues as best I could. There was no sign of progress whatsoever.

"This isn't working, Holmes."

"No, it is," said he. "Why, *by the boon that is owed to me by Kh'kath Harh Kugn*, I can feel my strength returning."

Outside the wind rose to howling force and the horses on the street screamed out all at once.

"You just cast a spell!" I said.

"What? Me? No, no, no. There's no such thing as spells—you said so yourself. Why, it is through the merit of your medical skill that I can now move my fingers again and no other reason."

"Holmes, I have asked you not to use your powers! You yourself have told me how detrimental it is to our world every time you do."

"Yes, but my sudden improvement is due to *your* powers, Watson, not mine. It's not as if *I pledge my troth to the fires of Mekzahn Greh-degh for greater life!* That is not why I am suddenly able to stand. It's because you are such a fine doctor. Shall we go?"

The sky outside grew black as night. The streets filled

with the panicked cries of those who rather wondered where the sun had gone off to all of a sudden. By the light of our fire, which flared first blue, then green, I could see Holmes standing by the sofa, looking at me expectantly.

"Holmes! Damn it!"

"Think nothing of it, Watson. I have the feeling that compared to any mischief Roylott may work, such transgressions are slight."

My protests continued, of course, but there was no sense in going without him. As we stepped out into Baker Street, the light of day was meekly returning as crowds of frantic Londoners ran this way and that.

Stoke Moran was not quite a castle. Dating from the period of the English Civil War, it was one of a particular breed of country homes that were constructed by people with guilty consciences or those who had reason to feel that if the war went one way rather than the other, they could expect a fairly large contingent of armed soldiers to come knocking at any hour. Thus, though it lacked an actual barracks, it did sport a high stone wall of some thickness, crenelated turrets and was positioned atop a high hill with a commanding view on all sides. It was a home, but it was a defensible one. Thus it did not surprise me that, as Holmes and I approached, Helen Stoner came out to meet us. Anybody watching the road from one of the turret rooms would see visitors more than a mile off.

"Don't worry," she called as she neared. "My

stepfather has gone to the city this morning and has not returned. If he was not on your train, he cannot possibly return before the next. We have some time."

"We shan't need much, I warrant," said I. "Chiefly, I wish to examine Julia's room and that of Dr. Roylott. Or... I mean... Holmes wishes to examine them."

I could have told her that Holmes and I knew perfectly well that Dr. Roylott had been in London, but chose not to alarm her. Holmes gave her a tired smile. Despite the invocations he had applied in our sitting room, he was still weak and unstable. I had allowed him to lean on my arm on the walk from the train station, but I practically had to drag him up the hill on the final approach to Stoke Moran.

Helen's, Julia's and Roylott's rooms were on the second floor, overlooking the road. Roylott had the corner suite, next to him was Julia Stoner's old room (where Miss Helen Stoner was supposed to now be lodging) and finally Miss Stoner's own room, which did not look as if it were undergoing nearly enough work to render it uninhabitable. It was furnished in a manner that bespoke a country estate in decline, but we found no clue of worth.

Julia Stoner's room was a different story. Even Holmes, lacking as he was in observational prowess, noted the difference immediately. "It's a lot nicer than your room," he said.

"Holmes! How rude!" I chided.

Miss Stoner waved me down and said, "Julia's room was redecorated just after her engagement was announced. We supposed Dr. Roylott did it to curry her favor."

"That is not what I suppose," I mumbled, casting an eye over the room. There were a number of peculiarities, apparent at the most cursory examination. "Miss Stoner, I think you said that your sister complained of the smell of Dr. Roylott's cigars. Can you see why she might?"

"Not offhand."

"Holmes, can you?"

"She didn't like cigars?"

"Look at the vent: it is of newer construction than the walls of the room—newer by far. It runs along the ceiling as vents often will, but do you note the peculiarity?"

"Do I ever?"

"It does not lead outside. It runs through the internal wall, towards Dr. Roylott's room. Why would you vent one room into the next? It's quite unaccountable. Not only that, but observe: the vent ends just touching this bell pull rope which in turn hangs down onto the bed, just beside the pillow. A strange proximity, I think."

I gave the bell pull an experimental tug, but was rewarded with naught but silence for my effort.

"Oh, that…" Miss Stoner said, with a blush, "that is merely for show."

"Show?"

"Yes. Dr. Roylott said we lacked the funds for a bell, but he did not wish us to live with the indignity of seeming unable to afford one. He therefore purchased a bell pull with the intent of purchasing a bell at a later date."

"I can see why he may have told you so," I harrumphed, "but I refuse to believe that such was his true motive. If it were so, he would not have gone to such extravagant measures to ensure this bed is never moved from below the bell pull."

"What good is a bell pull that cannot be reached from one's bed?" Miss Stoner asked. "I cannot think of a reason one would want to move the bed away."

"And yet, if you ever did encounter a reason, it still would not furnish you with the ability. Did you note that this bed has been bolted to the floor?"

"Odd," said Holmes. "Why would Roylott do that?"

"I suspect he wishes to ensure that whoever sleeps in this bed is forced to do so directly under that vent, with this bell pull coming down almost onto their pillow."

"Why? What does it mean?" asked Miss Stoner.

"It means you are absolutely not to spend another night in this bed until this situation is understood and defused," I replied. "I do not wish to be crude, Miss Stoner, but I think Holmes and I would very much like to rifle Dr. Roylott's room now, if you please."

"That may present some difficulty," Miss Stoner said, fretting with her cuffs again. "My stepfather is intensively secretive. He maintains that room himself and allows nobody inside; I've never had so much as a peep through that door. He keeps it always locked and wears the key on a chain about his neck at all times."

It seemed we were stuck, but Holmes—who had taken the opportunity to move down the hallway a few paces and examine the lock on his own initiative—reported, "Luck is with us! The door is unlocked."

"But that is impossible!" Miss Stoner protested. "He always… What is that smell?"

I tested the air and replied, "That, Miss Stoner is the smell of…" and here I paused to regard Holmes with an accusatory glare, "…sulphur and burning iron."

"By God!" Miss Stoner cried. "What is that dripping from the lock?"

"I suspect it is the inner workings of the lock itself," I said, unable to think of a suitable lie.

"Oh, no. Oh, dear me," said Holmes. "It seems as if this lock has been fiendishly booby-trapped to melt itself if someone should tamper with it. I've only just avoided being burned!"

"Nefarious! Ingenious!" Miss Stoner declared.

"I'm surprised to hear you think so," I said, rolling my eyes at Holmes in a manner meant to convey that he had just been extremely lucky. "In any case, we are in. Let us see what secrets Dr. Roylott keeps."

These secrets were of such quantity and clarity that even the unobservant Holmes spotted some the moment he pushed open the door. Before I had even the chance to look in, he asked, "I say, Watson, what do you suppose that pile of skulls is for?"

Pushing past him I entered into the lair of a mad fiend. Dr. Roylott did seem to have a penchant for bone-based décor, the walls being decked in shrines and ritualistic pictograms formed principally out of human bones. Several skulls had been set down into pelvises so that they looked as if they wore upturned collars of bone. The whole affair was decked in pale yellow bunting that draped the room from corner to corner along all four walls. Connecting this with the yellow scarf I had seen Roylott wearing and the fact he had held a medical practice in India, I made a connection.

"He's a Thuggee," I said.

"Hullo! I know those chaps," said Holmes.

From the hallway, Miss Stoner said, "Thuggee? What are you speaking of? I don't..."

She did not finish, for she rounded the doorway and encountered her stepfather's true nature. She gasped and fell back against the wall. It took her some moments to control her breathing—that dashed whalebone corset again, I think—at which point she muttered, "All those bones... Do you suppose... Julia?"

"Oh, no. No, I am sure not. No man can offer such disrespect to the bones of his own family member," I said, though in my heart I knew I was almost certainly lying. I further suspected that if Helen Stoner had not decided to hide in the pantry last night, her bones might now be here as well.

"I say, Watson, look over here!"

Holmes was bent over a table on which lay a number of instruments and concoctions that reminded me of his own alchemical workstation at 221B, though this one was more extravagant and possessed of a distinctly evil character. Curved knives and gleaming, silver-plated hypodermic needles lay in neat rows. Though this laboratory was of interest to me, there were two other matters of greater concern.

The first was the cobras. I found them in a glass terrarium by the window. They were sluggish in the cold, but gazed at me with all the malevolence their breed is known for.

The second was the vent, which ended just above Dr. Roylott's alchemical workstation. Though it featured a curved downspout, I could just discern light at the end where it opened above the late Julia Stoner's bed, some dozen feet away. It was certainly wide enough for a cobra—in fact I think all three could have slithered through abreast if they wished.

Turning to my compatriots, I said, "I have seen enough. I do not know exactly how Roylott has worked these crimes, but I am certain he is to blame. This is what I suggest: Miss Stoner, you are to give Dr. Roylott no indication that you have spoken with Holmes or me, or that you know his secret. I understand that this may be difficult, but it is of critical importance. Can you do it?"

"I... I think so."

"Good. You are to agree to sleep in Julia's bedroom again tonight. When Dr. Roylott has retired to his room for the evening, you are to signal Holmes and me with a lantern placed in Julia's window—Holmes and I will be stationed nearby. Make sure the front door is unlocked, then return to your own bedroom and wait there. When we see your signal, Holmes and I will sneak into Julia's room and endeavor to catch the good doctor at his mischief. Agreed?"

"Are you sure?" asked Miss Stoner. "Do you think

the two of you are enough to face such a monster as my stepfather has proved to be?"

"Oh," said Holmes, with a sideways smile in my direction, "I imagine we'll be all right."

"But isn't he—what did you say—a thug?"

"Thuggee," I said, "but you are correct in that we derive our English word 'thug' from their sect. They are an Indian murder cult, dedicated to Kali, the goddess of destruction and..." I had to choose my next words carefully, "...marital relations, external to the formality of wedlock."

"Well, if you are certain you can confront him," Miss Stoner said, "you could wait at the local inn. It's just at the base of the hill. If you arrive early and ask for a seat by the window, you will have a clear view of Stoke Moran."

"Capital. We must hurry, I think. Holmes and I took some time walking here and the next train must be arriving soon. Miss Stoner, you may want to splash some water on your face and take a moment to compose yourself."

She nodded her agreement and bustled down the hall, whereupon I turned to Holmes and whispered, "And as for you... Dr. Roylott must have no idea that his sanctum has been violated. This means his lock must be intact and fastened."

"Ohhhh..."

"Well, you should have thought of that before you melted it. Now put it back with as little magic as you can manage. I will say our farewells to Miss Stoner."

* * *

I soon discovered the chief flaw in my plan: it lay in Holmes's and my weariness, combined with the sheer amount of time we needed to bide while waiting for the occupants of Stoke Moran to settle in to slumber. The most felicitous remedy was to hire a room at the very inn where we were supposed to wait and sleep through the afternoon and early evening.

I woke much refreshed. Holmes looked better too, though a certain clumsiness remained in his limbs, which told me they were not answering to his will as they should. I thought some food might effect a partial cure, so we went down into the tavern to sit by the window, eat and wait.

In a country dominated by sheep and shepherds, mutton is not considered a delicacy. Yet when it is fresh and delivered hot from the oven, baked into a hearty country pie, it is difficult to best. I married mine with a pint of stout and rejoiced. Holmes pouted until the innkeeper agreed to make him a plate of toast. Once this was joined by a cup of their runniest vegetable soup, he settled in, happy as a cat. As we ate, he asked me, "So, what do you make of this case, Watson?"

Gazing around to be sure we were not overheard, I replied, "I feel sure that Dr. Roylott murdered his stepdaughter. I am unsure as to his exact modus operandi, but I have a theory: suppose he has trained his cobras to slither through the vent, down the bell pull and attack whatever sleeping unfortunate lies upon the bed below."

Holmes gave me a squinty look, as if he found this highly unlikely.

"No, think about it, Holmes! Remember the cobras? Remember their mottled scales? Can't you imagine a woman, surprised and bitten in the dead of night, crying out about the horrifying speckled band that had just worked her ill? That's what I think Julia Stoner was trying to say as she died, 'the speckled band'!"

"All right, I see your point, Watson," Holmes said, "but then again, might she not just say, 'Help, a snake?' It's got fewer syllables and the benefit of clarity too, don't you think?"

"But what else could she have been trying to say?"

"I don't know," Holmes shrugged. "Go through the alphabet. 'And' is a word. So is 'band.' 'Canned' also. 'Dand' and 'eand' are not, but 'fanned' is…"

"Yes, but how many words end in 'eckled'?" I said.

"Well I have been too much a gentleman to bring up the other flaw in your conjecture, Watson. Have you ever heard of a snake whose bite causes one's skin and musculature to fall off?"

"No," I admitted, "but then, I have never known of anything else that could either."

I fell silent to ponder that. I made no headway on the problem but I did notice we had another. Our supper was finished and the dishes cleared away, yet as I stared at the windows of Stoke Moran on the hill above, I realized it might be hours yet before our signal showed.

"You know, Holmes," I said, "we may need to order

a drink from time to time, else the innkeeper will take it amiss that we hold this table all night."

"As you say, Watson. Just be careful. We must be at our best tonight and you know how drink affects you people."

"*You people?*"

"Yes. Well, you know... everybody who isn't me. Alas, I shall never know the comfort of alcoholic torpor, since such draughts have no effect on my person."

"No effect?" said I. "Just as poison has no effect on you, I suppose?"

"Just so, Watson."

"Except that I have *seen* its effect on you, Holmes. Just last night you were completely overcome with it."

"Preposterous."

"When Miss Stoner came this morning, you were unable to stand."

"Or I chose not to, in order to make her feel unthreatened though she was entering the domicile of two unknown gentlemen."

"Ha! A fine explanation, Holmes, but we both know you could not stand."

"Watson! I am surprised at you. Just because I am immune to alcohol and other poisons and you are not, that is no reason to engage in envy and lies!"

"Lies? How dare you!"

"I am sorry, Watson, but you wear your envy as a Texan wears a hat: though it is a monstrous thing that would uglify any man, you seem almost proud of it."

I am sure I could have argued in circles with him

for hours but I had a more wicked expedient for proving my point. I cast about the room until I found the man I needed. He was at once the fellow who looked like he could least afford a drink, while also being the fellow who looked like he most often did. I beckoned a barmaid over to us and asked, "I say, miss, what is that slop-shirted shepherd in the corner drinking tonight?"

"Same thing as he does every night, sir."

"I wonder if you would be so good as to bring a bottle for my friend and me."

She hesitated, then said, "I'm not sure you'd want any of that, sir."

"Most nights, I am sure you would be correct. But tonight is special."

She shrugged and moved off to fetch our bottle of destruction.

"Bring four glasses," I called after her.

"You gentlemen expectin' comp'ny?"

"No."

I then turned to Holmes and asked him, "So you think you could drink more than any man in this tavern?"

"Any man?" he scoffed. "Any ten men! Any ten men and the horses that bore them here!"

"Very admirable. Let's just set the bar at three, shall we? I will drink a glass of... whatever it is I just ordered. You will then drink three and we shall see which of us begs off first."

The bottle arrived at our table with a heavy thunk. Its mottled brown glass was covered in a slick of grease.

I could not read the label as it was cheaply printed and had not profited by storage—by the looks of it, it had spent a century or so in the belly of a sunken pirate sloop. Nevertheless, the cork slid free with a joyous pop. I can only assume it was pleased to end its association with the foul bottle and roll off into the comparative cleanliness of the nearest pile of rat droppings. The smell that issued forth from the bottle was strangely familiar to me, yet at first I could not place it. At last, the dim recesses of my memory brought it forth. As a youth, I had spent one summer at the home of my uncle. While living, he had been a maker of stringed instruments. Ah, yes! Cello varnish! I poured a glass for myself and three for Holmes.

"To good health," said I, raising the glass to my lips and draining it in a single gulp. My eyes burned; my throat swelled; my stomach spasmed. Still, it was worth it to see the look on Holmes's face.

"Your turn," I coughed.

"Ah... yes... so it is, I suppose," he said. He grew visibly sick as he raised the glass, even before it touched his lips. He drank it down just as quickly as I had. He placed his glass back down and paused to let forth a high-pitched scream of distress. All eyes turned to our table. The slovenly shepherd in the corner raised his glass in salute. I imagine it was rare for him to meet someone who understood what he was going through.

I stared at Holmes, a smile on my lips, daring him to touch his second glass. He looked horrified at the notion of repeating his ordeal, but reached down with a trembling hand and grasped it. He held his nose while he swallowed it then cried out, "Aaaaaigh! Why? Why is it like that?"

I smiled and asked, "Well, Holmes, are you ready to admit..."

But he held up a hand to silence me and then—to my horror—drank down the third glass. This time he managed to avoid crying out, though only by clenching his mouth shut with both hands. He nodded that it was my turn and settled back in his chair, writhing slightly.

I must have grown quite pale.

I really hadn't thought it would come to a second round. Then again, I did not wish to return to Baker Street and spend the rest of my days being forced to admit that Holmes was immune to both poison and alcohol. Given the difficulty he'd had with his first three drinks, I thought it unlikely he could manage even one more. Thus, with doubtful hand and faulty courage, I reached down to refill my cup.

Some hours went by.

I'm not sure how.

I only remember laughing quite a bit. We must have invited the shepherd over, for he joined us in finishing two more bottles and I never did manage to get the smell of him out of my clothes. I think we must have engaged in a series of dares and forfeits. I cannot recall them precisely, but I do remember our best penalty: he who had erred had to reach down under the table with his knife and carve a chip from one of the table legs. He then had to eat it, without attracting the attention of the innkeeper. I do not remember who won or lost, but between the three of us, we ate one of the table's sturdy oaken legs and made pretty good progress on a second. I continually reminded Holmes that we must be ready when Helen Stoner signaled for us, but after a time it seemed as if he didn't know what I was talking about.

"Holmes, we have to stop. Stop. What will happen when the signal comes?" I protested, some time after midnight.

"What is this damned signal you keep talking of, Watson? It sounds like something you made up."

"No. I didn't. It's… it's a lantern."

"There are plenty of lanterns."

"No. In the window."

"Plenty of lanterns in the windows."

"Not our window. The house. The house on the hill."

"Like that lantern?" said Holmes, pointing to the light in the late Julia Stoner's window. "But that's been there for hours."

I was out the door in a flash, with Holmes close behind. The shepherd wanted to come too, but we eventually shouted him away. We staggered up the hill, along the muddy road.

"Shekels!" Holmes declared.

"What?"

"The money of post-Roman Judea! Don't you see, Watson, if someone was rich, he'd be well-shekeled! He'd be the Shekeled Man!"

"That's a bit of a stretch, don't you think?"

"Ah, but when a fellow is strangled or hanged, could he not be said to have been neckled?"

"Nope."

"Oh. Public speakers sometimes get heckled, though."

"That's true, they do," I admitted, "but keep quiet, Holmes. We're almost there."

I think we must have made more noise than we ought, sneaking into Stoke Moran and up the winding stairs. Luckily for us, our quarry was too distracted to note our approach; from behind Roylott's closed door, we could hear muffled chanting.

"He's started it," I hissed. "Quick, Holmes, into Julia's room!"

The room was in half-darkness, lit only by the lantern Helen Stoner had obscured behind the curtain to signal us.

"I don't see anything," whispered Holmes.

"Watch the vent," I told him. "That is where danger shall approach."

Even as I said it, there was a dull metallic bang from the vent, followed by the sound of an unknown, fleshy body sliding through the duct.

"Here comes the cobra," I said, but when our antagonist emerged from the vent, it was no snake. A human hand protruded itself from the edge of the vent and began groping about for the bell pull. Its spotted complexion and profusion of curly ginger hair proclaimed this to be the hand of Dr. Roylott. It used only two fingers to feel about; the others clutched something that gleamed metallic in the lantern's failing light—I recognized it to be one of his hypodermic needles.

The wayward human hand found the bell pull and

started down. As I had suspected, it seemed the pull was there as a guide to reach the pillow below. As unsettling as the hand was, what followed was even more horrifying. The hand was not disembodied. A long, prehensile forearm flowed out of the vent and began coiling down the rope. Certainly there could be no bones within, for it was rubbery and capable of bending in any direction at any point along its length.

"Disgusting!" proclaimed Holmes. He was alight with admiration.

In his shock and inebriation, Holmes quite forgot to keep his voice down. The creeping hand recoiled in surprise, then struck out in Holmes's and my direction with the hypodermic poised. We tried to get out of the way, but as I fled, the needle caught the flapping tail of my overcoat and pierced it. The back of my coat instantly disintegrated into a putrid brown liquid. Holmes saw this better than I could, and the fright of it caused him to cry out again. The hand turned towards him and pursued him about the room, striking randomly with the deadly needle as Holmes pelted back and forth screaming, "Ahhhhhhhhh! Watson! Help! The Freckled Hand! The Freckled Hand!"

In the fervor of its attack, the hand struck the pillow, the mattress and the easy chair with its murderous needle. All three melted into puddles of stinking slop. Holmes had the misfortune of placing his foot in one of these as he ran. He slipped and went down heavily. His trademark hat fell from his head and the contents of his pockets fairly exploded forth. His magnifying glass slid across the room towards me, but what caught my attention most was the metallic device that fell upon the carpet as he began to rise and renew his flight—his handcuffs.

As Holmes ran off, I dived in to recover them. I fastened one side to the stout lower rail of the bed, then waited. The next time Roylott's viperous arm passed, I lunged out and snapped the other cuff around it. In my panic, I fastened it cruelly tight. Roylott must not have been expecting that, for the arm jerked back and forth arhythmically a few times before it turned on me and tried to end my life with its bewitched poison. I flung myself to the far corner of the room and sat breathless against the wall. Holmes joined me and clapped a hand on my shoulder, crying, "Bravely done, Watson. I think we have him now."

The hand recoiled all the way up to the silver handcuff and feverishly attempted to pull itself through. I feared Roylott would manage to yank it free and resume his murder attempts, but the cuffs held fast.

I breathed a sigh of relief and asked, "What is it, Holmes? What has Roylott done?"

"One more trick he picked up in India, Watson. I think he must be a fakir."

I had heard of these mystics and recalled that they were famous for methods of manipulating their own bodies that seemed quite beyond the capabilities of mortal man.

"That makes some sense," I agreed.

"In fact," said Holmes, "he is a master of their art.

"Ahhhhhhhhh! Watson! Help! The Freckled Hand!
The Freckled Hand!"

A STUDY IN BRIMSTONE

I must say, I am impressed. Such transmutations are difficult to perform and even harder to maintain. Do you hear how much louder and more strained his chanting has become?"

I listened and agreed that I could note the change.

"In a few moments his spell will fail," said Holmes. "He will find himself returned to his normal shape, exhausted and unable to defend himself. He'll be helpless, Watson."

I nodded that this was good, but held that opinion only for a fraction of a second. Soon, the full ramifications of the situation occurred to me and I found myself shouting, "Keys!"

"Eh?" said Holmes.

"Where are the keys?"

"What keys? For what?"

The chanting reached a fever pitch, then began to fail. I could hear Roylott gasping for breath in the next room over.

"The handcuffs, Holmes! Quick!"

He patted at his pockets fruitlessly, and decided, "I must have dropped them when I fell. Look around, Watson."

But it was too late. Roylott's voice gave way to a fit of coughing, followed by a ragged scream. His spell failed. His body began to resume its normal shape and, as his hand was attached to the bed in our room, his body was drawn inextricably towards it. From his room came the shriek of tortured metal as the vent deformed. An instant later, the duct within our room began to bulge and shift. A number of rivets popped free and a second later the vent

319

over the bed became a spout. Several gallons of chunky gore erupted forth all over Julia Stoner's vacant bed.

Another case closed. Another success, we thought. True, I had slain a man, which offended my sensibilities and violated my Hippocratic oath. Yet this had been the result of an accident and the personality of the victim was such that nobody ever said to me that they missed his company. More to our satisfaction, Miss Helen Stoner was preserved from harm. Despite the sudden, strange death of Dr. Roylott, her fiancé's zeal to marry held and the couple moved away to begin their life together. They could have stayed at Stoke Moran, I suppose, but Helen Stoner was never happier than the day she packed her bags and left it forever.

In the Adventure of the Freckled Hand, we see one of my greatest failures. I allowed myself to be distracted. Our survival, our seeming victory and Helen Stoner's happy ending brought me such elation that I failed to consider the greater consequences of the case. I happily moved on to the next adventure and thought no more of Stoke Moran. How many men would have paused to ask themselves, "What will become of that house now?" Would a wiser fellow have worried that perhaps the next heir might be none other than Sebastian Moran? Would he have realized that—should Moran succeed in reconstituting his fallen master—Moriarty would now have a sturdy stone house with defensible walls and an

evil magical workstation already in place?
A better man might have.
I did not.
I apologize to you all.

CHARLES AUGUSTUS MILVERTON: SOULBINDER

THAT LADY EVA BLACKWELL'S ENGAGEMENT WAS
threatened did not bother me in the slightest.

I suppose it should have. She had, after all, come to
Holmes and me in the express attempt to save it. Yet, as
she spoke with dread about the prospect of becoming
unattached, it occurred to me more and more that she
was just the sort of girl I would like to marry some day.
If the worst should come to pass—if she should lose the
affections of the Earl of Dovercourt—how should she
replace him? With a doctor perhaps? Doctors are not so
well regarded as earls, I will admit, but they are a good deal
more practical. What if someone were to become injured
or sick? Having a doctor in the house saves a carriage ride.
And really, what *does* an earl do?

"Can you gentlemen help me, do you think?" Lady
Eva sighed.

Holmes clucked his tongue—indicating that this was
a matter of dread severity—and asked, "What do you
think, Watson?"

"Oh? Eh?" I said, rousing myself from my dream.

"Well, I suppose we might look into it. A blackmailer, you say?"

"Yes! A horrible blackmailer!" she agreed, nodding her chestnut curls. "He says I must supply him with seven thousand pounds by Friday, else he shall cross my match and see that Nigel and I never wed!"

"Seven thousand pounds…" I mused.

"The sum is extraordinary," she cried. "Why, you could buy a palace for that!"

"I would buy you a mansion in Dover," I said, "near the sea. A white one with a yard full of ponies…"

I became aware that Lady Eva was staring at me. So was Holmes.

"How would that help matters?" Holmes wondered.

"What? Oh… it wouldn't. I just… ahem… Lady Blackwell, I do not mean to be indelicate, but I must ask: what does this blackmailer have against you?"

"Nothing, sir."

"But he must have something," I insisted, "else how does he think he could foil your marriage? How does he intend to turn your fiancé against you?"

"He does not say! In fact, he writes that the particulars of my downfall will be forever unknown to me. Of course, I was inclined to throw the ridiculous letter into the fire, but he included these two lists, you see?"

She waved two pieces of paper at Holmes and me. Both were lists of names, but there the similarities ended. One was writ in a gilded hand upon stationery worthy of the queen. The other was done in filth-brown ink upon parchment so poor that a street urchin looking for something to scrawl his begging sign upon would have passed it by, saying, "Meh, I could do better."

She flourished the finer paper at us and said, "This first is a list of those previous victims who succumbed and agreed to pay him. I was shocked by some of these names, gentlemen! I called on some of them and asked if this document was true. Awkward as the matter is, they did confirm it. The blackmailer says that part of the price of his forbearance is that they tell their tale to the next poor soul to bear his letter, else he will work mischief upon them."

"Cad!" I declared.

"I spoke with four of the people on this list and they all admitted that they paid him. Some said they felt foolish for it, yet that was the worst complaint any of them could make; their lives and fortunes are all quite intact. *This* list, on the other hand…" here she waved the brown, feculent list at us, "…this is a litany of shattered dreams. There is not a soul on this list who is happy today. Broken marriages… lost careers… great artists whose works suddenly fell from public favor… It is unaccountable, the sudden trials and failures suffered by the people upon this list! And all of them whom I spoke to traced their misfortune back to the same man! All of them cursed the day they refused to pay this blackmailer and encouraged me to do whatever I could to save myself from his fury."

"An odd story," said I, scratching my chin. "I have never heard of a blackmailer who operates without having some sort of leverage on his victims. One wonders if it is not a ruse…"

"A ruse?" Holmes reflected. "How might he pull such a thing off, Watson?"

"I can imagine two methods, offhand. Either he has compiled these lists from people who had nothing to do with him, but whose fortunes were especially good or ill—"

"Yes, but that does not account for them telling Lady Eva that this villain's interference or forbearance made their fortunes or ruined them," Holmes said. "Keep in mind that they all verified his story."

"Did they? Suppose a man comes to you and says you must give him a pound or you will explode. You *do* give him a pound. You *do not* explode. Does it necessarily follow that your lack of unexplained detonation is due to the fact you paid him off? Is it not possible that you were never in any such danger and have just been conned out of a pound? Is it not also possible that you might blithely tell his next victim of your supposed escape and encourage them to pay as well?"

"It *is* possible," Holmes admitted. "In fact, some might say it is the basis of all religion."

"Ahem… yes… Well, the other possibility is that these witnesses are all in league with the blackmailer and stand to receive a portion of the funds."

"I do not think that could be the case," said Lady Eva, in a manner that all other ladies should study and endeavor to repeat, in order to render themselves irresistible to the mortal man. "Look at these names,

Doctor; they are well-known public figures."

"A good point, Lady Eva. I only mention it because I must consider all possibilities, even if they seem remote. Eliminate the impossible and whatever remains, however improbable, must be the truth."

Holmes rolled his eyes at me as if this were an extraordinarily naïve thing to say. I refused to be cowed and continued, "I think our next course of action must be to investigate the blackmailer himself and determine the true nature of his relationships with these supposed victims. Did he leave any clue as to his identity?"

"Oh yes," said Lady Eva, who would likely have made a fine mother to my children—caring and doting, yet stern when the occasion demanded. "He signed it. His name is Charles Augustus Milverton."

I laughed out loud. It was too good to hope that the man might be fool enough to begin such a criminal enterprise by signing his true name to a blackmail note. Yet my enthusiasm was dampened somewhat by Holmes, who said, "Milverton?" in the most disappointed way. He slumped into his chair and shrank like a beaten dog. Fixing Lady Eva with a look of both pity and apology for his own impotence, he mumbled, "Pay the man."

"Holmes!"

"I am sorry, Watson. And I am yet more sorry for you, Lady Eva, but his name is known to me and I have reason to suspect that he is more than capable of rendering the destruction he has threatened. If you wish to be happy in your marriage, pay him."

"But I can't!" Lady Eva protested. "Don't you see? My family has a title, yes, but that is no guarantee of means. It is not *wealth* that has allowed me to enter London society. It is only…"

She trailed off, for modesty does not allow a true lady to extol her own virtues.

"It is only your perfect grace," I said. "It is only your charm. It is only that, in you, the London aristocracy see what it is they aspire to become. They see their better, and yet the tutor is so winning that they cannot bring themselves to resent the lesson. Not to mention your cheekbones! Look at them!"

Lady Eva blushed. Holmes only watched me, waiting for me to make my point. I recoiled and mumbled, "Oh… I say, have you ever had one of those days where you find yourself thinking a thing and then—and you have no idea how it happened—you find that you have been saying it as well? I am having just such a day and I apologize."

"No, no, that was… kind of you, Doctor," said Lady Eva, fixing me with a smile that crushed my mind and my heart and made me wish beyond all hoping that I had been born an earl. "Yet, my trouble remains. Even by calling upon the support of my family and friends… even by putting myself deeply in debt to those who might wish me ill, I am sure I can raise nowhere near the sum. I think I can manage two thousand. Maybe a little more, but only very little. Oh, if you cannot save me from this man, could you at least negotiate with him on my behalf? Tell him to take two thousand—take it and leave me alone."

Holmes sighed, "I can try, Lady Eva. If you ask me to, I will. Yet, I warn you that more harm than good may come from my involvement. Milverton knows me well and I think he is not... favorably disposed."

"What choice have I?" asked Lady Eva with a sad shrug. "I cannot raise his fee and idleness dooms me. Say you will help, won't you? Say you will try?"

"I shall do my utmost," said Holmes. "I'm sure Watson will, as well. I only hope some good may come of it. Leave me his letter, won't you? Watson and I shall be in touch when we have news. In the meantime, it might be wise to begin raising the two thousand."

There was nothing left to do but say our farewells and see Lady Eva out. As I helped her down the stairs, she rested her hand in my palm and let me place my other hand beneath her elbow to guide her down. I drifted down the steps in dazed happiness, then let go of her perfect hand and turned back to re-mount the stairs to our rooms, to Holmes and to the life I had built myself. I was suddenly overcome with the feeling that I had let it all go wrong, somehow. This feeling was only reinforced when Holmes flung open the window above me and shouted, "Wiggles! Wiggles, I need you!" such that all the street might hear

Holmes fretted over his reply for almost half an hour, despite the fact that it was only three lines long. Wiggles and I waited by the hearth. At first I was uncomfortable in the company of the young wererat, but boredom eventually conquered fear. Soon, I sat suppressing my laughter as I watched him sniff the air, having apparently forgotten he was in his human form. In another ten minutes, I was tearing little hunks of bread and throwing them this way and that, watching him scuttle about to retrieve them.

Finally, Holmes approached. He handed Wiggles a letter, a shilling and a slab of beef that was just beginning to display that rainbow sheen which says, "You ought to have eaten me yesterday."

"Find the Soulbinder, Charles Augustus Milverton," Holmes said. "Give him this letter and wait for his reply. I am sure he will wish to set an appointment with me. Do not fail to bring his response or we may all find ourselves in some trouble."

"Soulbinder?" I wondered.

"Yes. Soulbinder," said Holmes. "Come on, Watson, let's go for a walk. Or something. I don't care; I just don't want to sit here thinking of him. I shall tell you more in the park."

He didn't. Shortly after reaching the park, he was accosted by a squirrel. It ran up his trouser leg and snatched a crust of toast from his hand. Holmes seemed quite content to chase the little blighter up and down the path, sometimes cajoling, sometimes threatening, always emanating the especial joy of one who has made himself a grand new friend. For my part, I was happy to let Holmes go. It left me free to think of Lady Eva and sigh.

And sigh.

* * *

As midnight neared, Holmes became ever more anxious. He paced the sitting room of 221B Baker Street, casting his eyes this way and that, but nowhere found relief. Time and again, his gaze was drawn to the clock on the mantelpiece, though I could not tell if he was impatient for the midnight hour to arrive or afeared of it.

"Warlock, sit down, won't you? You are making me nervous."

"You ought to be nervous," he replied. "Our guest is a dangerous man."

"And you are sure he will come?"

"He will come."

"But his note said to expect him at seven in the evening," I reminded Holmes, waving the return letter we had received from Milverton. It was written on lavender stationery and scented with a perfume that reminded one of musk ox and honey.

"I told you: that note is a lie. He's playing with me. He shall come at midnight. He always does." Holmes ceased his pacing, turned to me and muttered, "You really ought to go, Watson."

"I told you, Holmes: I am not going anywhere. Our client has engaged our services to save her from ruin and I will not meekly fall by the wayside and allow myself to fail her."

"What you mean is that you do not trust me to conduct this negotiation."

There was more than a little truth to that, but it was not my only motivation. In fact, I was worried for Holmes.

"Well… you know, Warlock… we've met a number of dangerous characters, but this is the first time I have seen you so unsettled. I can't help but wonder why you're so frightened of the man."

I could tell I had wounded him, but after a moment's reflection he said, "I suppose I *am* frightened. You know me, Watson. You've seen what I like to do with poisons and so you know I am a gentleman who is somewhat difficult to harm. Milverton, though… Milverton could hurt me."

"How do you mean, Holmes?"

Yet, he did not answer. He would not answer. He resumed his pacing.

"How do you know him?" I asked, attempting to start again on a different tack. "His victims are highly placed in the London aristocracy, yet I have never heard of the man."

"Oh, our paths have crossed before, Watson," Holmes said, then paused as if considering how much he ought to tell me. He must have deemed me worthy of further trust, for he added, "Milverton was often a pawn of Moriarty's."

"Moriarty!"

"Yes, my great enemy."

I thought a moment, worrying over one or two points until finally deciding that the only way to know was to ask. I said, "And yet you display more fear of this supposed pawn than you ever did of Sebastian Moran, whom you claim was Moriarty's trusted lieutenant."

"It is not his rank within Moriarty's gang that I fear," said Holmes. "It is his ability. Yes, Moran is a nasty fellow, but he has no leverage upon me. Milverton does."

I was going to ask what that leverage might be, but was interrupted by the chiming of our clock. Even before the first bell had faded, it was drowned out by a rapping on our sitting-room door. Warlock wilted. I rose to admit our guest.

If I had been hoping to find a looming specter clothed all in smoke—and I will confess, I rather was—I was disappointed. Milverton was one of those men who took every care that his dress and appearance shouted "businessman" yet every other aspect of his body, face and bearing declared "wheezy little bastard." He was in his early fifties, yet doing his utmost to appear in his late twenties. He wore a gray suit, tailored better than almost any other I had encountered. His teeth were straight and shining white. His skin, which I at first assumed to be deeply tanned, was revealed to be orange as he stepped into the light. The color was so unnatural that I wondered, for an instant, if he might be a demon. The thought was quickly chased away by the realization that it was more likely he'd been tempted by the tubes of orange skin-tinting goo one may purchase for tuppence at any of the less reputable pharmacies.

He swept off his gray silk top hat and threw his pale gloves within. He hung this on a hook and deposited his silver cane in our elephant's foot umbrella stand. His dark hair was slicked with some form of thick, pungent grease into long strands, which failed to cover his balding dome, despite the expert care with which they had been combed over it. Not deigning even to look at us, he cooed, "Soooooo sorry, chaps. I know I'm behind my hour, I know

I am. And yet, what is a fellow to do, eh? London, don't you know. Traffic, don't you know. I do hope you haven't been waiting long. Oh, I *do* hope not."

He turned to me, fixed me with a false smile and said, "*You* must be the estimable Dr. Watson, unless I am much mistaken. Oh yes, Doctor, I know quite a few unnatural fellows who would like to know more about you. Yes I do. Quite a few, indeed. They always get nervous if this one…" here he inclined his head in Warlock's direction, "… spends more than three weeks in any one man's company."

Behind Milverton, the wall discolored. Silently, it began to bleed. The spots joined together to form the word WRETCH.

"And Warlock Holmes!" Milverton continued. "How long has it been? A very long time, I think. Such a pleasant surprise to get your note. I must say I was a bit put out, for I *had* warned Lady Eva not to seek any outside aid. A man might be tempted to increase his fee in the face of such events, but seeing as it is you, Warlock—seeing as it is you—I think I can overlook this one indiscretion on her part. Only this one, though. No, since she has brought me back into contact with my old friend, her balance remains unchanged at seven thousand pounds. I trust you have it?"

"I don't have it, Milverton," Holmes growled. "*She* doesn't have it. You know that is why I wrote to you."

"Oh. Oh dear. Well, I only assumed she might have reconsidered by now."

"It is not a question of her consideration. She does not have the money."

Milverton shook his head and tutted. "Well she really ought to find it, you know. Such a judicious investment on her part. Why, her beau makes that in less than a year and a half! Can you imagine? Losing her love? Losing her position in society? Losing all that money for all of those years over the concern of less than a year and a half's income? She's cleverer than that. I know she is."

Above him, the word BETRAYER added itself to the wall.

"She hasn't got it, I say," Holmes repeated. "Take two thousand, Milverton, and do no mischief."

"Oh my. Oh, dear me. Now, you see, I *told* her not to bargain. I *told* her the price was not subject to debate. Now that is *two* indiscretions on her part. I cannot let that pass, Holmes, I really can't. I regret to inform you that Lady Eva's account now stands at eight thousand pounds."

Holmes's anger and frustration burst forth in visual style. His eyes lit up. Milverton, bathed in their terrible green glare, took a step backwards. Holmes took two towards our unwelcome guest; a grim smile spread across his features. But before Holmes could work any mischief, Milverton held up one hand to beg a moment's pardon and affected a terrific yawn.

"I say, such an hour… I think a cup of coffee is in order, don't you, gentlemen? Yes. Coffee, don't you think?"

Holmes stood staring at Milverton, with his fingers opening and closing slowly, as if he wished to grab something, wished to squeeze. Milverton stood his ground, but seemed to find a sudden interest in our furnishings. He regarded our bookcase for a moment, then stared at the picture of General

Lee. He seemed content to examine almost anything, as long as it was not Holmes's burning glare.

I smiled.

Much has been said of mutual benefit as the ideal foundation for bargaining. Good mention is also made of charity, civility and moral concerns, but to the student of history, these are laughable. He who has read of the Mongol hordes, of the South Sea pirates, or the might of Rome knows the ideal bargaining tool.

Fear.

I stepped in, saying, "Yes, coffee sounds splendid. I'll just make a pot, shall I? Holmes, why don't you take a seat on the sofa? Leave your armchair for Mr. Milverton, won't you? He is our guest, after all, and the night is cold. He will appreciate being close to the fire."

I moved to our small pantry to get the coffee grounds. Milverton took Holmes's armchair, though he seemed ill at ease in it. Holmes cocked his head to one side, until his ear was nearly upon his shoulder, and sat down on the sofa, smiling at Milverton hungrily, with his eyes still alight. I took my time fetching the coffee, sure that each passing moment strengthened our bargaining position, rather than weakened it.

As I returned and set some water to warm above the fire, I said, "So, what exactly is it you do, Mr. Milverton? Holmes described you as a Soulbinder."

"Did he?" asked Milverton. "Well, that is a misfortune. I have asked him not to, you see? I have asked him never to use that title and yet he disregards my wishes. Well,

I am sorry to say that Lady Eva's account now stands at nine thousand."

"You are not a Soulbinder, then?"

"Is there such a thing as a soul, Doctor?" he scoffed. "You have been through and through the human body, have you not? Have you ever encountered one? Have you ever slipped with your scalpel and nicked somebody's soul? I should think not. Is there a part of us that lives on after we are gone? Why should we assume so? No, I do not deal with such speculative fictions. My art lies in more tangible concerns. We each of us have a destiny, Dr. Watson. As we grow and interact, these human destinies intertwine with one another. I am one who sees these threads. I am one who can knot them closer together. Or, if I wish, I am one who can pull them apart. If Lady Eva is such a fool as to doubt my art, she may find her fiancé's destiny takes a very separate path from her own. She would not be the first, I fear."

I had decided I could make more progress with friendship than with threat. Let Milverton fear Holmes; in me he would find a helpful voice. "I have never heard of such a thing," I said. "It must be a rare gift, indeed. Can you change your own destiny, I wonder?"

"Every man can, Dr. Watson."

"How very droll. Can no one resist your tampering, Mr. Milverton? Even a fellow such as Holmes: could you work upon him?"

"Ha! Let me tell you something about your friend, Dr. Watson: the man is a mess. His destiny—his soul as you would call it—is one big knot. He has tangled himself with countless others in loops more intricate and more intimate than ever he should have. He is bound and bound again and has no power to unwind himself from some of his less welcome company, no matter how he might struggle. Oh yes, I can work upon Holmes's destiny, Dr. Watson. I may be the only man who can. Holmes himself is quite helpless to disentangle himself as I could do!"

He said it with a zeal so severe that I knew him to be attempting to comfort himself with it. I decided to hurry even less with the coffee and let him endure Holmes's green gaze a little longer. Yet this was not to be, for suddenly a deep, terrible voice burst from Holmes, shouting, "*Rache!*"

I nearly dropped the coffee pot in the fire. I could hear Milverton cry out in surprise. I spun round towards Holmes, to hear what Moriarty would say.

"*Rache! He that holds a hammer and will not strike away my chains—he is as good as my jailer! Charles's August has been long. He sows and sows, yet never reaps. Now, his harvest is nearing. That which he has grown shall be brought in to him at last. The crop is bitter; he will not taste it long. Rache!*"

Holmes fell silent and slumped to one side. For a moment I thought Milverton was going to fall over as well, in a dead faint. His lips moved ineffectually at first, then he gasped, "That... that's him, isn't it?"

"Him?" I said, feigning innocence. "Oh! Moriarty? Yes, that's him. I had quite forgotten you knew him. Yes, now I recall: Holmes said you used to be one of his minions, I think."

"Never!" Milverton cried. "No! Eleven thousand! For saying such a thing, Lady Eva's account stands at eleven thousand!"

"You *didn't* work for Moriarty?" I asked. "Well then, how do you know him?"

"I worked for him. I mean, I performed some work for him. But he came to me and hired me, you know, I was never one of his dogs. Let it be remembered: He came to me because I could do what he could not—even he, the great Moriarty—and he gave me gold in recognition of my skills."

"Well, that is high praise," I said. "The Moriarty I know never seems to give anything but ill news."

"Yes, he is greatly changed from when I knew him," Milverton said, then broke out in a nervous laugh. "But then, I suppose it's what he was known for. Step before Moriarty and you never knew exactly what sort of creature you'd be facing. As one body wore out, he'd find another. Change was his hallmark; the only constants were intelligence and malevolence."

Milverton had grown visibly pale, even through his orange skin treatment. I took the opportunity to say, "Of course you must know that my sympathy lies with Holmes and Lady Eva, so you will no doubt take my advice with a grain of salt. Still, I must say, these seem to be deep and dangerous waters, do they not? Might it be wiser to close Lady Eva's account and leave this matter behind you?"

"No! I cannot be seen to falter. I cannot let it be known that my net was ever escaped or my future clients will know there is hope."

"Yet what do you gain by hurting her? If nothing else, take the two thousand and let her go. Two thousand pounds in exchange for doing nothing? They are high wages, don't you think?"

"It's worth two thousand to me to see her fall. Let everybody see it. The more that is known of her fate, the more my next client will fear me."

"What a thing to say, Mr. Milverton! She has done nothing to deserve such treatment, has she?"

"She has! She has made bold to walk in circles high above her station. She was fool enough to hire a maid who sold me a lock of her hair for a mere five pounds. Ha! She who aims so high should have more caution, don't you think? Twelve thousand pounds, now! Twelve, for her folly!"

"Really, Mr. Milverton! If you go on like this for much longer, the queen herself would be unable to raise your fee."

"And yet we know Holmes, don't we?" Milverton asked. "We know he has ways of *making money*."

At this, Milverton stood up and fished around in his pocket for a moment. He withdrew a bar of lead, cast it upon our side table and muttered, "He knows my mind. I've plenty more of these when he's ready. If Holmes wants to free his pretty little debutante, he can call on me whenever he's willing to be reasonable. Now good night, sir."

"Are you not staying for coffee?" I asked. "I made it just for you."

"I won't! I am leaving!"

I tutted at him. Any man who does business in London

knows there are certain crimes that are unforgivable. Amongst them is asking for a refreshment and leaving before it is ready. Milverton turned back to me, saying, "Take a hundred, then, for your undrunk coffee. That's something, eh? Eleven thousand, nine hundred and Lady Eva can thank you however she will for selling a cup of coffee so dear."

He slammed our door, scurried down the stairs and was gone. Holmes lay half-conscious on the sofa and resisted my attempts to move him. As the hour was late, I simply threw a blanket over him and went to bed myself.

I awoke just after seven the next morning to the sound of Holmes puttering about the fireplace.

"Good morning," I said, walking into our sitting room.

"Hmm," said he and went back to organizing his toast racks. A few minutes later he muttered, "I'm not very clear on the events of last night."

I barely heard him—he said it as if reflecting to himself, but I realized he was awaiting an answer.

"Well, Moriarty had a few thoughts to add to the debate and after that you were somewhat insensible."

"That explains it. Was Milverton as glad to see his old master as Moran was?"

"Rather not!" I laughed. "He practically fled the place. I tell you, Holmes, I cannot fathom why you are so afraid of Milverton. I don't know if you realize it, but he is perfectly terrified of you."

"It makes sense." Holmes shrugged. "I nearly killed him, once. He knows I could end him in an instant. I know he has taken precautions. That's why we're so afraid of one another. The little bugger has bound his soul to me! Can you imagine, Watson? I have every reason to believe that when Milverton's soul flees—or his destiny comes to an end, as he would say—it will tug on some aspects of my own, ere it flies. I shall lose some very important connections and it wouldn't surprise me if I gain a few unsavory ones as well. Even if he should die of old age, I will suffer for it. Oh, I fear the day he walks into the street without looking both ways. But, enough of such concerns—what is the state of our negotiation, Watson? Did you manage to out-think him?"

"I fear not. In fact, Miss Blackwell's account now stands at eleven thousand, nine hundred pounds."

"Eh? What happened?"

"He was once defied, once affrighted, twice offended and then purchased an overpriced coffee. I am sure we must treat with him again before the matter is brought to a conclusion. If we achieved anything last night, it was only to weaken his resolve and introduce greater elements of fear and doubt into his thinking."

"Ugh," Holmes grunted. "I would rather be done with the man."

He went back to his toast racks and I to find the morning paper, but a sudden remembrance from the night before caused me to tarry.

"You know, there was one small thing…"

"What was that?"

"I found out how he gained his influence over Eva Blackwell."

In an instant, Holmes was upon me. He clasped me by the front of my dressing gown and shook me, demanding, "How? How does he do it, Watson?"

"He has a lock of her hair," I told him, struggling ineffectually to free my collar from his grasp. "He bribed her maid."

Holmes released me and began to pace. "Now we have something, Watson! Now we have something! So... he needs a token then... Is he making an effigy? Does he need the materials as ingredients for his spell or... By the gods! Does he cast the spell *upon the hair itself*? Are these tokens of his victims the medium that holds his enchantment? Are they like some form of phylactery? Oh, let it be so, Watson! Let it be so!"

"Why?" I asked.

Holmes turned to me and, in the tone a philosopher might use to address a moron, "Because if I could destroy his phylactery, I could break his spell! Don't you see? If I find out what he's done with Lady Blackwell's hair and burn it, his power over her is gone. More to the point, Watson, if I find he has a phylactery for me..."

"Oh! You could free yourself of his influence?"

"I could unwind that little blighter from my soul! I could live free of fear of what would happen to me if he should come to harm. What a relief that would be, Watson! Gods, it would be hard to keep from killing him on the spot, just to celebrate!"

"Holmes!"

"Oh, I wouldn't, of course. I'm just saying, Watson…
Oh, what I wouldn't give! Bless you, John; this is the first
ray of hope I've had in a long time. I have so much to do
now. So much to do…"

He ran to his bedroom and busied himself, clattering
around with his poisons and shifting noisily through his
closet. I made myself breakfast and settled in with *The
Times*. I had just decided on a second cup of tea when he re-
emerged. He was dressed exactly as a music hall comedian
might portray a tramp. He wore an oversized coat of a garish
color, patched and re-patched with theatrical abandon. One
trouser leg was shorter than the other. He had attached a
grand moustache that cleared his face by a good six inches
on either side. He grinned at his own artfulness and showed
me three gaps where his teeth were missing.

"Behold!" he cried.

"What… what am I beholding?" I asked.

"A clever disguise, of course. Dressed as a common
Irish working man, I shall seek employment in
Milverton's household, infiltrate and find where the
villain keeps his phylacteries!"

"No, you won't," I laughed.

"Why not?"

"Because you look like a clown, Holmes! You will be
spotted in an instant."

"I worked very hard on this disguise."

"Well, I can see that," I said. "There are elements

which are quite ingenious. How did you do the teeth?"

"Ha! The simplest illusion, Watson. I merely knocked them out with an ink blotter."

"You *what*?"

"They're on my desk. I'll put them back when I'm done. Really, this is a foolproof plan, Watson, you shall see."

"Don't go out like that, Holmes."

"I will."

"No. You're going to be caught. Let me help you."

But Holmes was too proud and too sure of his plan to let me interfere with it. He cast one hand towards the ground, shouting, "Escape gas!" There was a muffled boom and our sitting room filled with dense black and purple smoke. I coughed and spluttered, groped about for the window latch that I might vent the foul stuff. By the time I had cleared the air enough to see, Holmes was gone.

It was dark ere I saw him again. I had gone to the library and withdrawn the only two books I could find that concerned phylacteries in any context other than as a Jewish prayer box. The first book was useless; the second was interesting, yet they both laughed such creations off as quaint tribal superstitions. I was two-thirds of the way through the better volume when the apartment door swung open and Holmes stumbled in. He was spattered with mud. Half his mustache had been burned away and he stared about in utter confusion. Finally he announced, "Hello. I live here."

"You do," I confirmed. "How did the plan go, Holmes?"

"Ah! An unqualified success! Yes. It exceeded my every expectation."

"So you know what Charles Milverton is doing with his ill-gotten hair samples?"

"Oh… no. Better than that! I am engaged to be married to his housekeeper."

"What? How did that happen?"

"We are in love."

I looked him up and down. Even for Holmes—the most easily distracted man I ever met—this was quite an unexpected departure from his plan. I asked, "Who is this girl? Had you even met her before today?"

"I have not met her at all," Holmes said. "Yet, the importance of such trifles is greatly overestimated. I know all I need to know. Her name is Agatha and she is venerable."

"Venerable? That just means… old."

"Ye gods, Watson, it means so much more than that! It means that she has persevered in the face of nine murderous decades. Though time has robbed her of one leg and the vast majority of her teeth, still she refuses to surrender. Like a treasured heirloom, she has been passed from one generation of Milvertons to the next. And why not? On any given day, one can find her down on her one remaining knee, scrubbing Milverton's floor, turning in an honest day's work for an honest day's pay."

"That's all very admirable, Holmes, but you still have not provided me with an explanation as to why you should be so smitten with her—sight unseen—as to seek a betrothal."

"Well, I am not the only one," he said with a defensive sniff. "The court of popular opinion has already ruled on the subject and agreed with me entirely. She has seven husbands and three wives already and I fail to see how all ten of them could be wrong, eh?"

"Ah ha! Now we have hit on something, I think," said I. "Tell me, did you run into Charles Augustus Milverton today?"

"Er... yes, he intercepted me shortly after I got to his house. He says he's worked some fitting punishment for me, but the joke is on him for I made my escape free and clear and became engaged to his housekeeper."

I folded the book in my lap and took a deep breath. I knew my next words might fall heavily on my love-struck friend. "Do you think it might be possible that, when Milverton wants revenge on some fellow who has inconvenienced him, he binds that person's soul to the soul of his aged housekeeper? Might that not have happened before? *Ten times* before? Might you be the eleventh such person to be caught and treated thus?"

Holmes blinked a few times and cocked his head to one side, searching for a retort. "Well, that's... The thing is... Watson, can't you see..." He fell silent for a few moments, then moaned, "Well, I can't break it off now! What will become of poor Agatha?"

"Don't feel bad, Holmes. Ten spouses are considered more than adequate. I am sure she will survive. Though, from what you tell me, I am sure she cannot survive *very much* longer."

"Oh," said Warlock, shaking his head to clear away the remaining confusion, "so then, actually my plan…"

"…did not go so very well," I concluded. "Yet, do not despair. You have seen his house and have some idea of the lay of the land. I propose we seek a simpler expedient— let's burgle him."

"Watson! I'm surprised at you!"

"Well," I said, "we are running out of time. Tomorrow night will be our last chance. As negotiation and covert operation have now failed, we must turn to less legal strategies. Besides, the man is a colossal ass; I really don't mind burgling him."

"Oh no, I quite agree," said Holmes. "I didn't mean to imply that I was *unpleasantly* surprised."

"We are agreed, then," I told him. "Oh, and, Holmes, don't forget to put your teeth back in."

"Hmm? Oh! Yes, I shall. Thank you, Watson."

I spent the next day teaching myself the trade of burglary. The public is possessed of a morbid love of crime stories, so it was not hard to come across several ha'penny pamphlets that detailed the sort of cloak and dagger business I needed. Though it can be problematic to obtain the tools of such a trade, I was in the position to solve that difficulty with only twelve words: "Lestrade, please steal me the best thieves' tools Scotland Yard has confiscated." He didn't appreciate being given errands to run in the light of day, but he did come through. Two hours later, I found myself the proud owner of a dark lantern, a diamond-tipped glasscutter, a nickel jemmy, and a set of skeleton keys.

I was also privileged with access to medical supplies. Thus, one cab ride later, I had an assortment of anesthetics—courtesy of Stamford—that would make fine knockout drops. On the way home I stopped by a butcher's shop and gave him tuppence for a bag of gristly scraps. These I dosed with my homemade sleeping sauce, in case we ran into any dogs.

I packed my new tools and anti-canine meatballs into a dark leather satchel with my pistol. All that remained was to cut a few masks from black dressmaker's felt and wait. An hour before nightfall, Holmes and I set out for Milverton's house in Hampstead to begin our career of crime.

I was never much afraid of being burgled until I tried it myself and discovered how impossibly easy it is. I will confess I was afraid of guard dogs. I need not have been. All dogs love a good bite of fatty meat followed by a nap. I was happy to provide both. Milverton had only one dog and he was down and snoring happily in under a minute. The only response from his household to the dog's warning barks was one groom who shouted at the mutt to stop his noise.

Holmes and I made a quick half-circuit of the house, planning our best point of ingress. As some of the windows did not have their curtains drawn completely, we had a good many chances to look in at our targets. Fortune was with us; we found Milverton's ground-floor study unoccupied, unguarded and with the curtains open wide enough for us to view our goal.

"Look at that safe!" Warlock hissed. "It's as big as a wardrobe. No man has that many papers to guard in a home study, eh? Oh no, Milverton, I think I know what you've got in there…"

"How are we to crack a safe like that, Holmes?"

"Well… I'll have to take a look at it, I suppose. For now, let's just worry about getting to it, eh?"

I didn't even have to make a noise shattering the window. The back of my glasscutter had a sharp hook, whose use I soon guessed. It happened to be the perfect shape to work into the corner of a window and slice away the glazing that held the pane in the wood frame. I withdrew the entire sheet of glass intact. I then turned to the next window over—whose pane was the exact same size—and placed the pane I had removed up against its twin. I wedged its corners with sticks to keep it in place. Since glass is barely discernible from an empty pane, anybody who looked at the house would see no cut window, no broken glass and no pane leaning against the side of the house to hint that there were intruders about. Only the lack of glare upon the empty window frame could give us away. For my coup de grâce, I planned to simply replace the pane on the way out and let them puzzle over how we'd ever gotten in in the first place.

As we crept over the windowsill and across the study, I hissed, "I imagine you are planning on turning the door of that safe into a duck, or some such…"

"Oh! What marvelous fun! I hadn't thought of that."

"…but I really think we ought to try cracking it without resorting to magic."

"Then by all means, Watson, you attempt it first. If you succeed, all the better. If not, I will make short work of it, I promise."

"Fair sport," I said.

"Quack," said Holmes.

I stifled a laugh and said, "You watch the door."

The room was not entirely dark; the remains of a fire slowly burned itself out in the grate. I could see the safe well enough. It was an older model with three parallel dials, which spun towards the operator, displaying only one number at a time. The dials went from one to thirty. Despite its age, the mechanism turned smoothly and I could discern no click or pause when one of the dials was turned to any number. I shifted my attention from the dials to the safe itself, searching for any way to force the door, the top, or the back. Soon, I had to admit that my only hope lay in guessing the combination.

I wracked my mind, but could think of no combination that might be meaningful to Milverton—I barely knew him, after all. Holmes was beginning to get impatient. At last I struck upon a realization: assuming Milverton did not bother to turn the dials away from their orientation while the safe was unlocked, only the proper numbers would be exposed. I could therefore guess the correct combination by carefully noting which numbers were the most faded by the sun. I was about to call Holmes over with the lantern, when he scuttled over of his own accord and whispered, "Someone's coming!"

"Quick! Douse that lantern! Get behind the curtains,"

I said. "Stand upon the windowsill or they'll see your feet."

Holmes and I had scarcely reached our perch before the door handle turned. The door opened, but no challenge was shouted, nor did any sound of a search come to my ears. Whoever had come in walked about with lazy strides. He threw a few fresh logs on the fire, paced over to the desk, lit a cigar and then—judging by the creaking of wooden chair legs—came to rest himself in the armchair by the hearth. As I knew the occupant's back must be towards us, I ventured a peep around the curtain. With horror, I recognized Milverton himself. No other man would wear such a blatant comb-over lest he perish of shame.

My relief that he was not searching for us was tempered by despair that he seemed to have no intention of leaving soon. He sat in the fireside chair, enjoying the occasional puff of his cigar, perusing a long legal document. As the minutes slid agonizingly by, the awkward nature of my stance upon the windowsill began to work on my back. I began to cramp. I began to squirm. I feared I would slip off and be discovered.

I am sure I would have failed, if it were not for Holmes. I could see him by the moonlight that filtered through the window behind us. Though his features were concealed by darkness and the mask that covered him nose to chin, still his focus shocked me. He was not normally a patient man, nor a cautious one, yet he waited—still as a gargoyle and twice as stern. He made no sound and betrayed no fear, but stood with his face frozen in a purposeful resolve, staring hawk-like at Milverton's safe through the crack in the curtain.

I nearly jumped out of my skin when I heard a sudden footstep on the gravel path behind our window. Whoever trod there must have been no more than seven feet from us and I could not imagine how they had failed to see Holmes and me framed in the window. Nevertheless, this unexpected interloper's footfalls moved away and around the corner of the house. In a moment, I heard a knock upon the veranda door that led into the study.

"At last," Milverton mumbled. He stood and, as he did, I recoiled in horror to see what he was wearing. He had a claret-colored silk smoking jacket with a broad black collar and military-style epaulets fixed upon the shoulders. It was open to the waist, revealing a proud expanse of graying chest hair. On his legs he wore only gray silk shorts of a disgustingly sheer cut. I nearly gasped out loud when I realized what kind of appointment he might have arranged at this hour. I heard him unfasten the door and grumble, "You are late. I've been waiting half an hour."

A woman's voice replied, "Begging your pardon, good sir, it was all I could do to get away."

"Ha. Yes, I have heard the Countess d'Albert keeps a strict household. Lord knows she has reason to guard her secrets. Yet here you are, eh? Come inside."

"But... but, sir... I am unescorted and the hour is late, I fear..."

"Come inside, I say! You would balk for the sake of petty propriety? Do you not realize the scope of this endeavor?

What you proposed to me is criminal. If I wished, I could have met you here with a detective at my side; we'd have had your pretty little neck in a noose before the week was out. As it happens, I am intrigued by your offer. Come inside and let us be partners, eh? I am sure you will find it worth your while."

I heard her hesitate upon the threshold, but at last, with the soft swish of cloth, she stepped inside. She wore a long traveling cloak of dark green wool, which failed to conceal the burst of red curls that must have been either her pride or her bane. Her hair and her accent were enough to suggest her entire person to me. She was a shy, freckled Irish girl, employed as a domestic. She must be a basically good person, but struggling in the face of some difficulty—probably poverty—if she was forced into an alliance with Milverton. This was easy to imagine, but I blush now as I realize how much of my assessment was just that—imagined.

Milverton announced, "Now, you have these letters of the countess's. You wish to sell. If they are as good as you say, I wish to buy. All that is left is to discuss price and... terms."

He reached out towards her shoulder to guide her to a seat, but she shied from his touch. I didn't blame her. It could have been a friendly gesture, but from a man in shorts like those, how could anything but lechery lie beneath? She took a chair and huddled in it. Milverton launched into a clumsily prepared speech on the subject of morality and how they were now partners outside it. I was sure the evening's rendezvous would end with the promise of a substantial sum of money and an indecent proposition of another sort, but there was one surprise left.

A laugh. A woman's laugh. It was deep and rich and merry. It rang forth into the room as if its owner could no longer resist some perfect jest. It must have been half an octave deeper than the scared little Irish girl's voice had been and possessed of a confidence the trembling domestic could never dream of. I feared a second, unexpected woman had sneaked past my notice into the room. Yet when I peeped out around the curtain, I could see the woman in the traveling cloak's shoulders bobbing with rhythmic regularity. Indeed, it was from her that the laugh issued. She said, "Charles, do you *still* not know me? I am wounded, sir."

Milverton, who had just been turning back with the brandy he no doubt meant to ply her with, froze in his tracks. The color drained from behind his orange face treatment. "You," he said.

"Even I."

"How did you—"

"Escape that noose you put my pretty little neck in? Hangmen are easily fooled, Charles. They're nearly as gullible as you."

"Well," Milverton said, endeavoring to regain the friendly persona he used in all his dirty dealings, "so glad to see you came clear of it. I really am. Felt just terrible, you know. You know? What a bad business."

"Bad business indeed, Charlie. I told you not to cross

me. But you couldn't resist, could you? The first chance you got, you sold me out for a shilling, just to prove you could."

"I say, that's not fair."

"No," the woman agreed. "It wasn't. But this is…"

The room brightened with a sudden flash and my ears rang at the report from a gunshot. I had not seen her hand reach down within the folds of her cloak, nor did I spot the revolver, yet the tongue of flame that leapt from it was unmistakable. Milverton reeled, stricken. The lady's cloak slipped back just enough for me to see the slope of her jaw—pale and delicate. I would have said beautiful except that—in that moment of murder—it was drawn up into a smile. To gain pleasure at such a time—that is a thing only a monster can do.

And yet…

A thing can be horrible and beautiful at the same time. I have often wondered what would cross my mind if I were slain by a tiger. Fear, of course. Pain. Despair. And yet, I think, there would be an element of worship, too. Have you ever seen one—seen how its muscles move beneath the striped magnificence of its hide? It is a miracle beyond account that nature has framed such a perfect predator; married a thing's form so exactly with its wicked function. It would be a mark of pride, to be slain thus. I would want it remembered that it was no mere fever that had removed John Heimdal Watson from the earth, no cancer, nor the slow, rhythmic ticking of a clock. No. The agent of my dispatch had been a creature whose beauty was as irresistible as its force—the exquisite slayer. I think I saw the shadow of such thoughts play upon Milverton's face, too.

She fired again. And again. Milverton staggered back, trying to arrest his fall by grasping first at his chair, then his desk. It could not avail him. He fell. The air filled with screams. It took me a moment to realize that these issued not from Milverton, but Holmes. He sprang forth from our hiding place, crying, "No! What have you done? You can't kill him! Ye gods! Watson! Watson, save him!"

If our murderess was surprised, she didn't show it. She pivoted at the waist and her outstretched pistol hand sought another target, training itself upon the running figure of Warlock Holmes. It was then that my cowardice came in handy (I am humbled and amazed by how often this happens, by the way). In order to make myself feel less endangered, I had been fidgeting with the handle of my own pistol, which lay tucked into the bottom of my thieving bag. Thus, even as she spun to gun Holmes down, I thrashed free of my concealing curtains. I leveled the Webley at her and shouted, "Don't!"

Without a pause she changed targets again. Her pistol hand arched through the air, ceasing only when it pointed directly at my face. Now I was staring down her barrel, just as she stared down mine.

"Don't," I said again.

The hood of her cloak was down over her face still, but in the reflected firelight I made out two features. First: her eyes. They were nearly as green as Holmes's and alight with at least as much mischief. The second was her smile. It was not only confident but also pitying, as if she found me... cute. We might seem to be on equal footing, she and I, yet I came to realize that only one factor was even: our armaments. The weapons might be alike, but the warriors were not.

Look at you, her smile seemed to say. *Look at your wide eyes and your trembling hand. You, sir, are not a predator. Yes, you remembered to bring a gun to our gunfight. But you also brought a scrawny, sickly human to our tiger fight. How sad.*

Even as I recognized my terrible mistake, even as I realized I was about to die, Charles Augustus Milverton's chest gave its final, capitulatory heave. Holmes cried out in anguish and the room filled with...

...souls?

...destinies?

Thousands of delicate purple lines began to trace themselves upon the air. Like strands of hair. Like wisps of seaweed floating upon an unseen current. These destinies, I realized, had always been present, but invisible to all but the man who lay expiring on the ground before me. The murderess and I both stood agape as the purple threads traced themselves around and between us. They crawled through the air like violet vines, growing even as we watched. They emanated from my heart and Holmes's and hers. Even Milverton's. But whereas the vines that grew from the living hearts moved and stretched towards one another, Milverton's only fled from him.

I could see the purple lines of my fate reach towards the murderess's and tangle themselves with hers. And why not? It is a powerful thing, to come so near to killing another person, or to dying by their hand. I was sure I would never forget her after that.

Yet the thing that most impressed itself upon my memory was the glimpse of Warlock Holmes's soul I got that day. He was a mess. As Milverton had promised, Warlock Holmes was a magnificent, tangled knot. The number of threads within him was vast. Even given the speed I'd seen them grow between the murderess and me, it was hard to imagine anybody cultivating so many. Yet Holmes's threads had bound themselves within him in sickly tangles. They could not flow as they ought and in the tension of their arrested movements, one could not help but notice the mark of pain. Their torment was perpetual and unrelieved. It was—so strange to say it, but it was... obscene. So repugnant was the vast violet tangle of Holmes's soul that I recoiled with horror when I saw how many of those strands reached out to intertwine with my own. I reached out to try and swat them away, but my hand passed right through them.

If she had been less distracted than I, the murderess might have gunned me down with impunity. I was not concentrating on covering her. Nor, fortunately, was she paying much attention to me. Our eyes were fixed upon the same thing: the flame. Trapped within the tangled morass of Holmes's soul there was an angry blue fire. It bolted this way and that, striving to be free of him, but could not escape its ropy prison. As we watched, it became excited. It moved with an increased, almost gleeful energy. Soon, the reason for its joy became apparent. As the purple lines of Milverton's destiny that were intertwined with Holmes's faded, they began to release some of his tangles. Milverton, it seemed, had used certain threads of his own destiny to bind some of Holmes's into specific patterns. Now that Milverton's influence was gone, the bonds were struck away. The flame within Holmes bounded back and forth within its cage of tortured violet strands and at last burst free. It hovered in the air before him for a moment, changing in shape. It was a picture, I realized, or a word. Yes... in some language, it must be... a name? The burning name hovered a moment longer, then flew at Holmes and struck him on the forehead. He howled with pain and fury as the name branded itself upon his brow, then he crumpled to the floor.

The threads faded. I could tell they were still present, but as invisible to folly-prone man as they ever had been. Only firelight remained. Firelight and four humans: two upon the ground and two upon their feet, wondering if they ought to shoot one another. For an instant it seemed as if only one of us would be walking out of that fire-lit study, until I turned to my murderess and said, "Go. Just... get out. I'll... I don't know... I'll cover for us, somehow."

She stared at me as if she expected some trick. I could see her weighing the wisdom and the risk inherent in my offer. Eventually she gave a little shrug, turned and sped off into the night, out through the door she had come in. That was the first time I met *The Woman*.

If only it had been the last...

Even as she fled, I realized my present difficulties

were not done. The gunshots and our voices had raised the household. Even now, cries of alarm rang out in the hallway beyond. Holmes was still insensible, yet his pain seemed to have passed. He was slumped on the floor, limp and languid, laughing to himself. I did not see the burning name that had rested upon his brow, nor did it seem to have left any injury. Still, he didn't look as if he intended to be very helpful. I leapt to the study door and locked it. I threw a chair beneath the handle to wedge it, too, but in a room with so many windows and an outside door, how could I secure us?

My eyes flew about the room. The safe: no time to crack it now, but then the damage to Holmes was done and Milverton's threat to our client had likely died with him. The windows: most of the curtains were drawn, so I could not tell if some of the household were already out on the lawn, closing in on us. The fire: Yes! The fire!

I swept up the pincers from the stand of tools and, with them, grabbed the uppermost log off the fire. This I flung, still burning, against the curtains on the far side of the room. I followed it with another and then another. The long bolts of cloth did not disappoint me, but burst immediately into violent flames. That would give them something else to think about.

"Come on, Holmes, we're leaving."

From outside the study door, I could hear excited yelling. The doorknob rattled. I reached down to slip my arm beneath Holmes's shoulder to help him up. He regained his feet, but moved irregularly, as if he were unaccustomed to the length and function of his own limbs. He looked at me and laughed merrily. He attempted a few words, which ended in muttered gulps, as if his tongue would not answer to his command, then finally said, "Yes, Doctor. Let us depart."

We staggered through the veranda door and out onto the lawn. I could just see the murderess's dark green cloak disappearing over the wall to our right. I made for the wall to our left. Holmes moved uncertainly and tripped several times. I had to drag him along. It could not have been more than twenty-five yards to the wall, but it took us an age. Fortunately, the fire I'd started did seem to be distracting most of the people who spilled from the house. Unfortunately, it also illuminated Holmes and me. One of the men shouted and pointed at us. He and two others charged.

I cursed and hauled Holmes to the wall. He climbed like a drunkard and I had to pause to shove him over before leaping up myself. One of the men reached us. His hand closed on my ankle and he began to pull me down. He was larger than me and fitter as well. For a moment, I feared he would have me. Then I had a happy remembrance: I was holding a pistol. This I brought to his attention by firing a few rounds into the air. His zeal diminished somewhat and I made it over the wall to join Holmes. A few heads peeped over to watch us go, but one or two more shots just above the wall convinced them all to duck.

We made it across the street, through a hedge on the other side, across a neighbor's lawn, two more hedges and a back garden. Here I encountered a large ornamental

A STUDY IN BRIMSTONE

pond, which was welcome indeed. I stripped off my mask and Holmes's, which I deposited in my satchel with the dark lantern and thieves' tools. I added two large rocks and flung the thing into the center of the pond, to sink out of sight. My pistol I kept. This may have been inadvisable, yet I knew that—so long as we remained presentable—Holmes and I looked enough like gentry and little enough like the criminal class as to avoid most scrutiny on our journey home.

In fact, all the scrutiny we would suffer came in one dose, waiting upon the step of 221B Baker Street. As we neared, I could see Inspector Lestrade leaning against a wall, staring with frustration and dread into the gathering dawn. When he saw us, he made directly towards us.

"Good evening, Holmes," he said, then added, "Doctor."

"Good evening, Vladislav," I answered. Holmes nodded.

"I hate to inconvenience you at such an hour," Lestrade said, with a sniffle, "but it seems we've had a spot of bother out in Hampstead. Nasty business. Murder. Arson. The whole thing *reeks* of witchcraft. There were two suspects, spotted as they fled the scene."

"Oh... well... that is unfortunate..." I admitted.

"Let's see," said Lestrade. "Two masked men. Age indeterminate. One wearing a dark brown suit and bowler hat—much like yours, I think, Dr. Watson..."

"Er... there are so many, you know..."

"And a tall gentleman with striking green eyes and a

365

queer cap that folds down at the front and back."

"Yes but that might be anybody," I said. "Why that might even describe Holmes here."

"It might," said Lestrade. "It *very well might*. So, I suppose my question to you two is this: might this be a case we do not wish to see solved? Perhaps something that might be left on Lanner's desk, following a brisk evidence-destroying sweep?"

I heaved a sigh and mumbled, "By God, that sounds wonderful, Lestrade. Of all the friends I have ever had, I think you may be the most useful of the lot."

He smiled… sort of. He was not accustomed to compliments. Mine made him uneasy, I could tell. I saw him struggle, weighing his internal desire to obliterate anything and everything against the warm, yet unwelcome, glow he felt whenever anybody addressed him as "friend."

"I think that is all I needed to know," said Lestrade. "So sorry, Holmes, but I don't think Scotland Yard will feel the need to consult you on this particular case. Good night, gentlemen. Well… good day."

With that, the stunted Romanian turned and left, measuring each of his steps against the burgeoning pink glow upon the eastern horizon. Holmes and I went inside. We were both exhausted. I stumped up the stairs. Holmes, I noted, needed to drag himself up, leaning heavily on the bannister with his right hand. When we reached the landing, I suggested, "Tea?"

This had a visible effect on Holmes, who brightened and said, "Yes, Doctor. Thank you."

He had trouble getting his coat off once we were inside—as if buttons were suddenly unfamiliar to him. Once it was off, he seemed momentarily unsure which hook to place his coat upon. I deposited him in one of the armchairs and set about making the tea. I purposely put him in the one that faced the fireplace, hoping he would not notice that I took a moment to rifle his room as I bustled back and forth. I didn't need long; I knew just what I was looking for—the big brown package from our local dispensary.

I found it. I took it to the table with me, when I went to brew the tea. I returned to find Holmes sitting in the chair, opening and closing his hands as if practicing with them. On his face was an expression of pure triumph.

"Quite a night," I said.

"It was indeed, Doctor."

"Your tea."

"Thank you."

He reached out to take it with his right hand, then cradled it beneath his nose, treasuring the scent as if it were a long-forgotten familiarity—which I suppose it was.

I waited until he savored a long, slow sip, then asked, "Who are you?"

His green eyes flicked up to meet mine. "I'm sorry, Doctor?"

"Holmes calls me 'Watson' or 'John.' Never 'Doctor.' Nor does he drink tea. Even if he did, he wouldn't drink it in the same manner as you do, because the man who normally inhabits that body is left-handed. An easy detail to overlook, I suppose, yet all these things together lead me to deduce that the man who got up off Charles Augustus Milverton's floor was not the same man who fell down upon it. I shall ask again: who are you?"

"Well spotted, Doctor." He smiled at me, took a long drink of tea, shrugged. "It makes no difference, I suppose…"

Another sip.

"I am Professor James Moriarty, at your service."

He smiled at me again—the smile of a man who is about to take your bishop and declare checkmate. He held one of his hands palm up, just in front of his face. With a sudden whoosh, the gas lamps winked out. The fire in the hearth winked out. All their flames coalesced into a tight orange ball; a miniature inferno, hovering just an inch above his extended palm. His grin shone diabolically in the strange, swimming light and he chuckled, "Or, if we are to be honest, it must be said: you, Dr. John Watson, now find yourself in *my service*."

"I am Professor James Moriarty, at your service…"

WARLOCK HOLMES WILL RETURN IN

THE BATTLE OF BASKERVILLE HALL

MAY 2017

ACKNOWLEDGEMENTS

TO MY AGENT SAM MORGAN AND EDITOR MIRANDA JEWESS: thank you for having faith in me.

To Sean: thanks for illustrating, so beautifully, on nothing but a pittance and a hope.

To Douglas Adams and Terry Pratchett: thank you for your work. You proved SF/F humor could be done. You combined my two greatest loves. I wish I could have met you.

To... Who? Sir Arthur Whatsis? Who's that guy?

ABOUT THE AUTHOR

GABRIEL DENNING LIVES IN LAS VEGAS WITH HIS WIFE and two daughters. Oh, and a dog. And millions of micro-organisms. He's a twenty-year veteran of Orlando Theatersports, Seattle Theatersports, Jet City Improv and has finally figured out to write some of that stuff down. The sequel to *A Study in Brimstone*, *Warlock Holmes: The Battle of Baskerville Hall* will be published by Titan Books in May 2017.

SHERLOCK HOLMES
THE THINKING ENGINE
JAMES LOVEGROVE

It is 1895, and Sherlock Holmes is settling back into life as
a consulting detective, when he and Watson learn of strange
goings-on amidst the dreaming spires of Oxford.

A Professor Quantock has built a computational device,
which he claims is capable of analytical thought to rival
the cleverest men alive. Naturally Sherlock Holmes cannot
ignore this challenge. He and Watson travel to Oxford,
where a battle of wits ensues between the great detective and
his mechanical counterpart as they compete to see which
of them can be first to solve a series of crimes. But as man
and machine vie for supremacy, it becomes clear that the
Thinking Engine has its own agenda...

"An enjoyable read that respects Conan Doyle's canon."
Crime Scene

"An entertaining, intelligent and pacy read."
The Sherlock Holmes Journal

"The world of 19th century academia is brought to life vividly."
Baker Street Babes

TITANBOOKS.COM

SHERLOCK HOLMES
THE SPIRIT BOX
GEORGE MANN

German Zeppelins rain down death and destruction on London, and Dr. Watson is grieving for his nephew, killed on the fields of France.

A cryptic summons from Mycroft Holmes reunites Watson and Sherlock, tasked with solving three unexplained deaths: a politician has drowned in the Thames after giving a pro-German speech; a soldier suggests surrender before feeding himself to a tiger; and a suffragette renounces women's liberation and throws herself under a train. Are these apparent suicides something more sinister, something to do with the mysterious Spirit Box? Their investigation leads them to Ravensthorpe House, and the curious Seaton Underwood, a man whose spectrographs are said to capture men's souls…

"Arthur Conan Doyle was a master storyteller, and it takes comparable talent to give Holmes a second life… Mann is one of the few to get close to the target."
Daily Mail

"Our only complaint about is that it is over too soon."
Starburst

TITANBOOKS.COM

THE BURSAR'S WIFE

A GEORGE KOCHARYAN MYSTERY

E.G. RODFORD

Meet George Kocharyan, Cambridge Confidential Services' one and only private investigator. Amidst the usual jobs following unfaithful spouses, he is approached by the glamorous Sylvia Booker, who fears that her daughter Lucy has fallen in with the wrong crowd.

Aided by his assistant Sandra and her teenage son, George soon discovers that Sylvia has good reason to be concerned. Then an unfaithful wife he had been following is found dead. As his investigation continues—enlivened by a mild stabbing and the unwanted attention of Detective Inspector Vicky Stubbing— George begins to wonder if all the threads are connected…

"A quirky and persuasive new entry in the ranks of crime fiction."
Barry Forshaw, *Crime Time*

"An absolute delight—a gumshoe thriller that reminded me of Raymond Chandler."
Steven Dunne, author of *A Killing Moon*

"A controlled, artful crime story. A treat."
Conrad Williams, author of *Dust and Desire*

TITANBOOKS.COM

THE RUNAWAY MAID

A GEORGE KOCHARYAN MYSTERY

E.G. RODFORD

Private Investigator George Kocharyan is on the trail of a
runaway maid, the employee of a charismatic transplant
surgeon and his beauty-queen wife. The maid is accused of
stealing, but Kocharyan suspects that there is more to the story.
Throw in a Turkish drug-king, an ongoing investigation into
the death of a child, and the permanently unpleasant DI Vicky
Stubbing, and Kocharyan finds himself having to hide out with
his assistant Sandra…

AVAILABLE MARCH 2017

TITANBOOKS.COM

WRITTEN IN DEAD WAX

A VINYL DETECTIVE NOVEL

ANDREW CARTMEL

He is a record collector – a connoisseur of vinyl, hunting out rare and elusive LPs. His business card describes him as the 'Vinyl Detective' and some people take this more literally than others. Like the beautiful, mysterious woman who wants to pay him a large sum of money to find a priceless lost recording – on behalf of an extremely wealthy (and rather sinister) shadowy client. Given that he's just about to run out of cat biscuits, this gets our hero's full attention. So begins a painful and dangerous odyssey in search of the rarest jazz record of them all…

"An irresistible blend of murder, mystery and music… our protagonist seeks to find the rarest of records – and incidentally solve a murder, right a great historical injustice and, if he's very lucky, avoid dying in the process."
Ben Aaronovitch, bestselling author of *Rivers of London*

"The Vinyl Detective is one of the sharpest and most original characters I've seen for a long time."
David Quantick

TITANBOOKS.COM

THE RUN-OUT GROOVE

A VINYL DETECTIVE NOVEL

ANDREW CARTMEL

His first adventure consisted of the search for a rare record; his second begins with the discovery of one. When a mint copy of the final album by 'Valerian'—England's great lost rock band of the 1960s—surfaces in a charity shop, all hell breaks loose. Finding this record triggers a chain of events culminating in our hero learning the true fate of the singer Valerian, who died under equivocal circumstances just after— or was it just before?—the abduction of her two-year-old son. Along the way, the Vinyl Detective finds himself marked for death, at the wrong end of a shotgun, and unknowingly dosed with LSD as a prelude to being burned alive. And then there's the grave-robbing…

"Like an old 45rpm record, this book crackles with brilliance."
David Quantick

"This tale of crime, cats and rock 'n' roll unfolds with an authentic sense of the music scene then and now—and a mystery that will keep you guessing."
Stephen Gallagher

IMPURE BLOOD

A CAPTAIN DARAC NOVEL

PETER MORFOOT

In the heat of a French summer, Captain Paul Darac of the Nice Brigade Criminelle is called to a highly sensitive crime scene. A man has been found murdered in the midst of a Muslim prayer group, but no one saw how it was done. Then the organisers of the Nice leg of the Tour de France receive an unlikely terrorist threat. In what becomes a frantic race against time, Darac must try to unpick a complex knot in which racial hatred, sex and revenge are tightly intertwined.

"Engrossing. An auspicious debut for Darac."
Publishers Weekly

"A deeply satisfying feast."
Jim Kelly, award-winning author of *The Water Clock*

"Great plot, appealing hero, glorious setting."
Martin Walker, bestselling author of *Bruno, Chief of Police*

"A gripping, complex, and fluently told story."
Alison Joseph, author of the *Sister Agnes Mysteries*

TITANBOOKS.COM

BABAZOUK BLUES

A CAPTAIN DARAC NOVEL

PETER MORFOOT

Captain Paul Darac of the Brigade Criminelle is forced to abandon his jazz quintet mid-show by the call to a possible murder. He and his officers arrive on the scene to find a woman's mutilated corpse, although the cause of her death may not have been a sinister one. Initially routine, the case deepens and darkens into a complex inquiry that threatens to close in on Darac himself. But allegiances past and present must be set aside to unravel a tale of greed, deception and treachery that spans the social spectrum. It is among the winding streets of his own neighbourhood in Nice's old town, the Babazouk, that Darac faces his severest test yet.

AVAILABLE APRIL 2017

TITANBOOKS.COM

For more fantastic fiction, author events, competitions,
limited editions and more

VISIT OUR WEBSITE
titanbooks.com

LIKE US ON FACEBOOK
facebook.com/titanbooks

FOLLOW US ON TWITTER
@TitanBooks

EMAIL US
readerfeedback@titanemail.com